Broken

promises

By

H.M. Ward

LAREE BAILEY PRESS

www.HMWard.com

COPYRIGHT

LAREE BAILEY PRESS

First Edition: December 2015

ISBN: 9781630350833

Broken

promises

In memory of Jim, who knew life is beautiful.

CHAPTER 1

~MARI~

Katie kicks me under the table, shooting me a WTF look when I meet her gaze. She picks up her wine glass, smiling at her little dinner party consisting of me, my boyfriend, his younger brother, and the new girl from next door. I think her name is Amy, but I'm not sure because she's hardly spoken.

Katie lifts her glass. The red liquid sloshes within an inch of the rim. She grins and my stomach drops. I know that look. Crap. "To Mari and Derrick, the best boyfriend ever, with really awesome hair. May God bless you both with many years and lots of chubby babies for Auntie Katie to play with!"

They don't know Katie the way I do and start to sip their drinks as she says those last few words. There are never enough napkins when Katie meets new people.

"Holy shit!" Jared chokes out the words and looks at his brother. "You got her knocked up?" Tact isn't his thing.

Jared is tall and handsome like his brother, with dark hair, blue eyes, and a strong jaw. They both have lean bodies with hard muscles and broad shoulders. They're confident, both aware they have the looks, but Jared is more boyish than Derrick. Jared tends to act the cocky male stereotype—as if to be anything else would let us women down. Unlike Derrick, Jared has no filters. It's a trait he shares with someone else I know.

Katie is grinning.

I swipe my foot under the table trying to find her leg and miss.

Derrick and I start stammering explanations at the same time, "No, oh no. We're not. I mean." Our hands cross in front of us as if warding off evil spirits and our faces wear I-can't-believe-we're-talking-about-this expressions.

"Jesus, man! You scared me for a second." Jared leans back in his chair and relaxes. He's got Peter Pan syndrome up to his ears. Ever the lost boy, he'll never grow up or settle down.

Not that I'm ready to settle down either. I'm on the anti-marriage side of the fence at the moment. I like to keep my options open, so I'm not ready to stick a fork in the concept, but marriage holds little appeal for me. I've seen things, and, while I don't want those perceptions to guide my life, I understand how they've affected it.

Derrick is usually sweet and doting, but when his brother is around, their competing levels of testosterone frustrate me.

Derrick waves his hand at his brother, dismissing the fat baby fantasy. "Don't be ridiculous. There'll be a wedding before a baby." He laughs, intending his comment to end the conversation on a joke, but New Girl perks up at the word wedding.

Amy smiles at me. "Are you two engaged?"

It's one of the few times she's spoken tonight. She seems a little shy. Katie probably pried her out of her apartment with the Jaws of Life. After an evening with us, she'll never answer the door again.

Jared leans forward and slaps the table. "What! Why am I the last to hear about everything?" His reaction makes Derrick laugh.

I shake my head and look down to hide my face. Why am I blushing? "No, we're not. There's no engagement. There's no baby."

Katie idly swirls the wine in her glass. "And no sex. Got it."

Leaning close to Katie, I whisper, "Remind me to kill you later."

She holds up a second glass of wine and shoves it into my hands. Katie's my age—closing in on thirty—with long, dark blonde hair streaked with pale gold and cleverly cut to frame her face. She's about a head taller than me and speaks her mind without fail. "Will do. Seriously, though, you need to calm down. You know I'm kidding. And Jared, here, is going to have a heart attack soon."

He lifts his glass of Jack and Coke, "Damn straight. A guy has to sow his wild seeds first. Am I right, Aims?" He leans in and bumps his elbow into Amy's arm.

I make a face. First of all, I hate that expression. Secondly, Jared said it wrong—you sow wild oats. His use of the word seeds creates an unwanted mental image of Derrick spraying his stuff all over swooning co-eds in wet t-shirts. I shake the thought from my mind. I've spent too much time with Seth.

Amy slides down in her seat a little more, blushing fiercely. Her strawberry blonde hair and fair skin do nothing to hide that blush either. If she could discreetly jump out the window, she would.

"You don't have to answer him," I say, smiling kindly at Amy from across the little table. Everything in Katie's apartment is small. It's a rental on Long Island and costs a fortune, but she decided to stay put when Seth deployed. Her family is here, so I can't blame her. Her compact living room bleeds into a galley kitchen and breakfast nook. Five people can barely cram into the small space. A light fixture hangs overhead. Katie beefed it up with crystals and pale ribbon. Everything she has is reclaimed, recycled, and repurposed in a kaleidoscope of pastels. It gives the apartment a shabby-chic meets New Yorker character, and feels more like home than anywhere I've ever lived.

"Okay," Amy says, her voice an octave too high.

Jared laughs and swats a hand at us. "You two are no fun!"

"So, Playboy," Katie says addressing Derrick, "Seriously now, how many kids do you guys want to have? Have you talked about these things? Or are you waiting for the stick to turn blue so you can wing it?" She's smiling casually, her arm draped over the back of her chair.

Derrick nervously runs his fingers through his dark hair as he clears his throat. He's taken this kind of abuse from Katie before, but she's taunting him more than usual tonight.

Deciding to change tactics, he quickly asks, "Katie, how's Seth doing? I heard his tour is almost over. What do you plan to do for his homecoming?"

Oh, God! He gave Katie free range to blab about her and Sexbot all night. The nickname we gave Seth in high school stuck. I manage to maintain the plastic smile on my face as Katie responds.

"I'm pretty sure he plans on doing me—over and over again, upside down and right side up—it's been a while, you know?" Only Jared laughs. Katie stuffs a forkful of salad in her mouth and continues, her voice suddenly soft and sober. "I'm glad it's almost over. It's terrifying not knowing if he's all right." She looks around the room self-consciously, as if checking to see if anyone noticed the change in her voice.

Curious, Jared asks, "What does Seth do? Army?"

Katie shakes her head. "No, he wanted to go big or go home—he's a Marine."

"Wow, no kidding!" Jared seems impressed. I'm sure he's wondering about the man that could take on Katie.

She goes on, "Seth turned into a good man, but it wasn't for lack of trying. We hated each other when we first met. Mari was interested in his best friend, and you know how that—ow!" Katie's eyes snap to mine, silently expressing her displeasure at my shoe's collision with her shin.

I keep my voice calm, hiding the terror that's climbing up my throat. "They don't want to hear that story."

Jared seems to sniff out juicy drama. He looks like a tiger ready to pounce on a tribe of naked women. "Of course we do! Was he good in bed? Better than Derrick?"

My jaw drops and Amy's eyes turn to Ping-Pong balls bouncing right out of her head.

Derrick's gaze narrows, and he turns to look at me. "Which boyfriend are we talking about?"

"Do tell. Based on your expression, I'm sure it's a great story. Also, from the look on my brother's face, he hasn't heard it yet." Jared smiles so wide that his dimples might pop off his face and kill someone.

Everyone looks at me, waiting. I want to disappear. I hate this story. I never tell it willingly, I never admit we were together. Not to myself, not to anyone else. Every time I think of him it's like ripping open a half-healed wound. My stomach knots and I feel the words rising involuntarily up my throat.

But before anyone can say another word, Katie's phone begins to play "I'm Too Sexy," by Right Said Fred. She springs from her seat like a deranged Labradoodle. "It's Seth! I'll be right back." Katie bounds through the bedroom door and shuts it behind her.

"Your friend seems nice." Jared says it like he's in love. He watches her bedroom door as if he's hoping to hear an orgasm through the wall.

"She has her moments. She's very excited Seth is coming home and forgets to filter her thoughts. All in all, Seth is a good guy. He's been good to her. I suppose it is funny how things ended up." I bite my tongue before anything else can spill out, but the thought continues in my head.

It's funny how they stayed together, and Trystan and I broke up.

It's funny that Seth's promises meant something, while Trystan's didn't.

It's funny that I'm still mad, even though things ended a long time ago.

"You okay?" Derrick whispers, leaning in to softly kiss my cheek.

I nod. "Yeah, just lost in thought." I stand and start clearing the table, taking the dishes to the sink one by one, while Derrick and Jared talk.

I feel guilty whenever Katie mentions Trystan. I haven't told Derrick about him yet.

Guys react poorly when they discover I dated the sexiest man alive. Add in the rock star thing and they tend to jerk away from me, unable to compete with Trystan's ghost.

I have a stack of dishes in my hands when I hear it—a shrill cry that's equal parts terror and anguish. It's a small burst of suffering, followed by the sound of something hard hitting the floor.

An icy chill races up my spine from deep within me. With trembling hands and shaky legs, I step toward the table and set the dishes down. All eyes are on the door to Katie's room, but I'm the only one who can go in there.

Sensing the same thing I do, Amy stands and squeezes my hand. "Help her. I'll finish cleaning up."

The world around me freezes. Derrick's voice is a dull buzz as I pad across the room. Each step feels heavier, like someone strapped anvils to my feet. My heart beats harder because I know what's happened. I already know even though I've yet to hear the words.

I try to reassure myself that I don't know anything for certain. It could be nothing.

Maybe Katie dropped something. Maybe she stepped on a mouse.

Maybe it's worse.

Dread licks the inside of my chest, freezing me in place. Time shatters and falls to pieces around me. What will I say? How can I help her? I don't know. The door inches toward me until the knob is in my hand. I twist it and step inside.

Katie is lying facedown on their bed, her head turned toward the wall and resting on her arm. She's utterly still, staring at the paint with glassy eyes. Her phone is on the floor alongside her lamp.

Swallowing hard, I step over those things and sit next to her on the bed. She doesn't move when the mattress dips. She doesn't speak. Katie remains suspended in shock.

I touch her shoulder gently. "What happened?"

It's two words, two horrible words that won't have a good answer. I feel cold, and the air is thicker than before.

Katie is quiet for a while. I don't press her. I let her lie there, barely breathing, until she manages to speak. "Seth was there, talking to me, then the shouting began and the sounds of metal twisting and ripping apart drowned out his voice. Then there was nothing." Her lower lip trembles as she sits up and looks into my eyes. "I've lost him, haven't I?"

CHAPTER 2

I have no answer, but I'm afraid for her, with her. Seth's my friend. I've known him since we were kids. My eyes fill with tears, but I hold them back, blink them away.

I find my voice. It's too dry, too scratchy. "I don't know."

Katie leans against me, her body trembling as she tries not to cry. I wrap my arms around her and hold on tight. "He might be fine, Katie. There's no way to know right now."

She nods and sits up, pushing her long blonde hair out of her face. Wiping away the tears, she smiles at me. "Right. I shouldn't do this yet. I should wait until I know for sure, one way or the other. I should find his mom. We can wait together."

I nod. "I'll take you there. Don't worry about anything here. Amy is sweet. She's cleaning up. And if it will make you happy, I'll borrow a fat baby from the hospital for you." I'm kidding, but she manages a boogery laugh.

"No, it only counts if you do it the right way." She sniffles and grabs a tissue from her nightstand drawer. It seems as if she's going to say more, but doesn't.

"I know, get married. Like you."

She laughs, "No, have sex. Get married? I know you're against that. Proposing marriage is the fastest way for a guy to kill a relationship with you." She laughs and shakes her head.

"I'm not against it. I'm just not eager."

She dabs her face with the tissue and looks over at me. "I know you don't want to tell him, but if you think you guys have a chance at a life together, he needs to know about Trystan."

Normally I'd scold her for interfering, but I can't right now. Her red-rimmed eyes are puffy, and the sheen of freshly shed tears glistens on her cheeks. I smile at her and nod. "I will. Soon, okay? Please let me do it."

Katie stares blankly at the wall for a moment before fixing her eyes on mine. "I always thought we'd have more time—me and Seth. I thought we'd have kids. I wanted a super-cute baby girl with pudgy rolls, you know?"

"I know. No matter what, I'm here for you. During the good, the bad, and the ugly. Anytime."

As if on cue, my phone chirps with a new text message. I breathe in slowly, calming myself as I brace for what's coming. Please, not now. I glance at the sender and say a stream of mental curse words, before pinching the bridge of my nose.

"Is it work?"

"Yeah. I'll call in sick. I'll stay with you until you find out about Seth." I have my phone in my hand, ready to dial when I see the message:

WORK: HIGH-PROFILE CAR CRASH. P4 CLEARANCE. NEED YOU NOW.

I press my eyes together and wish this wasn't happening now. Dad will kill me if I don't show up. It's his emergency room. At the same time, I can't walk away from Katie, not now. She takes my phone away from me and types a reply.

ME: COMING

She hands me back my phone. "It's okay. I understand. You're a doctor and emergencies happen. I'll see you later, okay?"

My face crumples. I don't want to leave her. "I promised Seth I'd be here for you."

She rushes at me, throwing her arms around my neck. "You are. You are here right now. This was the worst part because I thought—" she gasps, trying not to cry, "But you're right. I don't know for certain."

Stepping back, she releases me from her bear hug and says, "He'll be all right." She says it out loud almost as much to convince me as to convince herself. "He promised he'd make it back. Seth always keeps his promises. I'll see him again."

I swallow hard. "Okay, I'll call after work and check on you."

Her big eyes glisten in the dim light. Before I leave the room, I pick up her things from the floor, placing the lamp back on her dresser and gently pressing the cell phone into her palm. "It'll be all right."

Katie forces a big smile and nods.

CHAPTER 3

I'm in a mental fog as I make my way to the hospital. It's a decent drive to the hospital from Katie and Seth's apartment—plenty of time to think nothing good. My foot is heavy, pressing the gas pedal as far down as it goes. I stare ahead, my eyes darting between cars as I think about things.

Life is too short.

It's too brief to be afraid to try.

The thing is, I did try—it was Trystan who walked away, and I still don't understand why. Out of nowhere, he was done with me. It didn't make any sense at the time, and I felt so hurt that I didn't chase after him. I didn't try to fix it. Shattered glass can't be mended. No matter what I do, those fractures are still there. Pieces remain lost or missing. It's not possible to regain what we once had, yet I still regret not attempting to mend things between us.

I wish things had ended differently, less anticlimactic. I wanted an explosion, a clear reason for the surprise end of our relationship. What I got was a pinhole in a balloon—a slow leak of air over weeks and weeks until there was nothing left—masking the cause of our destruction and hiding it from sight.

I blink and slam the heel of my hand on the horn. I'm flying down Sunrise Highway, trying to get to Montauk Highway. That's the fastest route, but some nut in a junker cuts me off. I slam on the brake and swear.

"This can't be happening," I mutter to myself. I wasn't even on call tonight, but I'll get chewed out for being late.

I wail on the horn again. The jalopy moves back into the center lane. I floor it and don't look back. A few moments later, I'm pulling into the hospital parking lot. As I press the brake and roll to a stop, I can't believe what I'm seeing. News vans, reporters, and cops are crowding the ER entrance.

Crap. Some socialite totaled her car. The hospital is going to be a madhouse.

I pull straight up to the ER doors and jump out of my car. A cop starts to scold me. "You can't park here. Hey! You can't go inside!"

I text Mitchell, a friend I know is working the waiting room this evening.

ME: HELP. NO PARKING. LATE.

A moment later my phone buzzes.

MITCHELL: YOU OWE ME SO BIG.

ME: DONE. TY.

The police officer is scolding me. "You can't park here. Get in your car and move it."

I look up at him. "Do you know who runs this ER?"

"Not you."

I ignore his response. "Dr. Jennings. He's a bit of a hardass. I wasn't on call tonight and yet here I am, responding to this emergency even though my best friend just heard her husband go missing in action over the phone. He's probably dead. I need to be with her. I don't want to be here. You don't want to be here dealing with this rich brat either," I jab my thumb toward the ER doors and whoever is causing this commotion. "Let me do my job so you can do yours."

"I.D." He barks. I hold it up. He reads it, and his jaw tightens. "Dr. Mari Jennings, as in the only daughter of Dr. Jennings, the hardass? As in the doctor who was in the paper last week for saving that kid at Yankee Stadium?"

"Yeah, that one," I say as I toss my keys at him. "A hospital employee in brown scrubs will be outside any second. Give the keys to him. He'll move it."

The cop shakes his head. "I can't do that, Dr. Jennings. Your car will be towed."

"Then tow it!"

Everyone around me is buzzing. It's that manic hushed whisper, the one that's so full of tension you know something bad is happening. The hair on the back of my neck prickles. I smooth it with my hand as I shove through the door and run into a mob of people. Every inch of the waiting room is full. I can barely move.

I push my elbows out, and start shoving. These people aren't sick. They're here to see the rich brat.

I hear them talk as I make my way through the sea of people.

"How do they know it's him?" A woman with wide hips and clingy clothing leans toward her friend. They're both wearing sweat suits. It looks like they rolled out of bed and ran here.

"I heard his car was totaled. He's already dead. They just don't want to say it." They continue whispering as I pass.

A few people away from me, a tall, thin man with dark skin laughs, his voice carrying over the roar of the crowd. "There are too many people in here to tell the truth. Imagine the shitstorm that'll follow that announcement!" He laughs and then shakes his head.

Who are they talking about? I need to get behind the doors and check in at the nurse's station. Rose is up there. I can hear her stern voice. After over thirty years in this job, she doesn't take shit from anyone. She snaps, "I'm sorry, but I can't give you information on his condition."

I'm too short to see what's happening. A man steps on me.

"Hey!"

He doesn't turn around. He's an ogre of a guy—as tall as he is wide. He's got rolls of fat down the back of his neck, clearly visible through the thinning black hair he slicked back and plastered to his scalp. He's wearing sweatpants, a comic book t-shirt and a pair of flip-flops. "He totally smashed the car. There's nothing left—and I mean NOTHING. They're saying outside that the cops had to cut him out, and he wasn't moving."

"Holy shit." The man he's talking to is enthralled.

"HEY!" I yell, elbowing him to no effect. The guy he's talking to looks around his wide friend and inclines his head toward me.

"Yeah I know, right? There is no way they can patch him up this time. Trystan's a dead man." He's smiling as he turns toward me. "Hey, girlie. I didn't see you there."

My eyes are wide. Trystan? He said Trystan. I blink, unable to pull the right words from my brain to my mouth. My mind is racing in a million directions at once, trying to make a rational connection—trying to think of another socialite with the name Trystan.

There aren't any.

I suck in three little gulps of air. My eyes water and I blink rapidly, cocking my head to the side like I'm hard of hearing. "I'm sorry, did you say Trystan?"

He jabs his thumb back toward the ambulance bay and glances down at my badge. "You're a nurse? Can you tell me if he's dead? That'll be news worth selling."

Before I know what I'm doing, I have my finger in the guy's lower ribs—he towers above me—and I'm poking him. I laugh like my brain turned to Jell-O and melted out my ears. My words come out broken, jumbled, my thoughts moving faster than my mouth. "That guy in the car wreck—what is his name?"

This can't be happening. Not tonight. My heart slams into my chest, threatening to burst. I stab him with my finger again, and he steps back.

"Yeah, it's the rocker—Trystan Scott. He got wasted and plastered his brand new Pagani Huayra into a tree. That's a two million dollar car. It crumpled like toilet paper." The man suddenly stops talking. He touches my shoulder a moment later. Our eyes meet. "Did you hear me?"

I shake my head. "That can't be true. He doesn't drink."

The guy laughs and rolls his eyes. "A fan, true to the end."

"No!" I shove my way past them as they laugh.

My breath freezes inside my body, and my lungs won't move. My heart is afraid to beat, terrified it might be true. My elbows connect with my ribs, and I no longer finesse the crowd. I race through the people, using my body as best I can, jabbing my pointy elbows as needed until I reach Rose at the desk.

"Get your skinny ass in here! Your father's going to tear us in half if you don't get back there. Like right now." She holds her hand under the desk and the door buzzes open. I push through, grab a clean pair of scrubs and shove myself into them in one continuous motion.

Another cop grabs me by my shoulders as he kicks the locking door closed. "Stop. I need to check your badge." I lift it for him to see, noticing for the first time that I'm shaking.

It can't be Trystan.

The cop scans my badge and lets me pass. "You can go. P4 rules, no pictures, no phones, no video. Talk to the press and you know the repercussions."

"I know, thanks."

I knew Trystan had a single drink after Tucker died. I saw him wrestle with one tumbler of whiskey for what seemed like forever before finally swallowing it. I don't think he saw me that night. Everything happened so fast. One day Tucker was watching out for Trystan, managing his career. Then we blinked, and the young teacher was in a casket, disappearing into a grave.

I can't do this again! I've already lowered two people I love into the ground. I can't lose Trystan, too. Not like this.

My chest feels like it's tearing in half as I race toward the board. Rose grabs me. "Room three, they've got him in there, and Dr. Jennings—"

As if bidden, Dad appears. "Mari, you took your time getting here." He's wearing an expression on his face that makes the rest of the staff wet themselves. I'm in for a verbal lashing.

"I wasn't on call tonight." It won't matter, for some reason he wanted me here.

"And you took your time to enforce your point?" He snaps his fingers and points to the floor next to him, indicating he wants me to walk with him.

Rose's eyes go wide, and she slams her mouth shut. She wants to tell Dad off like you wouldn't believe. We all do, but he has a right to be this arrogant—he's the best. That's why he's here. He never makes mistakes, and he runs a tight ship.
"I'm sorry, I—"

He flips through a chart that's attached to a clipboard as he walks. His white coat billows behind his long legs. "I don't care. When we have a crisis, and I want you here, you come. End of story."

"Yes, sir."

He scans the papers he's holding and grunts. "This isn't the correct report! Damn it, Rose! Where is it?" He rounds and slaps the clipboard down on the counter then keeps walking. He snaps his fingers in the air. "Get it. Now."

He barks orders at people, as we pass. The janitor sees him and quickly walks the other way, taking his mop with him.

"Mari, I'm sure you've heard about your idiot ex-boyfriend by now. He's lucky no one else was on that road. What he did was incredibly stupid." Dad continues talking about Trystan, but I tune most of it out. I learned to do that a long time ago, but it doesn't stop my stomach from churning like I've swallowed a bucket of acid. After everything that happened between us, it can't end like this.

But it seems it already has.

CHAPTER 4

NINE YEARS AGO

~MARI~

I'm sitting on the bed in my dorm room with Trystan next to me. His dark hair is long, and he tucks part of it behind his ear. He balances his guitar across his lap, smiling at me as he sings. His voice is mesmerizing.

He's working on a new song. His fingers slide up and down the neck of the guitar creating the music drifting through the air.

Leaning back against the pillows, I smile. For the first time in my life, I'm truly happy.

I'm in college, loving my classes, and dating the perfect guy.

Trystan stops suddenly and looks over at me. He doesn't say anything.

"What?" I laugh at the curious expression on his face. It's like he's hoping I'll buy him a puppy.

"You're beautiful. Everything about you is beautiful—your face, your body, your soul." The intensity of his words is palpable. I can feel them wash over me and connect inside me. That connection we've always shared is there and growing stronger.

Trystan's lashes lower as he watches my mouth. He keeps one hand on his guitar and leans in toward me. My pulse races faster as my body heats up. His kisses consume me, lighting me up from the inside out. I don't move. I let him come to me, pressing his body against mine. His free hand traces my lower lip with the pad of his finger before cupping my cheeks and pulling me close enough to press his lips to mine.

It's hard to keep things light with Trystan. Every kiss is heated, making me want more. I'm almost there with him, but I wanted to be sure. I want to be certain he loves me. I want to know he'll stay. He has a reputation that worries me, but he can't fake this, can he? What guy would go through what we've been through together for a quick tryst? I push the worry away. It's been too long, too much has happened to continue worrying about being a notch in his belt at this point.

The kiss ignites and soon my skin tingles all over wanting his hands touching me. I trace his jaw with my finger before dropping it to his waist. I slip my palms under his shirt, wanting to feel him, to slide my hands up his back.

Trystan's kiss deepens. The guitar slides off his lap and lands on the pillows where he'd been sitting on the floor earlier. It makes a musical thud. My eyes fly open, and I pull away, worried he'll be upset. "I'm sorry."

His eyes lock on mine. He doesn't give the guitar a second thought. Taking my face in his hands, he leans in close enough to kiss me, but doesn't. He licks his lips slowly, and I swear I can feel his heart beating. "Don't be sorry. I'd rather hold you."

I want this. I want him. I don't want to wait anymore. My lips press together a few times and tremble. He sees it. He knows what

I'm going to say. There's always been a connection between us—as if he could read my mind.

He kisses my cheek and whispers in my ear, "We don't have to, Mari."

Wrapping my arms around his neck, I pull him down, so his body presses mine into my mattress. I play with the hair that's falling into a frame around his face. "I know, but I want to. I want you. I've always wanted you. Be with me, Trystan?"

He remains slightly above me, holding me with one arm while leaning on his other elbow. The dark gray t-shirt he wears clings to his skin. There's a tiny hole near the neck on the right side, showing a soft spot of skin—a place I want to kiss.

Trystan's smile fades and his expression grows serious. "I love you."

"I love you, too."

Our eyes lock, igniting the rush of emotion flowing through me. He's nervous, but he wants this as much as I do. Threading my fingers through his hair, I pull his face toward mine. "Kiss me, and don't stop."

"Anything you want, my little kiss ninja."

His lips press to mine once more, and the floor of my stomach goes into free-fall. This is happening. I'm not going to say we have to wait anymore. I know him. I'm confident he's in love with me, no matter what the tabloids say—no matter what Dad says.

I push the thoughts away and reach for his shirt, tugging it over his head. He pulls it off the rest of the way and tosses it to the floor. When I reach for his jeans, he stops me, grabs both my hands and shakes his head. "Slow down. I want us to take our time. I want to learn every inch of your body, every curve."

Trystan slips his hand under my back and lifts me off the bed. Once I'm sitting up, he takes my tank top by the hem and lifts it up. After it's over my head, he tosses it on the floor with his shirt. His hands reach for me, and I suck in a sharp breath on contact. My eyes close as my head sways.

I love his touch. It's perfect, firm and possessive, but soft and gentle. It makes no sense, and yet it's completely divine.

His palm covers my breast as he leans into me. With one hand, he reaches around my back and unhooks my bra. My heart hammers harder at the thought of him finally seeing me, anticipation competing with uncertainty. My body isn't anything magnificent. I'm average everything, with mud-brown hair and matching eyes.

That's the last thought I have on the matter. When he presses his lips to my skin, I gasp. My back stiffens and I fall back into the pillows, pulling him down with me.

Trystan's kisses feel like he's worshipping a goddess. His mouth is all over me, tasting, teasing, and caressing me until my hips are bucking against him.

"Trystan, please." I call his name, begging him in a sultry voice that can't possibly be mine.

"Slowly, love. Slowly." He hooks his thumbs over the edge of my shorts, tugging them and my panties off with one swift move.

I lie back on my bed with him above me. His eyes trace my curves slowly, savoring them one by one before his hands do the same thing. He traces patterns on my stomach, forming swirls that lead to the tip of my breasts. He leans in and kisses me before doing it again and again.

I'm so hot. Parts of me scream to be touched. It's hard to be quiet, hard not to beg him for what I want. I press my eyes closed and bite my lip shut as he kisses my breast. His hand slips down my thigh, resting at the point where my legs meet.

My eyes fly open, and we watch each other. I'm breathing hard, trying not to make a sound when he strokes a finger over me. I can't keep quiet. I cry out, calling his name.

He grins. "There's my girl. Stop trying to be someone you're not. If you're into it and say things—beg, talk dirty, or whatever—I like that. I want to be with you, with Mari, with the woman who is all passion and promise. Don't hide her from me, okay?"

I nod and keep my gaze locked on his. He touches my face, gently pushing curls away from my eyes. He leans in and kisses me once more, before reaching for his jeans. He unbuttons them and slides them off quickly, tossing them to the floor. His boxers fall next, and soon, it's just us, skin on skin.

I let myself feel and love him the way I want. I don't worry about what I sound like or what he thinks. Trystan encourages me to take what I want, so I do. My timidity vanishes and, for the first time, we're together. I feel him inside me, as he presses against me, slowly until I can't stand it anymore. I feel wound too tightly, and every inch of me is on fire.

We're slick with sweat, and our bodies fit perfectly together. He pushes into me harder, faster. He's losing control, and I want to see his face. I want to watch those beautiful blue eyes flip from lusty to sated.

His hair is damp and sways as he rocks. My nails dig into his back as I try to hold us together, tighter. I thought I could outlast him, but I can't. The pulsing within me begins, releasing waves of lust. They wash over me, again and again, bringing Trystan to his climax.

I open my eyes and see the expression on his face. I watch as he loses himself in me and makes me his.

CHAPTER 5

The next morning, I'm smiling so much that I look like an idiot, but I can't help it. Nothing could ruin this feeling. It's light and carefree. It fills me with sunshine from head to toe. Every bit of me is happy and in love.

I grab my books and head down the hallway. I live on the third floor of an older dorm at the back of campus. Trystan left late last night, slipping out the window and running before anyone saw him. I know it's a matter of time until people find out how serious we are, but not having a roommate makes it last longer.

As I skip down the steps of the stairwell, I call Katie. She answers, "You suck. It's summer. Some of us need beauty sleep." She yawns and stretches, dropping her phone on the floor. I hear her swear and pick it back up.

The connection is sucky. I keep getting static, but it's good enough. Besides, if I have to keep this to myself all day, I'll explode like a piñata. "Katie! Guess what I did? Guess what? You'll never guess?"

She's quiet for a second and then her tone changes. "You did not." She squeals and I hear her bed squeak as she sits up. "You nailed Trystan!"

A mad blush spreads across my face. "Yes!" I'm too excited, so we both squee together.

"Details! I need them now!"

"Later, I promise. I need to get to class, but there's no way I could hold this in all day." I throw open the door leading outside and hear Katie laughing.

"Give me one little detail, Mari! Come on! Don't leave a girl hanging!"

I giggle and whirl around, throwing my arms out and letting my backpack swing around with me. The momentum makes it hard to stop.

When I do, I press the phone to my ear and say, "He's beautiful! Everything about him is completely and totally perfect. Be jealous. Very. Jealous."

I'm still giggling when I look up and see Dad. He's leaning against the Bentley, his arms folded across his chest. His eyes are wrong, devoid of emotion, red.

I forget the phone, forget Katie. I walk over to him. "Dad?"

We haven't spoken much since I left home. Though things are tense between Dad and me, I'm getting to see more of Mom. It's weird, but it's like I'm getting to know her all over again—differently this time. I really like her.

The best part is that she's really happy for me. She likes that I'm taking theater classes. She encouraged me to change my major from pre-med. And she even likes Trystan. She knows about us, about him. I wonder if she's always known how much I love him.

Daddy has had a rough time lately, and I know it's because of me—because I refuse to follow in his footsteps. For a second I think he's here to tell me off, but when his lips part he gives me the most god-awful look.

An imaginary anchor pulls down uncomfortably on my heart. I stiffen and hold my ground. I won't cry in front of him. It doesn't matter what he says.

"I need to talk to you, Mari." His voice sounds harsh. I'm not doing this in a parking lot.

I laugh bitterly, turning my back on him. "I'm not doing this now. I have class. Leave me alone, Dad."

Dad hesitates, then slams his fist into his car. I freeze and turn around. He loves that stupid car. I scratched it once and he nearly disowned me, but he created a hugeass dent on purpose? My eyes fixate on the indentation, then drift up to his face.

He swallows hard. "I don't know how to tell you this—"

The anchor is ripping my heart. I can't do this again. "Then don't, Dad. I get it. You're out of my life."

"Mari, that's not it! Damn it! Will you listen to me?" He's breathing fast. The color has drained from his face and a bead of sweat lines his brow. "It's your mother."

BROKEN PROMISES

"What about her?"
"She died last night."

CHAPTER 6

As Dad wrings his hands, nervously trying to find the right words to say next, I numbly focus on the details of his appearance. His shirt, normally neatly pressed, is wrinkled, and the buttons at his neck are undone. He wears no tie, no shiny shoes. His face is stubbled where it should be clean-shaven. The longer I look at him, the more I see. My gut tells me he's speaking the truth, but my heart can't accept it.

We stare at each other for what feels like ages before I manage to speak. My throat feels so tight, so dry. "What happened?"

"She was driving home from work at the hospital last night and got clipped by a tractor trailer. It crushed her car." He swallows hard, pauses, then continues in the calm tone he uses when delivering horrible news to the family of a patient. "They pulled her out and brought her back to the ER, but there was too much damage. They couldn't stop the bleeding, Mari."

My eyes widen as rage rips through me. "She died in the hospital?" Dad nods his head. "You didn't bother to tell me? Couldn't you text? You were there, and you let her die without saying a word to me! How could you?" My voice drops to a deadly low volume. My words are barbed and, at that moment, I want to hurt him. My hands clench at my sides—open, closed, open. I try to hold it together. I try to breathe.

He let her die without giving me a chance to say goodbye.

Students pass by us, averting their eyes and walking faster. No one stops. No one wants to see a father-daughter fight over losing a mother.

Dropping my bag to the ground, I charge at him, shoving him in the chest, screaming in his face, "How could you?" I push him again. My lips wrap around words laced with poison, words meant to destroy any relationship we have left. Yelling louder this time, I scream, "She's gone and I didn't get to say goodbye! You're such an angry, bitter, miserable, conniving little man to keep me from the last precious moments of her life! You ripped that moment away like it didn't matter! Like I don't matter!"

"Mari!" He snaps my name.

Passersby are stopping to watch now. The wind blows gently through the trees, stirring the leaves. The sun slices through the canopy, peppering the ground with golden shafts of light.

There are familiar faces in the growing crowd. I'm aware I look like a child throwing a fit, but this was over the line.

"No! Don't talk to me! Never, ever come looking for me again. Do you understand?" I'm in his face, snarling. "I never want to see you again, and when you die, no one will mourn you. I'll make sure you're as far away from Mom as possible. Even seeing you in the ground is more than you deserve." I suck in a deep breath, lean forward, swipe my bag off the ground, and turn the other way.

I have no idea where I'm going, but I have to get out of here.

Dad calls after me, "I tried, Mari. I called you."

I don't stop. He's lying, trying to save his ass. I feel no pity for him, only anger. He stole the last few moments of my mother's life so he could hoard her attention the way he always does. He never called me.

"The wake is tonight. The burial is tomorrow. Come and make your peace."

My shoulders tense, and my body shakes. Rage explodes from my mouth as I whirl around, screaming at him from across the parking lot, "Thanks to you, I'll never have peace—not ever."

I'm breaking. My mind is shutting down, unable to process anything due to the overwhelming waves of emotion raging inside me. There's a storm inside me, something that could rip me in half if I don't figure out how to calm it.

A crazed idea rushes at me—I suddenly want to dart across the highway and hope a car hits me so hard I can't feel this pain anymore.

The impact would be an injury I can comprehend. I understand broken bones and bleeding skin.

I can't understand this invisible agony drowning me from within.

I steel myself, knowing I need to find Trystan. I can't do this alone.

CHAPTER 7

I have no idea how I managed to get here—Madison Square Garden is a hike from my dorm—but I make it. Before I realize where I am, what I'm doing, I'm walking down an empty hallway toward the sound of his voice.

Trystan is singing my song. The acoustic guitar and his voice are the only sounds amplified through the sound system. I tug open the door to the arena, and keep walking. I pass the sound guys, but they don't notice me until it's too late to stop me. The security team Trystan hired is suddenly surrounding me. They're wearing uniforms—navy blue—with security badges on their left forearms.

Trystan is on stage, sitting in darkness save a single light illuminating him from behind, forming a perfect silhouette. It's like his YouTube video, the one that made him famous. His voice aches with longing, as he sings about wanting a girl who has no idea he's alive.

I was that girl.

I had no idea until he told me.

My lip quivers, and I'm lost in the past for a moment, remembering him in the basement of our high school—remembering everything we've been through to get to this moment.

That's when one of the guards takes my arm and pulls. He's a big guy with thick arms and a neck bigger than his skull. His nametag says BOB. "You can't be here, miss. Come with me, please."

Another one asks, "How'd she even get in here?"

"Let go of me!" I yank my arm back and scream his name, hoping he'll hear me over the speakers. "TRYSTAN!"

The men think I'm a deranged groupie—and why wouldn't they? His first concert is tomorrow night. No one knows about us. No one knows who I am or how much I love Trystan.

Tears sting my eyes when I realize he can't hear me. The guards are using their bodies to force me back. They're practically stepping on me, shepherding me toward the exit. We're near the doors. They're going to lock me out.

I scream again, "TRYSTAN, PLEASE!" Hot tears roll down my cheeks. If they lock me up, I'm going to miss the wake. I won't feel Trystan's arms around me. I'll be forced to deal with this alone. I can't do it. My voice is shrill as I continue to call his name, crying out into the darkness.

One guard speaks into his shoulder, "We're going to need to escort her out."

The walkie-talkie makes a static sound, and then a harsh-sounding voice replies through the speaker, "Broken glass on the north side of the building. Hold her for the police."

The guards are irritated—one rolls his eyes. The others speak to each other like I'm not there. They think I'm unstable and aren't sure what I'll do. Neither am I. Desperation is bubbling up inside of me. I feel like my body might plummet to the floor, seep into the concrete, and die. I can't handle this.

The ache in my chest grows larger, and my screams grow louder.

The music stops. The notes fade off until the only sound remaining is his voice. "Mari?"

Trystan doesn't wait for me to answer. He jumps off his stool, shoves his guitar into Tucker's hands, and moves to the edge of the stage.

A voice yells, "Don't jump!"

But Trystan doesn't listen. He launches himself off the scaffolding, lands in the pit below, and then climbs the railing. He rushes toward me. He's a beautiful blur of white in that clingy t-shirt.

He's next to me, prying between his guards, wrapping his fingers around my wrist. He looks at them sternly. "This didn't happen."

I'm shaking with tears streaming down my face. They won't stop. I lock my jaw and swallow my sobs. He's here. I want to melt into him. I want his hands on me, telling me it will be all right. I need him.

The guard who grabbed me shakes his head and points at me. "She's going to have issues with the cops. She broke in. There's broken glass on the other side of the building."

Trystan shakes his head. "I broke it. I'll pay for it. Tell them to bill me. As for her—she was never here—you never saw her."

"Yes, Mr. Scott." The man nods and walks away with the other men following in his wake. He picks up his phone and says they made a mistake. Then he explains how Trystan broke the glass. He doesn't mention me. I fade from the story.

Trystan keeps his fingers firmly wrapped around my wrist. He pulls me toward the back and suddenly Mr. Tucker is there.

His face is rosy, his skin is glistening, and he's out of breath as if he'd run over. "Mari, my God—what happened?" He reaches out and touches my shoulder, squeezing it for a moment before letting go.

I try to speak, but I can't. My mouth opens and moves. There should be words, but there are none.

He waves his hands and looks at Trystan. "Where do you want me to take her?"

A conversation goes back and forth quickly. "To your dressing room. Say she's your niece. Say her boyfriend dumped her, and tell people to get lost. I'll be there as soon as I can." Trystan tips his head to the side and looks at me. Our eyes meet. "Mari, listen to me. Whatever is wrong, I'll be there for you. I just need to separate for a second or people will see. Do you want them to know?"

I shake my head. "No." My voice is small, barely there.

"Me neither. It'll make everything a lot harder. I can barely handle things as they are. So stay with Tucker. I trust him, and I know you do, too. I'll see you in a few minutes." Trystan nods and runs off. When the workers around the stage ask what that was all about, Trystan flips into his charismatic mode. "Tucker's niece. Boyfriend problems. Plus I was screwing around earlier and broke a window. They thought she did it."

He shrugs like it doesn't matter and gets back up on stage. "Once more?"

The guy at the sound booth says, "From the top."

The chatter fades as Tucker walks me backstage with one arm draped over my shoulders. "Anything you need, Mari, I'm here for you. Remember that."

CHAPTER 8

Mr. Tucker was our English teacher in high school. It feels weird, sitting here with him like he's a friend. I guess he is, but the role he plays in Trystan's life is so much more. After everything that happened with Trystan's father, Tucker became the family Trystan never had, the family he needed.

When Trystan finally chose a record label and signed his contract, he asked Tucker to be his agent. That was only a few months ago. The two men seem to work well together, and their age difference is part of what helps Trystan find balance.

Trystan has always been afraid of damaging his life beyond repair. Tucker helps keep him focused and moving forward.

Tucker settles his massive body in a tiny chair and offers me the other one. His dressing room is more of an office. A computer sits on the ledge in front of the makeup mirror, with several pages of a legal-looking document taking up the rest of its surface. Several patches of highlighted text stand out against the stark white paper, and notes written in Tucker's handwriting litter the margins.

The room is simply constructed, with concrete walls and the same white flooring used in the emergency room where my parents work. The same emergency room where my mother died last night.

My eyes hurt. They're swollen, and my vision is blurry at the edges. I rub my eyes with the heels of my hands. I know I look like a train wreck, but I don't care.

Tucker leans back in his chair, pulls his keys from his pocket, and tosses them on the papers by the computer. "You guys can take my car and find someplace private to talk."

My head bobs, up and down as I stare blankly at a spot on the wall. I'm on autopilot, and my manners pop up because it seems like I should say something. "Thank you." My voice doesn't sound like me. I sound like a cat tried to claw its way up my throat. I swallow hard and try to clear it away, but that tight, raw feeling won't move.

Tucker folds his massive arms across his chest and watches me. "It's no problem. None, at all. We'll get you a badge for the future, so they'll let you in. I didn't think you'd come here. I should have thought of emergencies."

My eyes slide to the side, and I look at him. "This won't happen again, thank God."

"Either way, I'd rather you didn't have to crawl in through a broken window and get tased by security. I'll save that for Trystan." He smiles at me, joking, trying to ease the overwhelmed expression from my face.

We're quiet for a moment, and then he perks up and grabs a speaker. Tucker glances at me while looking for a button. "Would you like to hear him sing? He's almost done, but here—there it is."

And suddenly Trystan's voice fills up the room. He's talking, laughing. It sounds like he doesn't have a worry in the world—like nothing in his life is amiss, and yet I know that's not true. Trystan is all smiles and charm. He oozes charisma in waves. Women flock to him, wanting to be near him, while men wish they could become him. Most take the buddy seat and hope some of the chick overflow will spill in their direction.

"You know I won't say who it's about." Trystan says the words and I know there's a smile on his lips.

Another man is asking him, "Think about announcing it at the concert. Your fans will go insane. They've all been waiting to hear more about the girl you have a crush on."

Trystan laughs. It's that shy chortle that means he's uncomfortable. He'll deflect the question and redirect the man. I've watched Trystan charm his way out of anything. "Or maybe there is no girl and it's a marketing ploy? Where's my merchandising guy? He said something about having a mockup of this made."

"Your bracelet?"

"Yeah, it's unisex, and I'm always wearing it. The plan was to wear it during the concert and make a big deal out of it. There should be enough for the crew—and, of course, all the guys in the sound booth. I can't forget you guys."

"Awesome, man. I'll check on it and tell him to find Tucker."

"Great," Trystan says. "I'm on lunch break. See you this afternoon."

"Later!"

Tucker switches the speaker off. "He's something—a very talented young man."

"He is."

"He's also incredibly vulnerable." Tucker shifts his weight in the seat and leans forward, clasping one large hand in the other. "Maybe now isn't the best time to tell you, but I've hardly seen you over the past few weeks. Mari, I wanted to tell you I've been getting calls."

The look on Tuckers face worries me. "From who?"

He opens his mouth, ready to tell me when Trystan walks in. Tucker leans back and throws out his arms, beaming at his former student. "Here he is, the sexiest man alive!"

Trystan's cheeks redden as he stops in his tracks. His lips part and his eyes hit the floor. His dark hair falls forward, obscuring those gorgeous blue eyes. They're like sapphires today, radiant and bright. His mouth pulls to the side, and he looks up, pushing his hair out of his eyes. "This again? All right, but you can't keep asking, Tucker. Go ahead, bask in my presence."

Tucker chortles with that deep voice of his and pushes out of his chair. He grabs a stack of papers off the counter and steps toward the door. As he passes Trystan, he swats the rock star in the head. "Be back by two o'clock, smartass."

The corner of Trystan's lips pulls up into a lopsided grin. "Keys?"

"On the desk. Don't get a scratch on my baby, you hear me?"

I look at Tucker, not understanding. "Did you get a new car?"

"Nope, it's the same old Honda with the vintage rust and original peeling paint!"

"Now who's the wiseass?" Tucker laughs in response and heads out the door.

Trystan looks over at me and holds out his hand. I take it, and he pulls me into his arms and kisses my cheek. "Come on."

CHAPTER 9

We're sitting on the beach at Robert Moses State Park. The wind whips my hair and chills my skin. It's as if my senses are heightened and lessened at the same time. I feel everything and nothing at all. My mind doesn't know how to process all the conflicting sensations, or the anguish that continues to beat at me.

Trystan sits next to me on the sand, his arm wrapped around my shoulders. We stare at the leaves together and sit in silence. Trystan understands pain in a way most people don't. His childhood was short, and his father's anguish became his own. I rest my head against his shoulder. Trystan squeezes his fingers against my arm and holds me tight. He breathes deeply then releases it slowly before he speaks.

"I wish we'd known." It's as if he wants to say more, but doesn't know how—doesn't know what words to say.

"So do I." I managed to choke the words out even though they want to remain stuck in my throat. There's no way to undo the past, we both know that.

I watch as the waves crash into the sand, each crest appearing white and frothy before being obliterated. Each wave transforms from a complete high to nothing in a matter of seconds. My life feels like that right now. Last night was the best night of my life, and this morning was the worst morning of my life. It feels like I'm between two bookends and I don't know which way things are going to go for me. I thought I had more time to mend things with my mother. She was trying, and so was I, but now she's gone and it's too late.

Trystan takes his free hand and pushes his hair out of his face. The wind immediately blows it back, making it look messier than usual. His body has this lean, lazy way about it, but I know he's tense right now. I can feel it in his wrists, the way they feel tight, and the pressure of each finger on my arm feels as if he's trying to steady me, but also as if he's working to ensure I don't vanish.

"Are you going to the wake tonight?"

I stare at the sand and press my toes beneath the tiny grains. My gaze stays fixed on a point beyond my foot. "I don't know. I can't stand the thought of seeing my father. I don't want to talk to him. But at the same time I need to say goodbye to my mother. I don't know what to do."

Trystan is slow to reply, thinking over his words carefully. "There are times in life where we're forced to make decisions that affect everything. Now is one of those times, Mari. I know how hard you and your mother were working to fix your relationship. I wish I had a mom around to care so much about me." His voice catches in his throat as he says those words. "No matter what happens, no matter what your dad does, you know your mom loved you. Nothing on Earth can take that away from you. This is your chance to say goodbye, your chance to say the things you either weren't able to or always planned to say.

Mari, I'm not you, but I'm not sure I could pass that up."

I realize my face is wet, that tears have been streaking my cheeks throughout this entire conversation. I'm not breathless or sobbing, but I am crying. My soul is weeping, and there's no way to hide that. As much as I wish I didn't wear my heart on my sleeve, I do. I don't brush the tears away. I don't mind that Trystan sees them. I don't mind that he knows my heart is breaking. If there's anyone who can help me get through this, it's him. His childhood was an agonizing mess lacking things most people take for granted: a bed, warm meals, and a family that loves him. As a result, Trystan is incredibly sensitive to the things that make life worth living. It's not about having the most or the best, it's about the people in your life and the relationships you make. A big part of my trying to mend things with my mother is because of Trystan. I know I'm lucky to have him.

"Maybe I'll go in late after most people leave. I don't want to see all the people from dad's work using my mother's funeral to suck up to the boss. There may be a few people who cared about my mom there, though. I'm not sure who her real friends were. She was always with my dad, and he was always with her. They were so in love with each other they didn't see anyone else—me included. Nothing else mattered to them."

"You mattered to her. You can't convince me you didn't. I saw her face when she saw you perform on stage the night people found out my true identity." His hand drops from around my shoulders to find my hand and lace his fingers through it, squeezing hard. I feel his gaze on the side of my face. "That night people found out your true identity, too. They saw Mari Jennings, not the future Dr. Jennings, and your mother was there to support you."

I never thought of that night as a turning point for me, but it was. The night Trystan revealed he was Day Jones changed everything. I was there with him, standing on stage doing something I never thought I'd do, standing next to someone I was completely enamored with, but never dreamed I'd be in a relationship with.

Everything changed in the blink of an eye that night. The world discovered the true identity of the secretive Day Jones, and I found out I am so much stronger than I ever thought I was. He's right.

Trystan moves his long legs and pushes them out in front of him, as he threads his arm around my back and pulls me onto his lap. He holds me like that letting me be still, letting the peace of the moment transcend all my pain. I used to be afraid of how well he knew me, of how well Trystan could look at me and see what I was thinking. It's like he knew what I felt before I even said it. I was afraid of those things—I was afraid of him. In moments like this one, though, where I'm aching so badly I don't even know what I need, it's wonderful. His connection to me is a blessing. I used to fear he would sense my weaknesses and use them against me, but that was back before I knew who he really is.

I'm holding Trystan's hands, pressing the pad of my finger across his short nails. His calluses feel rough beneath my touch. My heart is swimming in my stomach. I open my mouth, still searching for the right words. "I never imagined I'd have to do this so soon. Trystan? Will you come to the funeral with me? I know it'll be a tight timeline for you, and I promised I'd be at your first concert, but I think it's best for me to say goodbye during the funeral and burial. I feel pulled in two directions at the same time. One is incredible, and the other is the most painful thing I've ever had to endure. It makes me feel totally crazy, but if you're there with me, I can do it. I feel like I can handle whatever is thrown at me with you by my side."

Trystan gathers me up in his arms and holds me tightly. His face is next to my ear, and he breathes words I need to hear so badly. "I will always be there for you. Through the good and the bad, all of it. I can promise you that."

_____

THE PRESENT

The memory of that day flashes behind my eyes, replaying like an old movie again and again.

I needed that. I needed to hear that promise. It's what gave me strength when weakness was consuming me. I put every hope on it, and ultimately that's what destroyed me—broken promises.

For years, I was angry and confused. I don't know what happened to us, why Trystan suddenly changed or why he never showed up. The funeral came and went with no sign of Trystan Scott. I faced the worst day of my life alone. He never gave an explanation for why he betrayed me. A few days later a picture appeared in Newsday that broke my heart. Taken the night of his first concert, it showed him in the arms of a stunning woman. The article said the two of them were a couple. There was even a quote from Trystan, claiming their new relationship held promise.

It was a knife in my heart when I was most vulnerable.

We never spoke again. All the things I never said suddenly bubble up inside me. I've kept those words tightly controlled within me for so long. Now I'll never get the chance to say any of it. I'll never know why he abandoned me. I'll never know for sure if he loved me.

My greatest fear with Trystan was that I was another conquest like every other girl before me. He seemed sincere. I thought so highly of him, and I was certain he'd never treat me like that—until he did.

The noise around me, the bustle of nurses rushing back and forth, attempting to avoid my father's fury, is muffled by the emotional tornado swirling within me. Part of me wants to scream at his dead body. I imagine myself standing over him, pounding my hands against his chest, and yelling at him for betraying me when I needed him most. The worst part was the "I told you so" from my father. He said over and over and over again that Trystan was a player, and I was the game. I never saw it coming.

My dad is still ranting next to me. He must've asked me a question because he's staring at the side of my face, waiting for an answer. "Are you listening to me? Do you think this is a joke? Do you think I get off on berating these people?"

"No, of course not." I make sure my face shows no emotion. I've learned that much over the years. The only way to handle Dad is to give him exactly what he wants, and for some reason he wants me for something now. "Where do you need me?"

The condemning look slips off Dad's face as he realizes he's in control once again. After Mom died, Dad's already cool nature turned colder. He seems only to find pleasure in controlling everything and everyone around him. Even his appearance is ruthlessly managed—his shoulders perfectly square, his spine perfectly straight, each hair falls perfectly into place on his head. My father would be an attractive man if he weren't so mean. People can't get past the condemnation in his gaze to see any good qualities he might possess.

That's what worries me. Right after I ask where he wants me, Dad looks at my face as if he's seeing me for the first time in forever. He's evaluating whether or not I'm up to this task. Part of me is annoyed, and part of me is surprised. Empathy is foreign to him, and sympathy is something he rarely exhibits. "Mari, I want you to handle the rest. Mr. Scott is in room four." He takes the clipboard he's holding and pushes it against my chest. Instinctively my arms come up and hold it.

My jaw drops open ever so slightly. I try to hide my shock, but this is cruel—even for him. How can he ask me to go in and do the postmortem paperwork on someone I loved?

It'd be like asking him to do this when mom died. Something cold comes up from within my stomach and freezes my ribs. I don't know if it's fear or loss, but it renders me silent. Dad can tell I'm searching for words, but before I can say anything, he points with one hand while pressing his other hand firmly on the back of my shoulder. He shoves me away, pushing me toward a reality I don't want to see.

I can't speak, but I managed to look over my shoulder at my father. He looks at me for a brief moment not filtering his disgust. I watch it appear and slip away like a thief in the night. That look straightens my spine and steels my nerves. I can't stand it when he thinks I'm weak.

I force one foot in front of the other and don't look back. A guard stands in front of the room, but he doesn't say anything. He saw my father shove me in this direction as did everyone else. It's obvious amongst the staff that I am the emergency room director's least favorite employee. Nepotism has no place here, and not a single person on this floor envies me. If anything, it's the opposite—they pity me for having such an asshole for a father.

H.M. WARD

I tell them it's not that bad. I tell them his apathy toward me is only here at work. I make them think he's a nice man at home, and his demeanor here is necessary for keeping the ER calm and running smoothly. I don't think they believe me. A few coworkers stop what they're doing and watch as I disappear behind the door. If they knew everything Trystan and I had been through they'd revolt. They'd attack my father with everything they could to prevent this. Rose senses something as she watches me. She knows my anxiety is higher than usual, but she doesn't know why. Her gaze meets mine briefly. I can't stand the look she gives me, so I push the door shut, creating a barrier between the rest of the world and myself.

My eyes scan the small room, studying the evidence of the fury of effort made to save his life. There are plastic wrappers, tape, and gauze scattered on the floor. On a rolling cart, in front of a pale, green curtain, I see a silver suture tray covered with the bloodied tools. I press my back to the door and breathe deeply. I never wanted this experience, but it provides the chance to say goodbye to my first and only love in private.

BROKEN PROMISES

Out of the corner of my eye, I catch the glint of metal amongst the discarded supplies on the floor. I lean over to pick it up and feel like I took a sucker-punch in the gut—it's the silver ring I gave Trystan back in high school. I run my finger across the bloodied Greek inscription, *η ψυχή μου είναι η ψυχή σου,* my soul is your soul. I blink back tears, and a sob escapes my lips.

I wrap my arms around my middle and take a deep breath. I'm suddenly very aware of my mouth and try to swallow, but the lump in my throat won't move. I slip the ring into the pocket of my scrubs and take a trembling step forward. My eyes stay fixed on that green curtain as I pull it open, pass through, and slide it closed again behind me. I want a moment with the rest of the world shut out to remember how it was once upon a time when we were a fairytale. Trystan saved me. I found myself when I was with him. He gave me a strength I didn't know I had, and he showed me what my life could be if I were brave enough to try. I hold the fabric curtain with my hand, clinging to it as if it were life itself, too afraid to turn around. I thought if given the chance I'd be angry. I thought I'd yell at him. That's not how I feel now.

My heart is racing in my chest, and I can't manage to get enough air in my lungs. My head droops, my eyes stare at my rainbow-colored Crocs, my lips part, and my heart pours out. "There are so many things I wish I could say to you, things about us, things about life. I didn't think it would be like this. I never thought..." Tears are stinging my eyes, threatening to fall down my cheeks, and my throat tightens, cutting off my speech. I can't find the right words to say, anyway. I hear ringing over and over in my head.

I never thought things would end like this.

I never thought I would lose you.

I never thought I would still love you.

I inhale and exhale slowly, feeling my body shake. I stand like that for a moment before I hear his voice, weak and soft, "You never thought what?"

CHAPTER 10

Startled, I swallow a scream and whirl around. I know that voice. I'd know it anywhere. I don't understand why I hear it. Part of me thinks I must be crazy, but my eyes tell me my ears are correct. I'm staring at a shirtless Trystan lying on a gurney with a towel draped across his hips. There's a gash on his forehead that still needs stitches. He's holding gauze to the wound to prevent the blood from dripping down his face. His pants and shirt, cut off him earlier by ER staff, lay discarded in a heap on the floor. One of his legs is in an Aircast walking boot, and the other one has a gash from his ankle up to his knee. His beautiful body is black and blue with bruises. In another lifetime, he was abused and battered. Those memories collide with this moment, and I want to scream, but can't force out sound around my shock.

Finally, I ask the obvious question because I don't know what else to say, "You're alive?"

Trystan blinks sleepily at me. "I didn't think you'd come."

I stare at him as if he'd said something absurd. "I thought you were dead!"

Trystan smiles but seems to regret it immediately. His face contorts with pain and his eyes close tight. "I'm afraid the rumors of my demise were greatly exaggerated."

My jaw hangs open and scrapes against the floor. I can barely blink, breathe, or think. Suddenly I'm speaking, no, yelling, and my arms flail wildly as my emotions get the better of me. "Don't you dare start bullshitting me! How could you do this? How could you do this to yourself and me? What other promises have you broken, Trystan? How far are you willing to fall?"

He winces before he opens his eyes. His gaze is intense, consuming, and I'm ensnared, unable to move. "You have no idea what you're talking about."

"I think I do. I was there, remember? I saw your father beat the shit out of you. I saw what he did with your stuff. I saw that you had no home, no food, no bed, no clothes—all because that crazy bastard drowned himself in alcohol every night. You said that wouldn't be you. You promised you would never drink anything, that you wouldn't turn into him, yet here you are."

"We can't stray from the paths on which fate places us. I can't be someone I'm not, Mari, no matter how highly you think of me— no matter what ghosts you think you see." He still speaks in poems. His voice is just as hypnotic as it was all those years ago, but I can hear the strain in his voice. Trystan is a survivor—he always has been—but tonight something sent him speeding into a tree. I want to know what it was. I want to know what spooked him badly enough to make the most stupid decision of his life.

"You have no right to talk to me like that. Don't spew fancy words at me and expect I'll drop my panties for you again. Fool me twice, shame on me."

"You were never the fool. I was." Trystan looks up at the ceiling, barely blinking, as he speaks. He keeps the bandage pressed against his forehead with one hand while the other rests on his side. His dark hair is crusted over with blood near the hairline. I'm surprised my father didn't shave it.

"I can't argue with you there." My voice grows colder by the moment. I don't want to have this conversation. I don't want to be in this room with him. Suddenly, things I wished for when I thought he was dead rush away with the tide of my emotions. I finally understand why my father sent me in here. I've grown especially skilled at suturing wounds. I've been studying methods of stitching skin back together in a way that diminishes scarring. There's no one here better at it than I am. That's why he asked for me. That's why my father called me here. He's not the bastard I thought he was. It's practical.

I grab the things I need and fall silent as I ready them on a tray next to Trystan's bed. As I move to examine the wound, Trystan releases the gauze, brushing his hand against mine.

"I still see your face when I close my eyes." He sounds tired and beaten.

Steel yourself Mari. Just fix him and walk away. Let his words roll off like the meaningless drivel they've always been.

I refuse to feel anything for him. I've been down this road before, and it ends with Trystan running the other way. I won't relive the past. We have different lives now. We're different people. Trystan stills as I work on him. I try to keep my mind on work, on the practical nature of this job. I try not to think about how nice his skin feels, to ignore the relentless charge between us. Every time I brush against his skin my stomach flutters. I ignore it and focus harder on my work.

Trystan can't seem to stay still or be quiet. He squirms again even though I know the anesthetic keeps him from feeling anything. "Stop wiggling."

"Sorry. Your touch is—"

I cut him off, "Don't."

But he doesn't listen. "It's the same. It's everything—darkness and light, stars and moonlight spilling down from the heavens into your hands. It's perfect." His gaze is fixated on my face, his eyes burning with intensity, willing me to look at him.

Resisting the urge, I continue to close the wound. "That's nice."

Trystan continues speaking in verse, saying things I don't quite understand. "Smooth, supple grace hides the turmoil brewing within, but it's there —it's still there— dusk after dusk, dawn after dawn. Doesn't that make you wonder?"

I refuse to catch his gaze. It's bad enough that I have to touch him, but if I look him in the eye, I have no idea what I'll say. In the past, when our eyes met and our skin touched, it felt like he could read every thought, every feeling moving within me. I still feel that connection sparking between us.

"There's nothing to wonder about," I say, finishing the sutures.

Trystan smiles and laughs. It's a familiar sound, one that makes me remember better times with him. I can't help it. My gaze lifts and aligns with those beautiful blue eyes. For a moment, I'm taken back to when I first realized he liked me. It took him so long to convince me he was sincere. I thought he was. I wish I knew why he left me when I needed him most. Minutes pass, but it feels like hours lost in each other's gaze, swimming in a sea of things that never were.

"Are you going to ask me?" Trystan's voice is soft and remorseful. I know exactly what he's referring to because I'm considering whether to ask or not.

My lips part and I want to speak, I want to ask him—but I can't. I already know the answer. He left me for someone else, which meant he was never sincere, he never cared about me, and—worst of all—he never loved me. Trystan can't help who he is. Women flock to his radiating confidence, to the poetic way he speaks. He's different than anyone else I've ever met. He always has been.

I shake my head and lower my eyes to his chest thinking that will break the spell, but it doesn't. It makes the sensation inside me grow larger. There's something at the core of my being that pulls me toward him. It has always been there and won't go away no matter what happens between us. Our souls are anchored together, and we are too close to deny it.

My eyes scan the toned muscles of his chest remembering the last night we were together. I touched every inch of his body, learned every curve of muscle. The pads of my fingers felt the rise and fall of his chest as he breathed. His strength, his passion, everything was mine that night. I shake my head to clear the thought from my mind. Walking down that path will be too painful, but that doesn't stop him from calling me back.

"It's not what you think." Trystan's lashes lower and then raise. He fights to remain focused on me, but I know the drugs are pulling him under. He won't be awake much longer.

I grab the rest of what I need and start to clean up some of his wounds. Trystan continues to speak, saying things I don't think of during daylight.

"Everyone thinks they know me, Mari. The truth is very few people know me in a way that matters. Even fewer people truly like me. It's been lonely since Tucker died. There are personalities in this world existing purely to do good, steering us onto paths too steep and narrow to climb alone. Tucker helped me take my life in a different direction, but I walked up the mountain alone. There are very few things that truly frighten me and being alone is one of them. I'm alone, Mari. Morning after morning, there's no one around me except people who want something from me. I'm at the top of this precipice alone. I don't even belong here and, since Tucker died, I've tried to stay on this path, but I can't. I'm not cut out for this."

I can't help it. There's no way for me to listen to him speak like that and say nothing. "You're not alone Trystan."

He lifts his dark lashes, his sapphire gaze meeting mine. He watches me for a moment, sensing my sincerity, before speaking. Taking a deep breath, he breathes, "I'm not?"

Inwardly I'm still battling my inner bitch who wants to castrate him for all the pain he put me through, but the kind girl living inside my brain kicks her ass and replies. "No, you're never alone."

I shift positions to examine his other wounds and check for a second gash on his hairline. Lifting a piece of sterile gauze dipped in cleaning solution, I go to wash the dried blood from his hair, but Trystan reaches for my wrists and stops me. My heart beats faster, and my breath catches in my throat. I've been touching him all this time, and feeling the pull between us, but when he touches me, it's a million times worse. I'm about to start shaking, desperate to pull away. The intense feeling of his touch has amplified over the years. It courses through my body, lighting me on fire and sending a spark across every inch of my skin.

Before I can move Trystan speaks. "I thought I'd never talk to you again. I thought I'd never see you again."

"Same here." My heart thumps one beat at a time. Why is it so hot in here? I can't think. His hands are on me. The memory of skin on skin, of our sweat-covered bodies moving together fills my mind. It's too much. It's like he's channeling the thought in me. Gasping, I pull my hands away and stare at him with my lips parted and my hands shaking.

"Mari, there's something I've been dying to tell you. For the longest time, I've wanted to say it, to explain—" he presses his lips together and swallows hard.

I want to know so badly. I want to know why he walked away from me. I want to know why he slammed his car into a tree. I want to know all the things I missed. Something within me is crying out for him, still craving his touch, still wishing the sound of his voice filled my ears. A shiver crawls up my spine, attacks my shoulders, and travels down my arms. My jaw hangs open with words ready to roll off my tongue. I notice the clock in the room ticking louder as my pulse roars in my ears. My chest rises and falls faster and faster.

Trystan watches me, looking up at me from the cold bed. His breath lifts his body making his beautiful chest rise and fall. There's a cut on his lip that's covered in dried blood. I don't know why I do it, but I change directions, leaning toward his mouth, carefully dabbing at the cut until it's clean. I'm so close that his scent fills my head. I wish I could stay in this place, I wish I could lie against his chest and feel his arms wrap around me once more. I'm frozen in time, staring at his mouth when the door to the room bangs open and someone barges through it yelling and cursing at Trystan.

I stand up straight and whirl around to meet the sound. Standing in front of me is a man in a black suit and shoes so shiny they look like glass. He's tall, thin, and twice my age. His face is red, contorted with anger, and he rushes at Trystan. Security is close behind.

"What the fuck are you thinking? Do you know what this means for the project? You dumb little shit! Do you have any idea?"

I stand there for a second, stunned, before I remember myself. "Sir, you need to leave!"

I step between them and put my hands on my hips, glaring at the man. He laughs. "Bedded her already, Trystan? Can't you keep it in your pants for five goddamn seconds to take care of work? This project," he says waving a folder of papers through the air, "starts next week!" I see something printed on the tab on the top of the folder, but the guy is waving it around so much I can't read what it says. "Tell me you're not the asshole I think you are. Tell me you know your fucking lines." The man is looking over my shoulder, glaring at Trystan.

I'm too short to block his view, and he ignores me like I'm the nobody he thinks I am. Fuck that. I snap my fingers in his face. When he looks down at me, I let him have it. I shove my finger into his chest and push hard. "No one talks to my patients like that in this ER. Get your ass out the door before I have security throw you out!"

He laughs. The dumbass laughs in my face. "Women always get this way around him. I hate to break it to you, honey, but Trystan Scott doesn't give a shit about you. He's talking about someone else. He always talks about her when he's like this, so don't think he's into you. That little shit isn't into anyone except himself." He screams over my shoulder again, yelling at Trystan, "You cost us millions, you little prick! You should have—hey!"

I lose it. I've never done anything like this in my life, but suddenly my clipboard is in my hands, and I swing right at the guy's head. I clock him with the backside of the clipboard above his ear. "I SAID GET OUT! LEAVE! NOW!"

He retreats one step with each word I say. He cowers as he backs away from me, covering his ear, which leaves the other ear wide open.
WHACK

I hit the other side and rise on my toes to scream in his face. "GET THE HELL OUT OF MY ER AND NEVER COME BACK!" My eyes narrow to thin slits and I'm ready to claw his face off.

Security arrives as the man crosses the threshold of the room. "You crazy bitch! You hit me! I'll tell your supervisor and have you fired before you can blink. Get a doctor in here now!"

Tipping my head to the side, I smile. "I am a doctor. Get the fuck out."

The man works his jaw and looks back at the security guards who are reaching for his arms. He shakes them off, angrily glaring at Trystan over my shoulder. "Here's the fucking script. You better show up, and if makeup can't cover that mess on your face you're in deep shit, kid!" He throws the folder over my shoulder into the room, papers flying everywhere.

"Enough of that," the guard says, pulling the guy by the elbow and turning him around. He's swearing, but I'm no longer listening. I slam the door shut and turn around, pressing my back to it, breathing hard.

Trystan is sitting up and looks like he's about to fall over. He must have tried to stand. His head sways in a circle as his eyes flutter closed. His hand touches his head, and he falls to the side. I rush at him, managing to get there before he falls to the floor. "Trystan, you can't get up. You've got a lot of medicine in your system. Don't sit up. Don't stand, okay?"

My arm is under his shoulder as I lay him back down on the table. When I pull away, he holds onto my hand for a second. "Thanks, for that."

I try not to smile, but I can't help it. "Dad is going to kill me. I hit that man with a clipboard."

The corners of Trystan's lips twitch as he adds, "Twice."

We both laugh for a moment, and when the room goes silent, I look down at the papers on the floor. Bending down, I pick one up. It's a script. Holding up the sheet, I ask, "What was this all about, anyway?"

Trystan sighs and closes his eyes. He presses a hand over his eyes and tells me. "That asshole was a representative of the studio filming a movie I'm supposedly doing. We start shooting next week. There was shit I was supposed to be at last week, but I blew it off."

"Why?"

His eyelids lower, and those long dark lashes obscure his gaze. He glances to the side for a beat and then back up at me, grinning. "I can't learn my lines." He shrugs, and then winces. "I haven't acted since high school. That was almost a decade ago, and I had help—Tucker and you. Agreeing to do this film was a mistake. I can't focus on the words, and nothing is sticking—not a single phrase. That's why he was pissed. Plus I ruined my face."

"Your face will be fine. You had the best doctor around stitch you up. They can cover that with your hair and the makeup department can hide any bruising still visible when filming starts." I'm quiet for a moment, thinking.

"That part doesn't matter as much. They needed me, and this isn't going to happen. My agent is going to be pissed." Trystan sucks in air and releases it swiftly.

Before I have too much time to think, I say it. "I'll help you. I'll run lines with you."

Trystan drops his arm and looks at me, stunned. His dark brows bunch together and his lips part slightly. He pushes up on his elbow a little, lifting his head off the bed. "Why would you do that for me?"

My stomach is in my throat. I don't want to think about why I said that. The answer is somewhere inside of me, but I'd rather not face it this second. So I smirk and shrug. "Because you need a friend, and so do I."

"You do?"

I nod. "Yeah, besides—if you don't listen, I'll get to slap you with my clipboard."

He smiles at me, lying back and closing his eyes. After placing his hands on his abs and lacing his fingers together, he opens one eye, and says, "You're such a badass, Mari. I like this side of you."

CHAPTER 11

Tired doesn't begin to describe how I feel as I get ready to leave the ER. My limbs feel as if they are made of lead—I can barely move. I'm stiff all over, and my feet are dragging as I hand Rose the rest of my paperwork, ready to head out.

"So," she says without glancing up at me from behind the desk or accepting my paperwork. Her fingers move swiftly across the keyboard for a few seconds before she lifts her gaze.

I know what she's getting at, and I'm too tired to get into it right now. "So."

"Are you going to tell me? Or do I have to dust off my sleuthing hat?"

I lift a brow at her. "You have a sleuthing hat?"

"It's metaphorical, and don't you dodge the question."

"I'm sorry. I missed the question, and I'm tired. I'm leaving, Rose." I force my folders into her hands and swipe my card through the time clock.

Rose stays in her chair and makes one of those old lady noises that makes me want to spill my guts. "Mmm-um. Well, you know where to find me when you're ready to come clean about your past with that boy."

I laugh lightly. "No one has called Trystan Scott a boy in nearly a decade."

"I'm old enough to be his mother, so he's still a boy to me. And you're a girl, and it's plain enough to see you two have a history. What happened after high school?"

My jaw drops and I slap my hands down on the counter. Another nurse looks up at me, startled. I lean in toward Rose and whisper-yell. "Did you Google me? Why would you do that?" My voice is way too high. I might as well confess. Whatever she's thinking will be way worse than what actually happened with Trystan.

"I did not Google you! I Googled him. Then I read his Wiki page and happened to see that he also attended your high school, which I recall because I already know everything about you. So, is there a juicy story there, Mari? A sordid love affair with the rock star before he became someone?" She's trying not to smile and folds her hands under her chin.

"Oh, God! Rose, you're off base here. And don't smile, your face will crack." I start looking for my keys. They should be on the counter, but they aren't. Damn it, Mitchell!

Rose laughs. "Come on, you know something about him, or you wouldn't be acting all squirrelly. Lay it on me. I'm an old lady and need to live vicariously through you young people." She tips her head to the side and grins. I know if I don't offer something she'll hound me until I crack, so I throw her a bone.

I make a sound in the back of my throat and flop my head on her desk. "Yes, we were in high school together. We got locked in a closet once. Fun times." I lift my head and grin. "I'll tell you about it sometime."

Her lips form a big O and her dark eyes nearly fall out of her face. "You did not do that to an old woman!"

"You're not old, Rose!" I turn and start to walk away.

She calls out behind me. "And don't I know it. I'm your younger, tanner sister from back in the day. We're twins separated at birth."

The corner of my mouth pulls up. I turn, walking backward as I say, "That means Dr. Hardass is your dad, too. I'll be sure to get you a seat at the dinner table, right next to him." No one likes sitting next to Dad when he eats. Everything has to be perfectly displayed—all outlines squared off to his napkin, plate, and placemat. When he eats in the cafeteria, he does the same thing—and yes, he brings a placemat, because he's him.

Rose frowns and wags a finger at me. "I meant to say step-sister. Yeah. That makes more sense, especially considering you don't like crawfish. Who doesn't like crawfish?" She shakes her head like it's weird.

"Good night, Rose! I need to find Mitchell before he leaves. The guy has my keys."

"Oh, he's already gone, honey."

I stop and look back at her. "And my keys?"

She shrugs. "He didn't give them to me."

"Crap." Annoyed, I rush outside into the early morning air. The sun isn't quite rising yet, so the sky is still that dark blue.

The cop that told me not to park at the entrance earlier is still there. He smiles and walks over to me, stepping lightly as if he were dancing. "Good evening, DOCTOR Jennings."

I stare at him for a second and then blurt out. "You towed my car, didn't you?"

He smacks his lips and makes a popping sound, before leaning in close to me. "I sure did. The Suffolk County police force is not your personal valet, Doc. I couldn't leave my station, and you were in a red zone."

"So I know whether or not to kick Mitchell's ass—did he come out here?"

He shoots me a wide grin, no teeth showing. The cop tucks his arms under his elbows and nods once. "I might remember someone trying to find the keys, but they weren't in the ignition. Damnedest thing happened after that, a tow truck just happened to show up."

I groan and stare at him. "Why do you hate me?"

"Why do doctors act like they're better than everyone else?"

"I didn't do that."

"You tossed me your keys like I was a servant. Word to the wise—if you're not careful, you'll turn into your old man."

I cringe. "Fine, you're right. I was an ass before. Let me make it up to you. There's a Dunkin' Donuts down the street."

He laughs. "Wiseass."

"Maybe. Okay, I'm headed home, right after I call a cab. And, I'm sorry about before. I didn't mean to come off like that. It's been a really weird night." As I finish the sentence, a limo pulls up behind me. The headlights shoot two narrow beams of light through the dark parking lot.

A tinted window slides down, and Trystan peers out at me. "Need a ride, Doc?"

The cop tenses, as if he were trying not to go totally fangirl in front of Trystan Scott.

I'm too tired to say no, and I don't want to call a cab to pick me up. Last time I rode home at this hour, the guy talked about pickles the whole time. I think he was trying to make innuendos, or maybe he'd actually pickled his thingy. Either way, I'd rather not live through another weird late-night cab ride.

"Yeah, that'd be great." I head over to the limo, open the door, and poke my head inside. "Do you have water or food or something?"

Trystan nods and hands me a brown paper bag. "The driver grabbed me breakfast, but I'm too queasy to eat it. Egg and cheese on a roll with a side of bacon." I don't mean to, but I smile. It's a meal he frequently ate in high school.

"Thanks. One second." I accept the bag and cup of coffee Trystan hands me, then walk it over to the cop. "Will you accept an apology breakfast? I hope you like bacon."

The man's face lights up as he peers into the bag. "Who doesn't?" He pulls out a crispy piece of greasy goodness and shoves it into his mouth as I head back to the car. "Dr. Jennings," he calls. I glance back at him. "Thanks."

When I slip into the car next to Trystan, I'm too tired to realize this should be awkward. I slump back in the seat and put my arm over my face. "I didn't turn into my father today. Wooh-eee." I twirl a finger in the air.

Trystan snorts. "Is that something you worry about?"

"Not until recently. When people start saying, 'you're like your father' and that's the last thing you want to hear, there's no way to ignore it, you know?"

His voice is soft. "I do."

I drop my arm and sigh in my seat, staring at this man, wondering about which ways he's changed and which ways he's the same. I know one answer to that question. The Trystan I knew wouldn't touch liquor—not even if his life depended on it. Alcohol was the antithesis of what he wanted from his life—he thought he might as well be chugging down poison. So, how did he get to this point?

The intercom buzzes and the driver asks where we're going. Before I can reply, Trystan says, "Home."

CHAPTER 12

~TRYSTAN~

What the hell am I doing? I touch my hand to my forehead, thinking I'll push my hair out of my face and wince. Stitches. I can't seem to remember they're there and my hand always goes to my face in front of Mari. If I don't cover my eyes, I swear she can look right through me. There's still that spark in the air around her, even doped up I can sense it. It has my skin prickling and my nerves on edge.

She blinks those beautiful brown eyes at me and stutters. "Wait, what? We can't go back to your place. Trystan." She scolds me, and that tone is everything I remember. If I didn't know better, I'd think she still cared about me, but after what I did to her—well, I'm certain she hates me. Mari was never one to leave a half-dead animal on the side of the road. She's a healer at heart and wants to ease the pain in the people around her. Maybe I took advantage of that while in the hospital.

"Don't Trystan me. Not right now." I slump back into the seat and try to ignore the pounding in my head and the dull screaming coming from my leg. Maybe I shouldn't have ripped out the IV before they gave me another round of pain meds. "I can't take you home, they'll follow us."

Looking between my fingers, I see her face scrunch up. There are little wrinkles around her nose when she does it. I've kissed that nose and held those hands. I wish I could feel her touch now and fall asleep in her lap. My time with Mari was the happiest time of my life. Since then, everything's gone to shit. Career or not, money doesn't matter if you have food in your belly and a roof over your head. Cash is a double-edged sword—it provides power, but it steals friendships. Half the people around me are only there hoping to make it big.

Fuck. I can't do this. Why'd I pick her up? I groan and pinch the bridge of my nose.

Her voice is soft, as if she thinks I'm close to breaking. "Don't do that. As it is, you have the start of a nasty black eye." I don't move. I remain slouched back against the Italian leather of the limo, my chin tipped up toward the roof, eyes closed. I can't look at her. Not now, not tonight. As the fog from the pain meds clears, that feeling comes creeping back. It claws at my neck and steals my air. My heart races like I'm running from a mob of fans and it won't slow down.

Her voice breaks through my thoughts. Her hand touches my forearm, and those small fingers delicately brush against my skin. Each hair feels her presence and stands on end, shooting an inhuman charge up my arm and into my heart. I jerk away without meaning to, without wanting to. I drop my hand and look at her. Those dark curls are wild, forcefully tamed into a sloppy ponytail, small ringlets escaping to hang by her temples.

She's the same, but she's changed too. Instead of soft round cheeks, her face has become angular and more defined. I remember her skin being freckled, but now I see only a spattering of light freckles across the bridge of her nose as if she'd been in the sun yesterday. Her neck is thinner and seems more alluring than I recall. My gaze drifts too far south and for half a beat I'm ogling her breasts, wondering what they'd feel like under those scrubs. They're bigger, rounder. I'm not too sure why since she's thinner than when we were together. I hope she didn't get a boob job because she didn't need one. Mari was already perfect. I lift my gaze to meet hers and realize I'm in deep shit.

I clear my throat and break our locked gaze. I don't want her reading me so easily. She'll figure out what I did and then all that pain will have been for nothing. "When we get back to my place, we can separate. The press won't see you leave. You can go home without having them in tow. I'm sorry about this." That last part comes rushing out, and I immediately wish I hadn't said it.

Mari snaps, "Sorry about what exactly? Nearly killing yourself? Potentially killing someone else? Or just being incredibly stupid?" She works her jaw as if she has so much more to say, but bites it back.

I stare at nothing and wish I felt nothing, but I don't. My heart is dying inside my chest. I've lost too many good people. I can't… I press my eyes together tightly and swallow the scream that's building inside of me. I reach for the crystal tumbler at the bar and the decanter filled with amber liquid.

Mari laughs and swats my hands. "Are you insane?"

"You don't understand." I glare at the dark carpet, trying not to yell at her.

"Then tell me. Talk to someone, but don't get drunk again. God, Trystan, what the hell happened to you? It's like you've lost yourself or something."

Nope, my heart is alive and still beating in my chest because her words put a knife through it. I didn't think I could hurt more than I already did. I was wrong.

Mari is sitting across from me on the long bench and scoots to the edge. She takes my hand in hers and rubs her thumb on the back of my wrist. She tips her head to the side until I meet her gaze. "What happened tonight?"

I sit there like that, wishing things weren't the way they are, but I can't change it no matter how much I want to—my first instinct is to lie, but I can't, not to Mari. My lip trembles, I feel it quiver as I try to grin and make up a bullshit story.

She sees it coming and squeezes my hand. "Trystan, don't lie to me. I feel it. I know something horrible happened. Telling me can't make it worse."

Our gazes lock and I can't look away. I can't lie to her or blow off her concern. I can't charm my way around her question either. She knows what I'm feeling. My emotions are hemorrhaging, and the physical connection between us only amplifies my pain. I rip my eyes from hers and pull my hand back. I can still feel her touch on the back of my hand.

"I can't. Not yet."

Mari is quiet. I can feel the words she wants to say drift through the air, but she doesn't say any of them. Eventually, her lips close. She makes a decision and moves into the seat next to me. "Come here." Her arms are open, waiting for me to fall into them. All I have to do is move toward her, or show that I want her here, but I'm frozen. I've missed her touch so much, craved it, dreamt about it, and lusted for her caresses long after I left her.

Now that she's here offering comfort, I can't accept. The turmoil within won't shut up. Part of me knows it's a fucking hug. Take it, moron! The other part knows it means more than that—to her and me. Say no! Don't put her through this again. It's beyond cruel to do this to her twice.

Swallowing hard I shake my head once and move away from her. Fuck, it looks like I punched her in the stomach. Her certainty fades as she shrinks back and presses her hands to the seat, backing herself into the corner of the limo. I'm an asshole, I know I am, and she shouldn't be here.

I look over at her, but I don't ask her to elaborate. I can feel it. The air is thick with remorse, regret, and pain.

She sighs and rubs her eyes. The look on her face makes me think she's going to drop an anvil on my head. "Promise me I won't lose you, too, no matter what's happening."

Lose me? She doesn't have me. She doesn't want me. Why would she even say that? Pity? Either way, she has my attention. I sit up a little. "Are you ok? Did something happen to Katie?" Our mutual love for Katie and Seth is the only bond we have in common anymore.

Mari shakes her head and swallows hard. She glances out the window, composing herself before looking back at me. "It's not Katie."

My jaw tightens as my stomach churns. I know what happened before she says it, but I can't hear this now. Not tonight. I double over to keep the contents of my stomach down and to hide the panic on my face. My pulse hammers in my ears, getting faster and faster. My body breaks out in a cold sweat, and I'm shaking. I try to hold still, but I can't. My chest feels too tight to breathe.

Suddenly Mari's hand is on my back, and her voice is warm in my ear. "I haven't heard for certain yet, but Seth was on the phone with Katie when something went wrong. I thought you should hear it from me before someone else told you. He might be alive, Trystan…"

Her voice sounds far away like she's at the other end of a subway tunnel. The buzzing in my head grows louder and drowns out her voice. I can't do this. I can't.

Before I know what's happening, she's shoving a glass in my hand and telling me to drink. I tip back the crystal cup and feel the liquor burn down my throat. I cough once as I realize what she did and glance over at her, shocked.

Mari shrugs. "Sometimes a drunk needs a drink. And sometimes his ex needs one, too." She takes the glass from me, puts it to her lips, tips her head back, and swallows the rest. When she finishes, she puts down the glass and claws at her face. "I've been waiting to hear from Katie. I wanted to go with her to Seth's mom's house, but then I got the call for you. I thought you were dead, Trystan! I got there, and they said you were gone." She looks everywhere except at me, trying to smile, but her eyes are too glossy, and her voice is too strained to be believable.

I lift my hand to reach for hers and hesitate. I can't touch her. It'll put me back in a place I can't be. I close my eyes for a moment and say the only words that will come. "I'm sorry. I'm so sorry, Mari."

The distance between us feels like a chasm. I can't stand it anymore. I'd jump out of the car to avoid it, and the pain that follows in its wake. I don't think before I speak. My heart gets ahead of my brain. "Stay with me until we find out. Being alone right now probably isn't good for either of us."

That's when I realize it—she's not alone. She has her Dad, Katie, and a slew of friends I don't know.

I feel her big brown eyes on the side of my face. I can hear her voice, timid and hurt, asking me over and over again—why did you leave me? Why did you hurt me? Why did you break my heart?

The same three things repeat over and over again, but then her voice cuts through the unspoken questions. "I can stay for a little while."

CHAPTER 13

Chills race up my spine as the elevator doors open, revealing the foyer of my penthouse. Mari remains behind me, standing in the spot my shadow would be if it were daylight. She twists her hands together nervously, not rushing into the room the way most of my fake friends do. Her gaze remains glued to the floor and her lips part like she wants to say something, but she doesn't speak. I swallow hard and step forward into my empty apartment high above Manhattan.

I don't come here very much anymore.

What once felt like a fantasy, now feels like a prison. The ornate furniture, million-dollar paintings, and reclaimed hardwood floor once excited me, but now they remind me there's no way out of this life. I don't complain—how could I? I'd seem like a total ingrate if I bitched about being rich.

I never wanted fame, though. People who knew me back when I was a kid remember a false version of me. They saw me as a showman, a charismatic speaker—that guy isn't me. He was an act, a mask devised to hide the pain surging through my heart on a daily basis.

Even though my mother left before I was two, my father always blamed me for her leaving. He'd get home from the factory at night back when I was in high school, pick up a bottle of booze, and get wasted. Nights were the hardest.

Mari was with me when life with my dad was the worst. It still shames me to think of what she had to do, of the situations I forced her into. But that was a lifetime ago—why are these feelings popping up now and mingling with the present? The anguish and remorse I felt then are still buried deep in my chest, trying to claw their way out.

I walk past an antique Paul Revere credenza, tossing my keys into the silver Tiffany bowl sitting on top as I pass. The old saying, 'once poor, always poor,' isn't true. There was a time I didn't have money for clothes, yet now I could build a bonfire out of cash in Rockefeller Center without feeling its loss.

Mari keeps her chin tucked as she walks into the room, hesitant to look around. She wrings her hands in front of her and swallows hard. I wish she weren't so nervous, that she could trust me like she used to, but that will never happen again. Not after what I did to her. Things are as they should be, and she has her own life now. She's not another casualty of Trystan Scott.

It's bad enough that Seth might be gone. The only reason he was in the Marines in the first place was because of me—it was my idea to enlist and get the fuck out of town. I thought it was my only chance to escape my dad, the only way out of the hell that was my life. But then my emotions got the better of me, and I wrote that song for her—for the woman standing next to me. After that, everything changed.

Fame has a price that no one understands until they're famous. My life isn't mine anymore. My life belongs to my fans. I traded one trapped existence for another. Each day I coax myself to go a little bit longer, a little bit further. I'm at the peak of my career and the middle of a contract, so there's no way I can walk away. It doesn't matter how much I want to fade into the background and disappear. That's not my life.

"Would you like a drink?" Startled, Mari looks up at me with those big brown eyes, and I wish I could hold her in my arms and tell her everything will be okay. Instead, I'm acting like a fucking hostess.

She offers a fake smile, as if it's painful for her to force up the corners of her mouth. "Water please," she says, finally managing to speak.

"I'll grab it. Please sit down." I extend my hand toward the charcoal gray couch. It looks like suede, but it's not. It's something that cost more and didn't harm any animals. It's also excessively masculine, like the rest of the place.

The decorator used warm neutrals, woods, and stone. Think of a rustic, pioneer cabin built with a billion bucks, and that's my apartment. Sometimes I long for my twin bed and empty room. Life was so much simpler then. If my Dad weren't a factor, I'd miss it.

I pad stiffly into the hugeass kitchen. Here the décor switches to French industrial—if that's even a thing. Everything is stainless, concrete, and hand carved stone. I walk over to a refrigerator case filled with Voss water and grab two glass bottles, before heading back to the living room.

As I pass through the doorway, I see Mari standing toward the middle of the room with her jaw dropped, caught between tears and a panic attack. Her eyes stare at a frame, glowing slightly in the dimly lit room. I didn't even think of that. Shit. There are Mari relics all over the place in here. It's the only thing that made this mausoleum feel like home.

I rush to stand between her and the frame, pushing the bottle into her hands. "Here you go. Water. In a bottle."

"Ah, the fancy kind."

"Exactly."

She doesn't step away from the frame and her eyes keep drifting over my shoulder to look at it. I twist off the cap and chug half the bottle, before placing it on a glass end table and flopping backward onto the couch. My intention had been to sit up, but today has sucked so hard that I lie back and cover my face with my arm instead.

I hear her voice from across the room. "You kept this?"

"Obviously." Dick answer, Scott.

"Why?"

"Why do I have half the shit that's in this room? Do you think I like all this stuff? The decorator found it and threw it up. That's it. There's not much of a story. Your paper was the right color, and she liked your handwriting." It's total bullshit, but I can't let her know anything. We'll end up back where we started, and I'm not doing that to her again. I already fucked up her life once.

Mari is quiet too long. When I slide my arm off my face, I prop myself up on one elbow. She has her phone pressed to her ear. She must have dialed Katie. "Who are you calling?"

The apartment is so still I can hear her breathe. Mari doesn't reply. Instead, she swallows hard and waits. That's when I hear it. A cell phone rings back in my bedroom. With each ring, Mari steps toward me. On the third ring, she turns her iPhone toward me so I can see the screen: MARI'S OLD BAT PHONE

Shit. How do I explain why I still have that?

Mari ends the call, and the ringing stops. Her dark brow lifts high on her face, and she sits next to me, her dark eyes cutting to the side to study me. "So, you either kept a throwaway phone from years ago, or you upgraded it and kept the number. That's an interesting thing to do."

"I'm an interesting guy." I laugh it off as if it has no significance, but it does. I kept that number because it was hers. She gave it to me when I had nothing, and I couldn't get rid of it.

"No one would say otherwise. I mean, you'd have to be pretty interesting to be THE Trystan Scott. I hear he's something else, you know?" She grins at me and almost rolls her eyes. Then that gaze drifts to the stitches on my face and her smile falters. "Why didn't you call me tonight?"

Sucker punch. Straight to the gut. I didn't see it coming. I drape my arm over my face and groan. "Not now, Mari. Tonight was bad enough without hashing out all our crap, too."

"No," she reaches over and pulls my wrist, jerking my arm upright. Mari pulls hard, but I don't help her, so I remain slumped on the couch. "I mean it. You were supposed to call me if things got bad, but I haven't heard from you once in all this time."

"Mari," I warn her, and my voice drops to that place where it nearly rumbles. She has no idea what she's poking, what demons could escape. I do. "I can't invite the past into the present. Not tonight. Not now. Leave it alone for another day, that's all I ask. The past few days have been overwhelming enough—what if Seth is dead? He's only over there because of me, Mari. If he's dead, it's my fault. This whole vat of shit is my fault!"

Her face pinches then softens. "No, it's not. Trystan, Seth is a grown man. He didn't follow you to a cliff and let you toss him off."

"Just because it's metaphorical doesn't mean it's not real."

"That's exactly what it means, Trystan!" She laughs and smiles at me. My wrist is still in her hand. The next thing she does is so far beyond fathomable, I nearly jump out of my skin. Mari takes that hand and pulls it away from my body enough to lie down on the couch next to me. When she's in the crook of my arm, we both stare at the ceiling like this isn't freaking us out.

The last time I was this close to Mari, I was with her. It was the only time we were together before I walked away. I press my eyes closed and suck in a jagged breath. She's going to notice the shiver that keeps drifting up my spine, but I don't ask her to move. I can't ask her that.

"Do you remember this?" Her voice is wistful, lost in the past. She's looking at the ceiling, a serene look on her face.

Her scent fills my head, and I swear I catch the scent of the strawberry lip gloss she wore in high school. "Yeah, I do." At first I think she's talking about the night we had sex, but she's not.

"I found you in the school basement, sleeping on the couch and you were freezing." She pauses a moment, and I feel her eyes on the side of my face. "Life hasn't been fair to you, Trystan. You've had to deal with more bad luck—no, it's more than that. You've had suffering dumped on you since we met. No one should be able to survive what you've been through, and somehow you've managed."

I open my mouth to tell her I didn't manage too well tonight, but she places a finger over my lips, stopping me.

"Everyone needs help sometimes, even you." She lays a hand on my chest and leans in, kissing my cheek before pushing herself up. She stops on the edge of the couch, opens her water, and downs the entire thing.

She starts talking about Katie and the dinner party she was hosting when Seth's call came in, but I'm lost in the memory of her hand on my chest and her kiss on my cheek.

I thought it would never happen again, but it did.

Mari kissed me.

CHAPTER 14

~MARI~

His New York City apartment is massive. It's the kind of place they film for television shows about how the one percent lives. At one time, Trystan was poor, and I don't mean can't-afford-brand-names poor. I mean he didn't have anything. His father didn't clothe him or feed him. Everything Trystan had, he earned himself.

Back then he wore a battered leather jacket, jeans, and a flannel or dark-colored t-shirt. Now I wonder how he managed to get through that time without anyone else noticing he had nothing. His friends certainly didn't know. His teachers didn't even see it—well, all but Tucker. That man saw everything. Sometimes I wonder if that's why he put us together in the first place. I didn't hang around Trystan by choice back then, not at first.

The heartthrob thing never sat well with me, and Trystan could have a gaggle of girls at his feet using nothing but that flirty smirk. People have always loved Trystan. It's a combination of his voice and demeanor. When he comes to life on a stage, it's impossible to look away. He pulls you into his story, into his world. It feels like he's speaking only to you, so how could anyone not love him?

My mind races through the past, leaping to predict what might happen in the future, but I shy away from those thoughts. At the end of the day, it doesn't matter how great he is, or how well we get along, there's one glaring problem I can't forgive—he failed me when I needed him most.

I thought about bailing on him now. Being here is stupid, and I'm already blurring the lines between us. For a second, things felt like old times, and my lips found his cheek. It was meant to be friendly and caring, but something flashed across his eyes a moment later. I know that look. I shocked him.

I don't know what to say, so I'm not talking. I've been wandering the room since that kiss, studying the knickknacks on the tables. My gaze leaps between the light fixtures, ceiling, and carpet. I smile and laugh, looking anywhere except at Trystan's eyes.

This isn't like old times. It's so much more. There's a river running between us with deadly rapids, and I still want to jump in and cross to the other side. What's wrong with me? I already know what's over there—a guy who's all charm and falsetto. Maybe we get along so well because we're two fake people trying to survive any way we can.

I should never have become a doctor. When my mother died, I tossed my personal dreams aside and didn't look back. I took help from the only person offering—my father. I emerged with a medical license, after completing medical school in record time. When you have no social life, it's easy to plow through school.

I reach for a glass object resembling a knot. It's not heavy. I lift the sculpture to my eyes and see a slender thread of silver. It runs the length of the knot, from one end to the other. It's an odd piece. I turn and ask about it. "Is this your selection or the decorator's?"

Trystan is in the kitchen fixing us something to eat. It's probably stuffed truffles or something weird. I wonder how much of the boy I knew is still in that body. He steps out, wiping his hands on a white dishtowel. He steps closer to me and lifts it from my hands. "Stylistically, it's not my thing. It's very post-modern, but the symbolic nature of the piece is interesting. So, yeah, I picked out that one. It was the least garish thing in a big store of ugly." When he hands it back to me, his fingers brush mine, sending an electric charge through my hand and up my arm. It steals my breath and causes me to jerk away.

How could that still be there? After all those years and everything he did to me? I don't want to consider how screwed up I must be to feel attracted to him.

It's not attraction, Mari, the little voice in the back of my head says confidently. I brush the thought away quickly, locking it up in the back of my mind.

"Yeah, I love shopping in Uggo Depot. You never know when you'll need a glass knot." I tease, following him back to the kitchen. I stop in the doorway and sniff the air. It smells good.

Trystan has that white towel tucked into the back of his jeans pocket. The contrast makes my gaze fixate on his butt. When he turns abruptly, he notices where my eyes have been. "Nope, you never know what the day will bring. I mean look at this—I'm slaving away in the kitchen, making us something to eat, and you're ogling my backside like a fangirl."

My jaw drops, and I straighten. "I am not! I was looking at the towel!"

"Sure." He winks at me, and continues, "I mean, of course you are. It's a beautiful towel. I'm sure there's not another like it, which explains its hypnotic powers." He turns his back to me, looks over his shoulder, and wiggles his hips, making the towel sway.

I grin and roll my eyes. "You're an idiot."

"Maybe, but I have a great ass." He takes the frying pan off the stove and points to a cupboard. "Grab a couple of plates from there and follow me. I've made a dish of culinary amazingness."

I grab two plates and follow him into the dining room. It has a single long wood table surrounded by silver chairs. It's reminiscent of dining on a log while it goes through the saw at the old mill. His decorator must have been on something because this place isn't him. Not even a little bit.

Trystan sees my face when I enter the room. "Yeah, I know."

"It's nice." I try not to laugh, because I'm so totally lying, but the corners of my mouth twitch. "No, really. It's got a style that's really unique, and—"

"And it came from the other side of Uggo Depot."

"It really did. What were you thinking?"

"That I wanted the designer out of my house. I needed to be alone, and that was the fastest way to get rid of her." He puts the frying pan on the table and points to a chair opposite him. "Sit. Mangia, Mangia, and all that."

I pull out the chair and slip into my seat. Trystan makes a show of the grand reveal of his dish. He presses his hand to the lid and says, "I've been taking cooking lessons—don't laugh—and this is my best dish." He pulls back the lid theatrically and smiles.

A rush of steam comes out, along with the sweet scent of herbs and onion. When the little cloud clears, I can see what he made.

It's Hamburger Helper.

I laugh and sit back in my seat. "Thank God! I was starting to think you went all nuts on me."

Trystan's lips twist in a boyish expression he rarely wears. His eyes dip to the side and then he grins. He lets out a rush of air and reaches for my plate while lifting the frying pan. He tilts the pan on its side and the noodles and meat slide onto my plate. It's very Trystan. Hamburger Helper was his go-to meal when he was in high school. He made it for me a few times when we were dating. It means something because I know the stories that go with it—to him, this was the crème de la crème of what he could afford to eat. And it was never the brand name version, and he usually couldn't afford the meat. This dish was a highlight in dark times. I'm surprised he still makes it.

As if he can read my thoughts, he explains, "It's comfort food and always has been. Some people like Kraft Mac & Cheese, while others like—"

"Hamburger Helper, now with real meat!" I finish with a laugh, smiling broadly at him. "You don't have to explain, seriously. I'm relieved you're not trying to feed me something your decorator made."

Trystan is dishing up his food and laughs so hard he drops the plate. The noodles and meat slosh off the side. He uses his hand to shove them back on his plate, then grabs the towel from his pocket, and wipes his hands off. "Well, after spending ten grand on cooking classes, I discovered the most important thing I'll ever learn about the culinary arts."

"What's that?"

"I suck at it," he blurts out, then stuffs a forkful of food into his mouth.

I didn't expect him to say that. I already have food in my mouth and nearly choke as I start laughing. I put my fork down and chug some water. When I look up, Trystan is watching me. Those dark blue eyes seem pensive, and I wonder what he's thinking.

There was a time when he told me anything and everything. Now, I have no right to wonder what's going on behind those sapphire eyes. He's not mine anymore.

I look away and the moment breaks.

Our meal continues with a comfortable chatter. Trystan must be running on adrenaline. He doesn't complain about his sore body, even though I know he must be hurting by now. We're in the middle of cleaning up when my phone rings.

Time suddenly slows, and seconds take minutes. I reach for the phone and press it to my ear, watching Trystan and noting the desperate hope in his eyes. It's not until that moment that I realize I'm the one who will have to tell him if Seth is dead. I'll be the bearer of bad news. I'm the one who will break him—he can't handle this, too.

I turn my back on him and place the dishes I'm holding in the sink. "Katie, hey. Are you all right?"

Her voice is scratchy as if she's been yelling… Or crying. "Yeah, as good as I can be when something like this happens." Her voice sounds strained and tight.

My stomach sinks in response, and I grip the counter, noticing how cold the stone is under my fingertips. "What happened?" That's the question I need to ask, yet I don't want to hear the answer. The hairs on the back of my neck stand up, and a chill rushes over every inch of my skin. I already know what she's going to say before she speaks.

"He's gone, Mari." Katie's voice cracks and she swallows a sob. She steels her voice and starts again. "The entire convoy is gone. What I heard on the phone was the end of the attack. Their phones shouldn't have worked at all, but each of them managed a single short call out. It's as if they knew, Mari. And Seth," her voice cracks as she says his name. "He didn't even tell me. He let me laugh, and…" Katie breaks down into sobs, and I wish I were there to put my arms around her. I hear her mother-in-law speaking to her softly, and I know she's not alone. Katie gasps and clears her throat. "Anyway, I wanted you to know."

"Okay. Listen, I'll let Trystan know." Katie agrees and disconnects quickly. I place my phone in my back pocket.

Dread fills me from top to bottom, and I don't want to turn around. How am I supposed to say this to him? But then I feel his warm hand on my shoulder. A wave of emotion floods through me, sadness, grief, dread—all colliding with my desperation for this to somehow be a mistake. Katie can't be a widow. Trystan can't lose his oldest friend. I can't watch the two people I love most be destroyed by this.

The thought rings clearly in my mind, and with his hand on my shoulder, I know he heard it. I don't know how or why this connection is there between us, but it is. I want to lean into the sink and scream, but he's pulling me back.

Trystan's hand finds my waist, and he turns me slowly. I face him with glassy eyes and a fake smile. How am I supposed to say this? I try to look up at him, but I can't. I can't find the words.

Before I can speak, Trystan's arms are around me. He holds me tightly, kissing the top of my head. "Is he gone?"

I press my face to his chest, tears streaming down my cheeks, but I manage to nod. My throat feels too dry to swallow. "He's gone, Trystan. Seth died in combat."

CHAPTER 15

The rest of the night is a blur. I remember time ticking by slowly, and my face damp with tears. Trystan's body is near mine, but his mind is miles away. We start out sitting near each other on the couch, but we're soon lying down, tangled together. Trystan has his arms around me, with my head tucked under his chin.

It's as if holding onto me will make losing Seth less real, less painful. Trystan already lost so much it's hard to find words to comfort him in times like this. What do I say to him? Can I tell him he's not alone? Can I even promise something like that? I won't say it without meaning it.

And if I do make promises to Trystan, what does that mean for me? I have a boyfriend—a very sweet boyfriend—who will flip out when he finds out I spent the night in the arms of rock star Trystan Scott. I blink hard and swear I hear my eyeballs moving inside my skull. My head hurts, and everything is amplified. Even Trystan's soft breathing sounds like a rush of warm wind as it washes over my cheek.

At some point during the night, I made a decision. I wasn't aware of it until now, but it's there all the same. I'm not the kind of person who will desert a friend when they're suffering. I could have said no. I could have gone home and cried on my boyfriend's shoulder, but he didn't know Seth. There's something comforting about being around people who knew him—even Trystan.

During the night, both of us told random Seth memories, and the loss didn't sting so much. Now, in the morning light, this all feels too intimate. I'd have a stroke if Derrick spent the night with his ex, for any reason, wouldn't I? Can I justify this? Do I need to?

Nothing is going on here. Trystan might as well be my brother for how much he came on to me last night—he didn't. It wasn't like that. He cried and buried his face in my neck. He held onto me tightly and mourned the loss of his friend. I couldn't walk away, and I didn't want to. Is that bad?

Who am I becoming? I don't know. I want to be trustworthy and dependable, but the lines are so blurry with this.

I pause for a moment. When did being trustworthy and dependable become my priority? I sound like a Cockapoo. Seriously? Those are the attributes I strive to be? What happened to me?

I roll out of Trystan's arms and sit up on the edge of the couch. I stretch and feel the morning air kiss the skin of my midriff. Trystan props himself up on his elbow and watches as I stand and walk over to the huge windows overlooking the city. In the distance, wispy puffs of white smoke billow into the sky. Directly below us, the city looks peaceful.

I sense Trystan behind me before I hear him. It's strange, but that man feels like a part of me. I don't know how else to describe it. It's as if he were the other piece of my soul and when we're near I feel it. It's like putting two drops of water too close together. They merge into one. I don't mean that in a sexy way, either. It just is. I don't question it anymore. At first it terrified me, but not anymore. If I keep my guard up, if I keep his hands off me, we're still two drops of water.

Last night you were one, the little voice in the back of my mind reminds me.

That sounds way too intimate for my taste. I wish I could figure this out.

Trystan chooses that moment to speak. "Sometimes there isn't anything to figure out."

I round on him. It feels like he suckerpunched me. My jaw drops and quivers. I feel so exposed at that moment. Was that luck or something else? He wasn't touching me! He didn't see my eyes, so how did he know what I was thinking? "What?" My voice is shaky.

Trystan shrugs as if he has no idea what he did. He steps up to the window and reaches for a hidden lever. When he presses it, the piece of metal pops out. Trystan slides the expanse open and steps onto the balcony. The air is crisp and whips me in the face. He's still wearing the dark clothes he left the hospital in last night. He leans on the railing and stares out at the city. "Sometimes there's nothing to figure out, nothing to do. You have to take what life throws at you in stride and keep going."

I'm next to him, at the railing. The wind blows my curls across my cheek, but I don't move them away. I don't even blink. I can't tell if he's responding to my thought, or if he even knows I didn't speak out loud. Trystan seems pensive and somber, so maybe it's me.

When he glances at me out of the corner of his eye, the connection solidifies. I can feel it lace down from my heart and tug in my gut. My shoulders tingle and the skin on my face feels warm. There were times I convinced myself I imagined this, that this pull to him wasn't real. But here I am, and it clearly exists.

I swallow hard, not breaking eye contact with him. Not this time. I want to know the truth, once and for all. "Is that what you did? When my mother died? You promised you'd be there and then," I shake my head, "nothing. You vanished."

Trystan steps away and I swear I hear his pulse pounding in my ears. His body tenses as a lie forms on the tip of his tongue, but I can't understand why. Without thinking, I reach for him. My fingers wrap around his wrist, and I hold on tight.

A rush of sounds, sensations, and images flicker through my mind like an old movie. Parts of the memories are missing, burned away as if overexposed. Everything floods my senses in a rush, out of order, and the only thing that I feel for certain is his remorse. It's a massive storm I'm unable to navigate, one emotion transcending all others, impossible to miss.

Trystan jerks his hand out of my grip and steps away. A deafening silence fills his wake until I hear my own heart thumping in my chest again. I blink rapidly, trying not to cry. I don't understand. Why did he leave me? If he left me because he'd finished with me, why would he feel remorseful?

Trystan sucks in a jagged breath and shakes his head. "Don't do that to me."

Anger springs up from inside me. There's so much I don't understand about him, about us, and he's hiding the truth. I'm suddenly sick of the lies. "To you? Don't do that to you? You do that to me every time you touch me! You can look at me and know everything!"

I search for the right words to navigate such a strange situation, but there aren't any. Tears prick my eyes, and a scream builds inside me. I finally land on the one thought I want him to hear most of all. "You hurt me. You left me when I needed you most, and it's difficult to stay here with you now, but—."

"Then leave." Trystan turns his back on me and pads inside. He gathers my things and shoves them in my arms. "No one is holding you here, and I don't need your pi—"

I drop my things on the floor between us and shake my head, "That's not what I'm saying, and you know it!"

"You said you don't want to be here, now go!"

"Trystan," his name comes out in a growl, and I reach for both his hands and hold on tight. His anger is hot and itching to strike. It's surging through him, hiding old wounds, and this invasion fuels the fire, but I don't release him. "I'm saying I can't hide from you. I don't know what this is between us, but it's always been there. Sometimes it's good, but most of the time it's terrifying. You know my thoughts before I say them. You're so tuned into me that you can sense how I feel, and I swear it's more than that. It's not possible, but here we are, and—whether it's a gift or a curse—the one thing I want to know most is hidden from me. No matter what I do, I can't see why you left me. It's been nine years! Tell me. Please."

By the time I stop speaking, my hands have slipped from his wrists. I'm spent. For some reason, confessing those things sucked all the emotional strength out of me. My knees feel ready to buckle, and my stomach twists into knots. I can't stand the silence following my plea. It's as if I didn't speak at all. Trystan just stands there staring at me. Apathy feels so much worse than if he'd confessed he'd cheated or done something even more horrible. It's like a knife in the back, in my heart, and in my eye. There's nothing that hurts more than realizing he never cared about me.

To keep my lips from trembling, I bite down on them once and avert my gaze. I don't want him to feel anything, to know anything about me. Not anymore. Without a word, I bend over and scoop my things off the floor. I head to the door hoping he'll say something, wishing he'd stop me. I can picture the smile on his face as he finally drops his guard completely and tells me what happened that night—why he failed to keep his promise to be there with me—but that doesn't happen. Trystan remains still, his lips pressed firmly together, his strong arms folded across his chest, his jaw locked.

I cross the room and pull open the door, thankful his apartment doesn't connect directly to the elevator the way most penthouses do in the city. When my fingers touch the handle, I turn back to look at him. I can't help myself. I have to say the words that are burning a hole on my tongue. "Out of everything I gave you—my heart, my body, my friendship, my trust—this hurts the most. I helped you tonight, more than once. I did it even though it ripped open old wounds, scars that never healed because I couldn't understand why you would sleep with me then bail. After everything we went through together," I shake my head and look at the wooden floor. When I glance up at him, I force a smile to my lips. "For the longest time, I thought people couldn't change—that it was impossible. Congratulations, you proved me wrong. People can change. They can become calloused enough to lose the spark that made them unique. You had that spark, Trystan, and now it's gone. Have a nice life."

CHAPTER 16

I don't think after that. I run. Tears well up in my eyes and before I can wipe them away, the elevator doors slide open. I shove through the front doors before the doorman can speak. His hand is in the air, and he calls after me, but I don't stop.

I should have stopped.

When I'm on the other side of the glass doors, a barrage of camera flashes blinds me. Confusion pinches my face and my arm instinctively darts up to cover my eyes. They hurl questions at me as they take my picture.

"What's your name?" One man calls out.

A woman with huge dark hair shoves a microphone in my face and bumps it against my mouth. I try to push it away, but she doesn't back off. "Are you in a relationship with Trystan Scott? Or was this a one-time affair?" I turn away from her and slam into another guy. I expect him to shove a microphone up my nose too, but he doesn't. The guy takes my arm and elbows his way through the crowd with me in tow until we're in front of a limo. He opens the door, and I jump inside. The man closes it behind me and gets into the drivers seat. Within seconds, we're driving through the empty streets of New York City at god-awful o'clock in the morning.

I rub my eyes and feel like scream-crying. I haven't done that since I was six years old. My dad slapped me across the face because it was inappropriate. I don't care what's appropriate right now. I bury my face in my hands and lean forward in the seat.

The driver is quiet for a little while, before asking, "Do you want to head home, Dr. Jennings?"

I glance up at him, surprised he knows my name. The man has a big build, a thick neck, and a shaved head. His skin is dark and tattooed. I don't recognize his appearance, but his voice jogs my memory. "Bob?"

He grins at me in the mirror. "The one and only."

"Wow, you look different. Very kickass." I try to sound light and carefree, but I don't pull it off.

"I know what you did for him last night, and it was nothing like the paparazzi implied."

I watch a few cars go in the opposite direction as we head into a tunnel. The yellow lights whiz by as I settle back into my seat. Jumping into a car was nuts, even for me, but I didn't have much of a choice. "Did he tell you to rescue me, or did you just happen to see me walk out?"

Bob gets a sheepish smile on his face, and I know it wasn't Trystan. "Dr. Jennings—"

"Call me Mari—unless you want me calling you Mr. Bob."

He snorts a sharp laugh and looks in the mirror at me. "Mari, he's not been himself lately."

"If lately covers the past decade, I'll agree with you." I fold my arms over my chest and slump down in my seat. My head is screaming.

I close my eyes and tip my head back against the seat.

"It's not my place to say, but with your showing up when you did—well, I wondered if he pulled that stunt last night hoping to see you again."

I open my eyes and sit up a little. "That's insane. Why would he do that?"

"Like I said, he's not been himself lately."

I shouldn't tell him, but Bob is one of the last few people who care about Trystan. "Oh, Bob, it's going to get a lot worse. Seth died last night."

Bob swears under his breath. We spend the rest of our drive in silence.

As we emerge on the other side of the tunnel, I wonder if Trystan is flaming out. He's been in the public eye every day for nearly a decade. He's been showing signs of distress for a while. It's like watching the hull of a ship get laced with hairline fissures. One day they'll cut too deep, the waters will come rushing in, and he'll be over.

I hang my head between my shoulders and regret saying the things I said as I left. No matter what happens between us, I don't want Trystan to lose it so badly he takes his life.

Damn it. I screwed up. We're not the same. He doesn't have the luxury of wearing his heart on his sleeve, not anymore. I pressed him for the one thing that would make it easier for me to be around him and didn't consider how it would affect him.

What if he did crash to get my attention? What if he wanted to say something and I didn't give him a chance?

I want to pull my hair out. I can't live with 'what ifs' crashing into my skull all day. I have to work later. I need to pull myself together, but I can't help feeling like I tugged at a string on someone who is coming apart at the seams.

CHAPTER 17

Bob drops me off at Katie's apartment. I want to check on her before I head home. I knock on the door, but there's no answer. I wonder if she's still at Seth's mom's house or if she's in bed. I don't want to leave without checking on her, so I knock again. "Katie?"

If she's there, she won't open the door if she's crying. Katie hates crying in front of people, even me. I turn around and lean against the door with my back while fishing my cell phone from my pocket. I pull up her name and text her.

ME: So, I spent the night with Trystan last night…

KATIE: WHAT?!?

She races through the apartment and yanks open the door so quickly, I fall backward and slam my butt on the floor. I shriek, and my phone goes flying.

A moment later, Amy opens her door from across the hall. "Are you two all right?" She's wearing pink slippers and a matching bathrobe.

Katie's face is glistening with freshly shed tears, but her eyes are wide with curiosity. She gives Amy a thumbs up. "Yup. Mari's just a klutz. Sorry."

"Hey!" I protest, but I'm too tired to get up. "My butt hurts."

"You dirty girl!" Katie bellows as she closes the door on Amy.

I groan and cover my face. "Dear God! You know that woman now thinks I like butt action, right? Jeeze, Katie!"

She smiles and blinks her wet eyelashes at me innocently. "Get up! Spill your guts and all the glorious details of your sexy night with your ex!" She grabs my wrist and starts pulling me across the floor.

I laugh so hard I can't get up. Katie finally plops down and sits on me. I make an oof sound as Katie laughs. "TELL ME!"

"Fine! I slept with him after patching him up at the ER."

She bounces on my stomach twice and protests. "That's not dirty details! You can do better than that!"

"There are no dirty details."

Katie's teasing dissipates, and she slides off of me. Katie's always had radar that could focus with pinpoint precision. "What happened?"

I give her the highlights, starting with thinking Trystan was dead and ending with Bob rescuing me from the reporters and bringing me here. When I finish, my head is against her shoulder, and I want to cry.

Katie listens quietly then wraps her arms around me, giving me a tight hug. "Yesterday sucked."

"Yes, it did."

She takes a deep breath and adds, "Thank you for talking to Trystan about Seth. I was so scared to call him and tell him that myself. I know that put you in a weird spot, and I can't thank you enough. I could barely talk last night, and I didn't want him to find out from a reporter or something."

I shrug as if it didn't matter. "That's what friends are for. Do you need anything today?"

She shakes her head and pushes up off the carpet. "No, I don't think so." Katie looks so forlorn, which is strange for someone like her. Normally, she's all bounce and smiles—a human version of Tigger. I wonder who she's going to be when she gets through this. I hope I can be there for her, and figure out what she needs.

I get up and follow her into the kitchen. Katie pours a cup of coffee and offers me one. I take it and sip the hot liquid slowly. "My schedule sucks, but I think I can get a few days off work. I'll go with you to the funeral home and whatever else you need. Just tell me where and when."

"Thanks, Mari. What I really need... Well... Could you stay here tonight?" Katie asks uncertainly. Her brows scrunch together as she stares at her coffee. "I don't think I'll sleep, but I don't want to be alone right now. I feel strange—like this is a dream I can't wake up from." She tucks a piece of hair behind her ear and glances up at me.

"Of course I'll stay, Katie. I'll help you however I can, but the thing that helps the most is time. Sometimes the only thing you can do is breathe. These days will come and go, and I can stick around as long as you'd like, okay? Don't be afraid to ask."

Normal Katie would give an over-exuberant response, but this time she just nods. After chugging the cup of coffee, she looks at me from over the rim. "I missed something in your story. How did you end up at his place last night?"

"What?" Her question catches me off balance.

"You ended up at his place, right?" I nod, not seeing where this is going. "How'd that happen?"

"I don't know," I say, thinking about the lack of parking, followed by the rule-following cop, and finally Trystan pulling out of the parking lot at just the right time. "It was weird, like fate made it impossible to walk away."

Katie lifts a brow and tips her head to the side. "You don't believe in fate."

"No, but last night was different. It was like a series of events lined up to prevent any other outcome." I'm squirming inside. She hasn't asked, and I haven't mentioned feeling that same strange connection with Trystan even stronger than before.

"What about your Trystan clone? Derrick?"

"Stop calling him that. He's not like Trystan at all."

"Of course he's not—they just look like brothers. You don't have issues." Katie turns around and places her cup in the sink. She's a little more direct than usual, probably because she's emotionally raw.

"I'm ready to tell Derrick about Trystan, though. It's time he knew."

Katie leans against the counter and folds her arms over her chest. "Oh, he knows already."

"What do you mean?"

"Mari, I knew you spent the night at Trystan's penthouse before you got here. Look." She turns up the volume on the TV that's been silently glowing in the corner of the kitchen.

They're showing pictures of me with the caption:

TRYSTAN SCOTT'S LATEST
CONQUEST

CHAPTER 18

I blink at the screen, ready to totally flip out. Katie points the remote at the screen and changes the channel. "Don't freak out, yet. That one runs on smut titles. Most of them are inferring you're an item. See?" She stops at another station. The host is a young twenty-year-old blonde with a high-pitched voice better suited for a pre-K classroom than the news.

"And it appears rock legend Trystan Scott has become seriously involved with this young woman seen leaving his New York City penthouse early this morning. Scott's chauffeur helped her navigate the press without speaking, leaving us all wondering," the woman looks directly at the camera, "Was this public display intentional? It's rare to see a woman leaving Trystan Scott's Manhattan penthouse."

The other co-host bursts in, "Rare? It's like seeing Santa Claus having brunch with the Easter Bunny. We're in new territory, Lisa. Is it possible this bad boy is finally serious about someone?"

"It appears so, Todd—" her voice vanishes as Katie hits the power button, plunging the room into silence.

"So, what are the odds that Derrick watches the morning news?"

"I didn't have sex with him! I didn't cheat on Derrick! And I didn't—awh, crap!" I can't even make words anymore. Garbled noises flow freely from my mouth.

Katie walks over to me and puts a hand on my back. "You're losing it, Mari. Use your words, honey. Come on."

I'm pacing, circling, pulling at my hair and sputtering half thoughts. "He'll see it!"

"Yeah, he will. The question is what are you going to do about it? Mari, this isn't horrible. You're not an asshole. Trystan lost his best friend. You're his only friend left that goes back that far, possibly his only friend at all. What were you supposed to do? Leave him alone to jump off his terrace? Everyone knows Trystan's been acting out. You were a friend last night."

"But the press! H—"

"The press doesn't know what the fuck they saw. If Derrick loves you—and I hate to admit this, but I think he does—he'll believe you. And if he doesn't, then he's the asswipe I've always claimed he is." She smiles at me like Mr. Potato Head. "See? No problem."

I manage to pull it together and wonder how she's so strong. "I'm sorry, I shouldn't be dumping this on you now."

She swats a hand at me. "Please, dump. It gives me something to think about." Katie presses her lips together, and her voice drops. She picks at her nails and swallows hard. "That's why I want you to stay here tonight. When it gets quiet, my mind wanders to his last minutes, and I can't stand to think about him dying like that—that he knew." Her eyes are glassy, and she forces a smile. "If we talk about things I can take longer to let it sink in, you know? It doesn't change anything, but it'll give me more time and make it a little less painful."

The lump in my throat is the size of a melon. I can't fathom what she's going through. Losing my mom was hard, but this has to be so much worse. Katie thought she'd share a life with Seth, babies and lots of years together. Instead, it was all ripped away.

"Well," I walk over to her and bump my shoulder into hers, "it's a good thing my life is so screwed up. I can keep you talking about other things for as long as you want."

She nods a few times and looks over at me with tears in her eyes. "I thought we'd have a fat baby Seth or Katie. We'd even picked out names, you know? How can I let that go?" Katie's bottom lip quivers as tears stream down her cheeks. "I didn't just lose Seth last night, I lost all our dreams, too. What am I going to do?"

I don't know what to say, so I wrap my arms around her and hold on tight. Katie sobs against me and I feel the tears rolling down my cheeks. I wish I could take her pain away. I wish I could fast-forward to a year from now, so she doesn't have to endure this, but I can't. "We'll figure it out."

CHAPTER 19

My heart feels full of lead. The weight of Seth's death, Katie's pain, and Trystan's whatever that was all pull at my heartstrings so violently I think my chest may rupture. I know I carry things too close to my heart. I take on other people's pain as if it were my own. Coupled with my personal grief and suffering, it becomes too much. I know I'm headed to a dark place, so I need to batten down the hatches and hold on tight. I have to be there for Katie. Not only was she there for me when Mom died, but she was there for me when Trystan left me heartbroken, and when I threw myself into medical school, and during my residency from hell. She encouraged me when I decided to change back to pre-med in college, and didn't judge me for ditching my new art path. She didn't tease me the way Dad did, either. Katie's always been there to put a smile on my face, and I am going to be there for her.

It took a lot of arguing with Dad to get the rest of the week off, but he finally caved when I started shouting. Family drama in the middle of the ER is his idea of a nightmare. Chaos and public spectacles overload his senses. I understand that I torched any favors he owed me by calling in all my chips now. With all the crap in the press about me being with Trystan, he wants to disown me, but he won't. Part of his pride dwells in me being a kickass doctor. Pride is a double-edged sword, and I've learned to swing it both ways to get what I need.

When our conversation flips to Trystan, I cut him off at the knees. "You set that ball in motion when you called me to work at your whim, and if you don't want your name in the press, then drop it. Nothing happened. Nothing will happen. I'm not seeing him. I'm dating Derrick. End of story." I think I growled the last few sentences. It worked, though, because he did drop it.

The next person to handle is Derrick—and the "my ex-boyfriend is a mega rock star" conversation never goes well. It has to be in person, so I head over to our favorite spot to have lunch at Villagio. The little Italian restaurant is quiet—so he can't throw a fit—and it overlooks Central Park. I love the Park and the trees. I'm not a hippie, but there's something about trees that makes me feel steady. They've been here longer than me and will be here long after. They've endured seasons of change, wild weather, and they're still standing strong. I want to be a tree.

Wow, random thought. Okay, I'm too tired to do this. I'd postpone it, except for the fact that I think the press will figure out who I am, where I live, and make my life hell. They may piece together that I'm the girl from his high school by the end of the week, and then there will be no more secrets to keep. No, I need to tell him now.

Derrick walks in as if on cue and glances to the corner where we usually sit. "Hey, babe." He waves at the maître d' as he strides toward me, kissing me on the cheek before sitting down at our little table.

"Hi." My voice doesn't come out right.

Derrick sits across from me and his dark bushy eyebrows meet. "What's the matter? Are you okay?"

Before I can reply, the waiter comes over. "The usual?" We eat here at least twice a week. I'm in love with their ravioli and manicotti.

I nod and Derrick answers for us. "Yes, that'd be great."

The waiter takes the menus and disappears into the back. The restaurant has a few people here, but it's not bursting at the seams. My gaze wanders to the park and into the trees. The wind ruffles the canopy of leaves and a few drift to the ground.

"Mari, what's going on? You look beat." Derrick picks up the glass of wine I ordered before he arrived and takes a swig. He's not a sipper.

"I need to tell you something possibly unpleasant."

His lips curl up, and he laughs. "I'm sure it's nothing."

I hate it when he does that. "It's not nothing."

"Unless you had a random hookup last night, I'm sure it's nothing. You always think every little thing is going to break us up, Mari. Have some faith in me. Now, come on and tell Derrick what's wrong." As he speaks, he picks up a piece of bread, dipping it in the oil and spices on the white plate between us.

Band-aid. Rip this sucker off in one yank. I don't like that Derrick thinks it's nothing, that he's not braced for it, but his ego is too big to accept that some things may faze him.

I clear my throat and glance out the window. "A long time ago, I dated someone. Last night he was in a car wreck and visited the emergency room."

"Was the asshole drinking? I know how much you hate that." He smirks, as if this is funny, dips the rest of his bread and shoves it in his mouth.

"Derrick, please let me finish." He holds up his hand and leans back into his chair. I glance around at the other couples enjoying their lunches. I've done this before and with some guys it doesn't matter that we are in a public place—they still flip out. No one wants to be compared to Trystan Scott. It creates an ego issue the size of the Titanic.

"Tell me, babe." He prods when I've been quiet for too long.

I take a deep breath and dive in. "You know I've known Katie and Seth since high school, right? Well, I've known this guy that long, too. We were all friends a long time ago. Anyway, when I left the ER I discovered my car had been towed, so this guy gave me a ride. I was going to go home, but it became obvious he didn't know about Seth, so I decided to wait for the confirmation with him."

Derrick's smile slowly falls off his face as I list the events of the night. His arms fold across his chest, becoming tighter and tighter. It's obvious by now I'm intentionally not saying this guy's name. Derrick isn't a total ass, so he asks about Katie and Seth. "Is he all right? Seth, I mean? I know Katie will be devastated if something happens to him."

I glance away blinking rapidly and feeling tears spring into my eyes. "He didn't make it."

"Oh, God. Babe, I'm so sorry."

I nod and keep going. "Thanks, but that's not the end of the story. I stayed with the guy until we heard from Katie. I left early this morning and ran into some cameras. They took my picture, and it's only a matter of time until they figure out my identity. I wanted to tell you before now, but from experience, guys act weird when they realize my ex is famous."

His arms drop and he leans forward as he says, "Famous? You dated a celebrity?" He scoots closer, laughing, not taking this seriously. I'm sure he thinks that the guy is a micro star, someone he can ridicule and tease me about later. This reaction always leads to a yelling mess I can't fix.

"It was a long a time ago before he was famous. We were kids." I shrug and glance to the side when I see the waiter coming with our food.

He serves me first and then Derrick. Each plate is beautifully pristine and smells wonderful, but I'm suddenly not hungry. Derrick makes small talk, complimenting the dishes, and when our waiter leaves, he leans in and teases, "Well, spit it out. Tell me the name of this long lost lover I should be so worried about." Derrick cuts his steak and shoves a piece in his mouth.

"No, you're right," I'm taking this in a different direction. I refuse to let this blow out of proportion and at the rate I'm going, we aren't going to be able to come back here.

"He's not important." Or he wasn't important to me until last night. Or maybe before that. I have no idea. I stare at the ravioli thinking they look like little pillows and wish I could put my head down on the table.

"Then spill, Mari. If the guy doesn't matter, tell me. Unless you're ashamed you did one of those Hollywood pussies. If that's the case, it's okay. We all did stupid things when we were younger." He winks at me and bites off another piece of steak.

The belittling comments piss me off, but I knew he'd be like this, so I tread carefully. "How's your steak?"

"Excellent, as always. Come on, tell me his name. That's why you wanted to come here, right? You thought I'd go batshit crazy when I heard you had some Hollywood asshole as a boyfriend five years ago?"

"It's more like ten years ago. Almost."

His smile drops. "Almost?"

"Yeah, it was nine years ago, ten in the summer."

"You keep track?"

"Not really. It's just bookmarked in my brain because I changed my major to pre-med after we broke up."

He puts his fork and knife down, and then reaches for my hand. "This is obviously important to you. I'm all ears."

"I don't want you to be mad. I didn't tell you in the beginning because I didn't know how this would turn out, and—"

"Mari, you don't have to sugarcoat it for me. Just tell me." He sounds so open, so sincere that I let the name slip off my tongue.

"Trystan. Trystan Scott."

His fingers slip from mine, and he gets that look in his eyes. His head tips to the side as his jaw drops the tiniest bit. That's the look—the verbal ball-kick. Shit. He's going to come out swinging.

Derrick picks up his glass of wine, swallows the rest of it, and places it back on the table. He licks his lips, and one eye goes squinty as he tries to fathom this. "You dated Trystan Scott, the musician? As in the guy Forbes claimed earned 600 million dollars this year? That guy? That's your ex?"

Crap, crap, crap. "Derrick, he wasn't making big money while we dated."

"You dated him when he had nothing, so you're like thick as thieves, right?" he shakes his head like I betrayed him. "And Katie knew? She never said anything, and she knew. Unbelievable."

"Katie dropped hints the size of the Hindenburg on a daily basis, and even if she should have said something to you, now isn't the time to remind her." I'm suddenly playing defense for Katie.

Anger ignites across Derrick's face. "So, what then? Should I have guessed you dated the biggest pussy-hunter around? That asshole is a player and always has been. How the hell did you fall into his bed?"

His words feel like a slap in my face. "What, because Trystan Scott couldn't possibly want someone like me? What the fuck, Derrick? Is that really what you're leading with?"

"Yeah, Mari, that's what the guy who's been with you for months says when you drop a shit-bomb the size of a nuke on him. I thought we were serious. I thought we weren't keeping secrets like this, and you know what? The worst part is this." He pulls something out of his pocket and slams it on the table so hard that it bounces. I hear a clink as it falls to the floor and skids under a table. "I never saw it coming."

He shakes his head, muttering to himself, drops a hundred dollar bill on the table and walks out.

The waiters watch in horror, as do the other customers. I've sat through this enough times that I no longer hide under the table afterward. I just gather my things and get ready to go. That's when the manager comes over and picks up whatever Derrick threw at me. He walks over, looking like he wishes he were anywhere else.

"Signorina, I believe this was meant for you." He places a ring on the white tablecloth and backs away.

It feels like someone is stepping on my throat when I lift the ring. It's a platinum band with a satin finish. There's a single stone—a princess-cut diamond—in the center.

Derrick was going to ask me to marry him.

CHAPTER 20

~TRYSTAN~

"Your story is fucked up," Jonathan Ferro says from the end of my couch. He's slouched against the pillows with his hands tucked behind his head. Jon's been my best friend for years and stayed that way. As a Ferro family member, Jon understands what it's like to be in the limelight, to have the world constantly judging you. It's been an easy friendship, especially before Bryan Ferro died. The three of us would tear up the town clubbing or hop on a jet and hit Vegas—you name it, the three of us were together. It's been harder to enjoy life since Bryan died, but his death has only solidified my friendship with Jon.

I'm at the bar grabbing a drink, but now that the scotch is in my hand I don't want it anymore. I stare at the glass, swirling the amber liquid around for a moment, then abandon it. Sitting down across from Jon on a wood and leather chair, I nod and slouch back into the cushion. "Tell me something I don't know."

"Do you know that you're completely and totally—beyond a shadow of a doubt—utterly pussy-whipped? Because I don't think you took that into consideration at all."

"Fuck off, Jon. Now's not the time."

"When will be the right time? Five years ago, you did this thing for days where you stared at that shitty old phone wondering if you should call her."

"I didn't call her."

"I know. You nailed my brother's girlfriend instead. Great choice, by the way. That made him love you even more—because you know how much Sean likes you already."

"Sean can go fuck himself." Why are we hashing out the past? Jon has this way of making his words fake a left followed by a right before he sucker-punches you in the gut. I brace for impact.

"He probably has, several times, but that's beside the point. The thing that has your junk in a bunch is this girl. She's the same fucking chick from ten years ago! You nailed her. Move on!"

"It was nine years ago." I realize I shouldn't have corrected him after I say it.

Jon smirks and sits up, leaning forward to the edge of the couch, and slapping his hands down on the table. "That's my point. You're marking the days and pining over some bitch you can't have. Get over it already!"

"I can't. You don't know what she does to me."

"She's not fucking here! Trystan, you have everything you ever wanted, and you drive your fucking car into a tree? That was for her, right? Damn man, you're messed up. Get some Prozac or something before you do something more stupid."

"Jon, it's not like that."

"Then what's it like, Trystan? From here you look fucking nuts."

I lean forward in the chair and run my hands through my hair. I press my lips together hard, take a steadying breath and smile. I lift my hands and speak as calmly as possible. "Mari is the girl that got away, but I made her leave. I pushed her away. I burned any bridge between us and I did it on purpose."

"What the hell for?" His voice raises an octave as he speaks. He can tell how much Mari means to me, so my actions make no sense.

"Because, I couldn't be there for her. When she needed me most, I couldn't be with her without bringing the fucking press along. How am I supposed to have a life with her like this? I thought one day it would die down, and everyone would forget about me."

"You're not a one-hit wonder, dude." Jon laughs and sits back into the cushions on the sofa. We sit silently for a moment, both staring out the window before he shifts his gaze back to me. "So that's why you stabbed her in the back? You didn't know how to handle the press?"

I nod and hold my head in my hands, staring at the floor. "It was right before my first concert when her mom died. It was the only way I knew how to deal with it—what was I supposed to do? Show up at the funeral with paparazzi? That's wrong on so many levels."

"Trystan, this is part of your life. It might die down from time to time, but it'll never go away completely. There will always be someone who wants to see the human side of you, and you're right—they would have crashed her funeral and fucked it up. But that doesn't mean you should have left her."

I put my hands on my knees and push up. I pace the floor in front of the terrace. "I can't keep talking about this. I made the decision a long time ago, and I can't undo it."

"But you wish you could?"

"I don't know. The same shit will go down at Seth's funeral. I can't do that to Katie."

"But you can explain it to her and let her decide. You didn't give Marie that chance." Jon stands up and walks over to the bar. He pulls a bottle of Coke out of the mini fridge under the bar and pops the top.

"You're saying her name wrong. It's Mar-ee, not Marie."

Jon is chugging the soda. When he comes up for air, he apologizes. "Sorry, before today you've never even said her name. The point here is that Mari never had the chance because you never gave it to her. If you care about Katie, talk to her."

"Of course I do. I told Seth I'd watch out for her if anything happened to him."

"Good," he says as if I'd just had a profound understanding of something.

"What's good about any of this?" Jon is usually pretty straightforward, literal, and loyal. He'd give you the shirt off his back without a second thought.

"You may have lost one friend, but this situation gives you another chance—a chance you blew the first time that won't come by again. You don't make promises lightly, Trystan. I know that. Everyone knows that. But you can't stop living your life because the press is on your ass. They're part of life for guys like us, and if I know anything about it, it's that you need to let the people who love you decide shit like this. You belong to the public—you make your money because they like you. For them to like you, they have to have access to your life and all the shit that entails. I can tell the press to fuck off. You can't."

I don't know what to think about that. I've heard it for years—I belong to the public, my life isn't mine, it belongs to the people who put me in this penthouse high above the city. I miss the silence, the quietness of an empty theater, and the anonymity that comes with walking down a street where no one knows my name. Those days have long passed. My friends from that era of my life are few. After the way I treated Mari the other night, I don't know if she'll ever talk to me again.

Jon catches my mood and walks over to me. He looks down at the city with me and slaps a hand on my back. "You're not going to want to hear this, but I think you need to. The press has a way of destroying everything they touch, but you destroyed this on your own. You gave up before you even tried. Guys like us don't get many real friends, Trystan. She was there for you back when you had nothing, and she would be there for you through all this, too—assuming you didn't put a knife in her back."

When I glance up at him, he knows I already did.

"Shit," he says quietly. "So what are you going to do now?"

"I don't know."

CHAPTER 21

I take the Aston Martin onto Ocean Parkway, heading away from the city. I floor it once as I pass the lights and feel the salty sea air clinging to my skin. I breathe in deeply, letting it fill my body. I hope I'm doing the right thing, and not dumping more shit on my friend's widow. I head toward Katie's place, hoping to find her alone. It feels wrong to have this conversation over the phone. My gut instinct says I shouldn't attend Seth's funeral or burial, but I need to say goodbye. I need to see the casket lower into the ground and read the headstone. It still feels like he's alive and about to walk through the door at any second.

I need closure, but I can't take it at Katie's expense. I promised Seth I'd watch out for her and I will.

When I'm closer to her apartment, I voice-dial her phone number. Katie picks up on the second ring. "Hey, Scotty. What's up?" Her voice sounds so somber and not bouncy like it usually is.

"I'm headed your way. We need to talk, and I prefer to do it in person. Are you home?"

"Psh, yeah. Where else would I be?"

"Okay, I'll be there in a little bit."

"Sure. Just come in when you get here. The door is unlocked. Walk through the bedroom and I'm sitting on the back balcony."

"Okay, be there in a few." I end the call and floor it. The rush of wind in my ears drowning out the beat of my heart.

No one knows why I hit that tree the other night, and I don't intend to tell them either. I'd rather they think I was drunk than know what really happened.

I pull up in front of Katie's apartment, put the top up, and rush inside before someone sees me. A Yankees cap covers my face, and I keep my head down. I skip the elevator and bound up the steps, taking them two at a time. When I get to her door, I try the knob. It's open like she said. I step inside and place my cap and keys on the table at the entry.

"Katie?" I call out to her, but I guess she can't hear me outside. I walk through her bedroom to find her on the balcony, slouched in a plastic chair, wearing a hot-pink baseball cap with her hair tucked underneath.

I put a hand on her shoulder and crouch down next to her, expecting to see Katie. But it's not her.

Mari jumps and nearly falls out of the chair. "Trystan! What are you doing here?"

The touch blasts me with a jolt of calmness followed quickly by shock. I jump back up and take a step back, feeling how desperately she wants to get away from me. I don't even need to touch her to feel that. The look on her face says it all. "I'm sorry, I didn't mean to startle you. I was looking for Katie. She said she was out here."

Mari's lips bunch up, and she frowns. "About ten minutes ago, Katie suggested I sit out here and read this amazing book." She holds up a Kindle and smirks. "She's not here.

She went to the funeral home to work out the rest of the details with Seth's mom."

"But I just talked to her on the phone ten minutes ago."

"Yeah, like I said, she's not here."

It takes me a second, but I realize what Katie did. "She thinks we should talk, doesn't she?"

"Apparently." Mari is too quiet, and it unnerves me. She's hurting, I can feel it course through my gut, her pain flowing into me.

I'm not sure if I caused this or if it's the aftermath of losing Seth. Either way, I'm not going to add to her suffering. "I'll just head out, then." I walk quickly back toward the front door and grab my things, not turning to look at her for fear of what she'll say.

I made such a big mistake with her. If I had everything to do over again, I'd do it differently. I was so young and stupid back then. I didn't know how to handle my life, and the casualty was my relationship with the only woman I ever truly loved.

Just as I reach for the knob, someone knocks. I pull it open and am standing face to face with a guy of my height and build, with light blue eyes, dark hair, and a frown on his face. "What the fuck are you doing here?" He says, pushing through the doorway and shoving me back in with him.

Mari steps between us. "Trystan is here to speak with Katie."

"The fuck you are," the guy says to me over her head. He's working his jaw like he's going to unhinge it and swallow me whole. He's a snake. Everything about him screams slime. I want to know why he's here, but I don't have to ask. If he hates me, he knows I had a relationship with Mari.

"I don't believe we've been introduced," I say stepping around Mari. "I'm Trystan Scott, Mari's ex-boyfriend."

The guy swings at me.

Mari screams, "Derrick!"

I dodge his fist, grab his wrist and yank him forward. The guy does a face plant on Katie's carpet. "Sorry, I don't fight pussies." I step past his spread-eagle body and flop down in a chair next to the sofa.

"Trystan." Mari scolds me the way she used to when I was pissing off Tucker on purpose. The flecks of gold in her eyes make them look like they're on fire.

I fold my hands in my lap and don't move.

Derrick is off the floor and standing in front of me. He pulls Mari into his arms and practically pisses on her to mark his territory. "You had your chance asshole. She's with me now and always will be."

I don't get it until he lifts her left hand. There's a diamond ring on her finger.

Reality hooks my gut and rips it from my body. My breath vanishes from my lungs, and I can't speak. Mari's big brown eyes soften, and I know she didn't want to tell me like this, but she didn't have much of a choice.

I smile at them, grateful I can act. "That's awesome, dude. Why don't you go fuck her now, too, just to make sure I don't try anything? You've marked her in every other way possible since you walked in the door." I smirk at him, adding, "Psychotic jealousy doesn't look good on you. Also, if you want her to forget me, you should try to look less like me. Go to the GAP and buy something else to wear, cut your hair—see if she still likes you then."

"Trystan, stop." Mari's voice has a razor-sharp edge to it. She glares at me, and I look away. Her fiancé starts to say something, but Mari glares at him, and he swallows it. "Derrick, now isn't a good time for us to talk. Katie is at the funeral home. The funeral will be in the morning, followed by the burial. I'll be riding with Katie, but I'd like you to meet me there. Please?" Her voice is so passive it kills me.

She thinks she has to beg him to show up? Fuck. That's my doing. She's probably afraid he won't show up at all.

Derrick-the-Dick pulls her into his chest and kisses her clumsily before replying. "Yeah, of course, I'll be there. Why wouldn't I be? You need me."

I say nothing, silently wondering if he knows how things ended between Mari and me. Instead, I smile and wave at him as he leaves. When the door is closed, Mari turns around and presses her back against the door as if she's relieved.

"So, a ring?"

"Yeah." Another one-word answer. She doesn't want to talk to me.

"When's the wedding?"

"Why? Are you going to promise to come and then not show up?" I don't like the tone of her voice. Mari isn't cruel, but I deserved that.

I smile at her, but it fades quickly. "I wish you every happiness, Mari. I truly do."

The anger on her face fades and changes into something else. I have no idea what she's thinking—which is weird because I usually know. Maybe she doesn't know what she's thinking or feeling? But that look—what is that? Indifference? Annoyance? Resignation? Did she say yes to this clown because she's tired of waiting? Did I push her to do it?

"Thank you." Her voice is soft, barely there.

I stand and walk over to her. "I shouldn't have said those things the other night. You were right, and you deserved to know."

She shakes her head, almost frantically, and tries to step past me, but I don't let her. I block her path and trap her between the door and my body. "No, it was none of my business. The past is in the past, and I should have left it there. I shouldn't have said those things to you, and I regretted them the instant I walked out the door."

The corner of my mouth wants to pull up into a smile. I feel my body wanting to resume old habits. My feet want to rise on the balls, and my hands want to go behind my back. I want to tease her and make her smile. I want back everything we lost, but now it's too late.

"It's all right. I deserved it."

She shakes her head. "No, you didn't."

I glance down and then back into her eyes, careful not to touch her. I never want her to feel like she has to be afraid of me invading her thoughts. "I did. I deserved that and more. I was a shitty friend and have been for a long time. You've always been kind to me, Mari, and believe me, I know. It seems like everyone wants something from me, but you never have. You took me as I was, and that was good enough for you. I'm the one who fucked it up."

Her lips part and I think she's going to say something about the past, but she doesn't. Her cheek twitches and her lips tug into a crooked smile. "Do you still need help running lines?" I didn't expect her to say that. The shock must show on my face because she laughs. "A promise is a promise. And Derrick already knows. Why do you think he's so pissed?"

"Mari," I'm looking down at the floor when I say her name. Our shoes are inches apart, but she steps closer to me. I choke on my thoughts, and nothing comes out of my mouth. When I look up, she's close enough to kiss. "I, uh—" I'm stuttering. Holy shit, what the hell is wrong with me?

She smiles and rolls her eyes. "Are you teasing me?"

"No, I uh," I swallow hard, wishing she'd step back. I can't think while I'm so close to her. "I don't want to cause problems between you and what's-his-name. I can find someone else to help me out with the script."

"Trystan, it's fine. I took the next few days off to be here with Katie. You can hang out here as much as you want, and Derrick or Katie will be in and out, so it's not a big deal."

"Mari, your fiancé didn't act like it was nothing. Seriously, I've put you through enough already. I don't want to add this, too."

Her eyes are locked on the coffee table when she speaks. "Normally, when something like a funeral pops up, I'd drown myself in work, but I promised Katie I'd stick around so she wouldn't be alone. It was her idea to run lines here. She wants to hear people talking and slow down the emotional assault that's about to attack her life. I can't blame her. It would help her to hear people, and she could help read the script, too. The distraction would be good for her."

"You're using Katie against me?"

"I'm not against you, dork." She throws a pillow at me.

I catch it and hold it at my side. What the hell is she doing? I don't understand why she's being so nice. "Then what are you doing? I was an asshole the other night. You should be pissed at me."

"I was. I'm over it. Life is too short to be mad at people I care about and, for some reason I can't fathom, I still care about you, you lucky bastard. Derrick agreed to suck it up, and Katie wants to pretend we're going to sing a Bette Midler duet together. Let her live in la-la land for a while."

I stand there, stunned at the direction things have gone. "And you?"

A confused expression crosses her face. "What about me?"

"I'm serious, Mari, I don't want to hurt you more than I already have. I know I can't fix what I did, but—"

She cuts me off, "How do you know? Did you even try?" She stands suddenly and walks toward Katie's room, about to shut me out. "These are strange times, and I'm going with the flow. Anything for Katie. I won't be able to stay up running lines all night with you if I don't lay down for a little while now. Get your script and come back. I'll see you later." She closes the door without another word.

CHAPTER 22

What the hell just happened? I run my hands through my hair and head down to the car, but when I walk outside the paps are there. Damn it. I can't come back here.

I jump in the car, elbowing my way through the press—knowing Bob will kick my ass later for ditching him—and peel out before a guy with a camera can jump on my hood. You have no idea what the press will do for a picture until you've been on the other end of their lenses. Those bastards have broken into my house, contacted my father, even jumped in front of my moving car—they're desperate. I can't blame them for acting that way. One shot of me is worth ten grand—minimum. Ten years ago, I would have done the same thing had I owned a camera.

I laugh and floor it as I hit the expressway. Nah, I would never do that. Even though I worked every day, I never purposefully stole something from someone else. In this case, they're stealing my privacy. Bits and pieces of my life get snapped away until I don't want to walk outside anymore. Imagine walking past a row of commission-based sales kiosks in the mall, all manned by people trying to sell you crap. Now imagine that each product equals a ten thousand dollar sale. The value increase makes each salesperson that much more aggressive. They don't care what happens to me. If I run into the street trying to evade them and get hit by a car, that just means they'll get paid even more for a shot of rock star Trystan Scott's demise.

I let out a rush of air and wish my life weren't so fucked up. I voice-dial Jon.

He picks up on the second ring. "Hey, Trystan, what's going on?"

"The press found me at Katie's. They're going to camp out there waiting for me to come back. I can't do that to her. I need a distraction. Any ideas?"

"Give me a little bit. I'll draw them away, for tonight at least. They'll probably head back by morning."

"I'll take anything you can offer. Mari's talking to me again, and Katie needs me. I can't ditch them, and I don't want Katie to come home from the funeral home and run into the press. Anything you can do is appreciated." I grip the wheel tighter and wish I hadn't driven there. Someone probably spotted the plates.

"I've got this, Trystan. I've been attracting and evading the press since I could talk. Give me an hour and they'll be gone." He disconnects, and I drive on in silence.

———

I ask Bob to meet me at Battery Park with the script. He's already there when I arrive, and he looks pissed. With his eyes hiding behind metallic sunglasses and his black wool suit, he looks like a Men In Black character on steroids. Tucked under his massive arm is the yellow envelope containing the script.

Bob pushes off his old Caprice Classic, with oversized tires and chrome rims, and walks over to me. "I can't protect you if I don't know where you are, Trystan." He hands me the envelope.

"Sorry, I had to take care of something personal."

"Uh huh. And I've only been with you for a few weeks so I understand why you'd ditch me." He's being sarcastic. Bob has been by my side for nearly a decade.

"Bob, don't. Not right now." I tuck the script under my arm, feeling like a dick. I'm about to ask him something, and he's going to punch me in the face. At least, he'll want to, before replying appropriately. "I need a favor." I tip my head forward, indicating that I want his car. "Can we switch for a few hours?"

"Awh, hell no! The paps found you, and you've cooked up something stupid with that Ferro kid again."

"Jon's almost thirty."

"Yeah," he grabs his face with his hand and pulls down as if he were wiping it off. "I know. Twenty-nine and three-quarters. You're both kids compared to me. If you have to use my car to get away with it, this idea has dumbass written all over it."

I glance around, making sure no one is watching us, and then lower my gaze to the asphalt. I resist the urge to kick a rock. Bob's right. I need to stop acting like a kid, but this isn't what he thinks it is. "I may have accidentally led the press to Katie's house. Jon is going to do something Ferro-ish to draw them away for the night. I need your car to go back."

Bob folds his arms over his chest. "Fine, but I'm driving you."

"You can't. I'm trying to mend fences with someone, and I'd rather be alone."

"Trystan, you're killing me. How am I supposed to do my job?"

"Help Jon?" My voice is too high, and the command comes out as a question.

Bob curses under his breath while pacing in a circle. When he comes back, he points his sausage-sized finger in my face. "If you fucking drive into something again, I'm going to kick your ass." His nostrils flare angrily, but his hand drops and he steps back. Bob fishes the keys out of his pocket and tosses them to me.

I catch them and nod my head in thanks. "That was an accident. I promise I won't wreck your car."

Bob puffs up into my space, lowering his face until his chin lines up with my forehead. "A man's car is everything, but I'm talking about you. If you do some other dumbass thing—and I don't care if it's drinking, parties, drugs or what—I'm done with you, Trystan." His dark eyes are firm, and I can tell the crash rattled him.

If I could tell him what happened, I would.

There's nothing to say, so I just nod. I rush over to his car, pull open the door and toss the script on the seat. It's going to take nearly an hour to get back out to Katie's—that's just long enough for Bob and Jon to do their thing.

Before I pull away, I notice Bob is still standing there, studying me as if evaluating me. I slide the window down, thinking I'll reassure him that I'm fine, but he walks over and holds out an envelope—a small white envelope that looks like it came from the Hallmark store.

I take it from him. "What's this?"

Bob checks my mail, sorting out the fan mail and sending the rest of it to my accountant. He's never handed me mail directly before, so this is weird. "It's something you should open when you have friends around, and not before."

"Bob, you're shitting me, right? Is it blank?" He's freaking me out a little bit with his behavior.

The man shakes his massive bald head. "No, it certainly is not, and it checks out. Like I said, wait until you're with friends. Don't open that alone."

"It's my father, isn't it? Is he dead?"

"Trystan." There's a warning in his tone, and he reaches for the letter.

I jerk it back and stuff it in my jacket. "Got it. Open it at Katie's, not a moment before—also, there's some bad shit in there that may or may not be about my father. Great. Sounds like fun."

It sounds horrible. I haven't seen my dad since I watched the cops drag him away. I assumed he was in prison or maybe on parole by now. No one told me he's dead, so maybe that's what this letter contains. I'm not sure how I feel about that since the man hated me.

BROKEN PROMISES

Why does bad news come in threes? First Seth died, now this. That means there's still one more piece-of-crap disaster still coming.

CHAPTER 23

That letter is burning a hole in my pocket. I can't keep my mind off of it. Mari's got to think I have brain damage based on the way I'm reading my lines.

Katie is lying on the couch, staring at the ceiling. Mari is sitting on the floor with a script, still feeding me lines from scene one. It's pathetic.

She finally puts the manuscript down and pushes up off the floor. She makes a beeline directly to me. I have no idea what she's doing until she reaches into the inner pocket of my leather jacket. I swat her hand away, and she frowns. "Trystan, you can't concentrate not knowing so just look at it already."

I try to laugh it off and turn up the charm. I offer her a full-wattage smile and dance away from her hands. "Look at what? Your beautiful face? I am, and it's very distracting."

"Barf." Katie makes the most unenthusiastic vomiting noises I've ever heard. She looks over at me. "You always take your jacket off."

"So?" Both women are staring at me. Mari's fiancé is about to show up, and I don't want to do this now. "I'm badass. I need to impress Mari's future husband." I grin at Katie, but she throws a pillow at my head. It misses me and rolls over the carpet.

Mari is staring at the side of my face, and I'm pretty sure there will be burn marks on my skin in a moment. I round on her. "What?"

She sighs with her entire body and her shoulders go slack. "You're as impossible now as you were in high school. Just read the letter!"

"What letter?"

"WE CAN SEE IT." Katie sits up and glances at Mari.

I don't realize what they're doing until they both rush at me from opposite directions. Mari slams into my side as Katie rushes at me head-on and knocks me to the floor. The next thing I know, Katie is lying across my legs and Mari is sitting on my chest. She flops backward, slips her hand inside my jacket, and pulls out the envelope. "Shit."

They're both laughing, and it's nice to hear, but I'm not ready to open that note yet. "Mari, don't." My voice comes out breathy because she's on my chest. The touch isn't skin on skin, but I feel her concern for me anyway. She rolls onto her stomach and props up on her elbows, waving the white envelope between her fingers as I try to get Katie off my legs.

She meets my gaze and stops. The smile falls from her lips, and she realizes the letter contains bad news.

Before she can say anything, the door swings open, and Derrick walks through with a pink bakery box. He stops, drops his jaw, and blinks. He snaps out of it, and mutters, "Oh, good. The orgy started without me."

Mari pushes up, walks over to him and kisses him on the cheek. "Awh, you brought dessert."

"Yeah, I got those mini cannoli you like."

Katie suddenly jumps off my legs and rushes at the box. "Dibs! This is my dinner, bitches! Get your own." She grabs the box and disappears into the kitchen. Before anyone can say anything, she stuffs one in her mouth and smiles. Cream oozes from between her teeth.

That's the thing with Katie—she puts herself last, always trying to make other people forget their troubles, even when she's drowning in them. No wonder why she didn't want to be alone tonight. I laugh, I can't help it. She looks disgusting with saliva and crème oozing from her mouth.

Katie puts up her hands like a zombie and frankenwalks toward Mari. "Brains! Brains!"

I fold my arms over my chest and tuck my chin, hiding my laugh. Mari scowls at me. "Hey, I'm just glad she's not coming at me."

"You suck! Stop!" She backs away from Katie, laughing until she's trapped in a corner. Katie kisses both of Mari's cheeks, sliming her with cannoli filling.

They're both laughing hard, and even the douche is chuckling. I need to try and be nice to him, for Mari. I walk over and hold out the metaphorical white flag. "Did you get a cake?"

His gaze cuts to mine and his smile falters. He's suspicious. "Yeah, why?"

"Is it a cassata cake, by chance?"

Mari hears me through Katie's slimy kisses and they both turn around and look at us. "That's not funny, Trystan." She waves a finger at me.

"It's not a good idea. Derrick brought the cake." I glance at her and notice a blur of white tucked into the front pocket of her jeans under her oversized sweater.

Derrick doesn't miss a beat. He's got the cake in his hand and scoops up half, dumping it in my palms. Maybe he's not an asshole? He nods at me and indicates we should rush them, making a Katie and Mari cassata cake sandwich.

Both women scream when they see us coming, but they're trapped in the corner with nowhere to run. I cream Katie, pushing the cake into her cheek while Derrick gets Mari. They both shriek with laughter. Katie rounds on me and jumps. I could escape her bear hug, but I let her get cake cream all over me until she sticks out her tongue.

"I'm going to lick Trystan Scott!"

"I don't think so." I try to escape, but Mari grabs one of my arms and Derrick grabs the other. They slam me back against the wall, and Katie licks the side of my face, leaving a trail of slime.

When they release me, they're all laughing so hard they can't breathe. I act like it's gross, but I'm smiling, too. Mari's doubled over with tears in her eyes. She's leaning against Katie, and they're both covered with white cream. There's a blob of cake in Mari's dark hair, but she doesn't seem to care. The two of them slide down the kitchen wall, caught in a fit of giggles until they can't laugh anymore.

Derrick heads off to clean up in the bathroom. I grab a kitchen chair and sit down, still covered in cake and Katie slime.

She's too young to be a widow. Grief rushes back, and suddenly I feel hyper-aware that Seth isn't here. This is the kind of thing that would have happened with him. I know Katie and Mari are thinking it, too, because the mood suddenly plummets.

I grab a cannoli from the box and lift it in the air. "To Seth, and all the times he made us laugh. As long as we keep going and don't take life too seriously, we'll do him proud."

Mari smiles. She grabs a cannoli from the box and lifts it. "To Seth, and all the times he grinned and said, 'do me.'"

Katie snorts and grabs a cannoli. She lifts it into the air and all three of us tap them together as if they're champagne glasses. "To Seth, wherever you are, know I'm thankful for all the laughter."

CHAPTER 24

~MARI~

Something weird is happening—Trystan and Derrick are getting along. You know, maybe Katie's right—they do look similar. I didn't see it until they were sitting next to each other at dinner. Oh, God, now I'm 'that' girl, the crazy one who dates clones of her ex.

I don't want to think about it. I'm happy with Derrick and, after the initial shock of it all, he's taken the whole rock superstar ex-boyfriend thing pretty well. They seem to be talking easily, which feels weird. I expected them to hate each other with a little more gusto.

Maybe they're being nice for Katie's sake. Whatever the reason, I'm glad they're not fighting.

Even though the envelope is folded in half, it keeps poking me from my pocket, forcing me to remember it's there. I don't want to push Trystan to open something like this in front of Derrick. His mind is somewhere else tonight like he's looking over his shoulder. I've glanced out the window a few times without seeing any reporters. I'm sure he's worried they'll camp out at Katie's apartment, but they haven't so far.

Trystan is leaning back in his seat in the kitchen chair with his legs kicked out under the table. He seems comfortable even though I know he's not. He isn't finished grieving Seth, and whatever is in this note is going to be bad. Trystan glances at me across the table, smirking, before tapping me with the tip of his boot. I smile back and avert my eyes. I don't want him to know I'm thinking about him, worried about him, or anything else.

I don't know how to fit him into my life or if I want to. For the next few days, he'll be around for the funeral, and after that it's only a few days to learn the script, and he'll be gone again—if that's what I want.

That's the one thing I can sense from Trystan. He doesn't know what I want. He can't read me, and I know why. It's because I haven't decided. I don't know if I can let go of the betrayal and the pain he caused, or if I even want to. How do I erase something that completely crushed me?

Katie kicks me under the table and offers a toothy smile. She's still wearing cake in the ends of her hair, although she's washed off her makeup and slicked her hair into a ponytail. She lifts a glass of milk in the air. "To you guys. Thanks for hanging out with me tonight. I know it feels like a bipolar emotional roller coaster, which isn't fun. To friends—old and new." She tips her head toward Derrick. "Thanks for not screaming when we destroyed your cake."

He shrugs. "Some cakes are created for eating. Other cakes are created for fun."

I glance at Derrick from the corner of my eye and then at Trystan. He's nodding and holding up his cup of milk as well. Katie dumped all the liquor down the drain before Trystan came back, unwilling to aid in his self-destruction. No one seems to notice its absence—not out loud at least—and the cake tastes better with milk than alcohol, anyway.

"Well said," Trystan agrees with a nod. I should be happy, but I'm not.

I glance at Katie, but she doesn't seem to notice. Something isn't right, but I can't put my finger on it. Maybe I'm mental? Today has been insanely long. I brush aside my apprehension and help clean up the kitchen. After every last bit of cake is cleaned up, I follow Derrick to the door while Katie and Trystan finish loading the dishes.

Derrick pulls me to him and slides his hands down my back to rest just below my waist. His voice is soft and deep. "I had a good time tonight. I love you." He lowers his lips to mine and kisses me slowly. His hands press on my back until one lifts to my bra and presses harder, forcing my breasts into his chest. It's a passionate kiss for him, and for a second I wonder why, but then I feel it—Trystan is there, and he's watching us.

Shyness floods me, and I pull away. My face flames red, and I look at the carpet, trying to hide it. Trystan doesn't say anything. He just flops down on the couch and turns on the TV.

Derrick gives me a look and then his gaze cuts to Trystan before returning to me. He leans in and kisses my cheek, seeming to understand that I don't want to make out with him in front of people. Before he pulls back, he whispers, "You never pulled away in front of Katie, but I understand if you want to give him some time. I can respect that, as long as it's not forever."

"It won't be." My hands splay across his chest, and I look up to see uncertainty in his icy blue eyes. I wish I knew what he was thinking, but I don't.

He smiles. "Good." Derrick kisses me on the cheek again and heads out.

By the time he's gone, Katie has snuggled into the chair, and the only spot left to sit is next to Trystan. Stop acting like a child. Adults can be friends with their exes. Get over it already and stop being stupid. I plop down on the cushion next to him, careful not to touch him, and feel the letter stab me. I'm about to pull it out when I look up at the TV. "What the hell is that?"

Trystan is grinning and staring. Katie's mouth forms an O and is hanging open.

Trystan laughs. "It's Jon Ferro. In Times Square."

"I see that. What the hell is he doing?" He's standing next to two women covered in body paint. It looks like they're wearing leopard leotards, but they're not. It's an intricately painted design. I wouldn't have realized they were naked had the station not blurred their girlie parts—which was silly because you can't see them under the paint.

Jon appears dressed for a safari, wearing light-colored clothes, a fedora, sunglasses, and he's holding what appears to be a rifle. With a grin on his face, he proudly tells the reporter he's going on an expedition.

"Yes, Tina, I'll be hunting on the African Savanna next month, and I plan to shoot as many exotic animals as possible. The mansion needs new décor, so it's not entirely for sport." He laughs and smiles as if he hadn't said the most politically incorrect thing imaginable.

I blink at the screen. "Did he just say he's going to shoot endangered animals and hang them on his walls?"

Trystan nods and sits forward. "Yeah, he did."

Katie finally mutters, "Holy fuck. He's insane. Every reporter within a hundred miles is going to blast him for that."

Trystan glances over at me and then back at the TV. It makes me think that he knew about this. I frown, watching Jon say more insane things before lifting the rifle and aiming it at one of the naked women. Without hesitation, he shoots her, and the camera pans to show her side covered in dark red paint.

"Holy shit." Katie stares, shocked.

Trystan is trying not to laugh. I slap him, playfully, with the back of my hand. "Okay, spill. Why is your BFF making an ass out of himself in Times Square? He's pissing people off on purpose." The crowd is getting rowdy, and that's before a big man in a black suit hands Jon another paint gun. I blink at the screen in disbelief. "Is that Bob?"

Katie glances over at us. "What'd you do?"

"I didn't do anything," I say sharply, "this is all him."

Trystan sighs and looks up at the ceiling, stretching his neck. I catch a glimpse of a silver chain before it dips below his shirt again. Does he know he's lost the ring yet? Has he looked for it? The movement forces out Trystan's Adam's apple and I see him swallow hard. When he looks at us, he presses his lips together and parts his hands. "The press followed me here earlier. I asked Jon to draw them away, but I didn't know this was his plan."

I fish the note out of my pocket, realizing we're on borrowed time. "Did he owe you a favor? The press is going to slaughter him for this."

"They'll report it was a prank in the morning when he donates a million bucks to an animal shelter and adopts a panther. Jon is sly that way." We sit, silently staring at Jon's antics for another minute, before Katie spies the letter in my hand.

She grabs the remote and shuts off the TV. "Don't waste the distraction. Rip open that letter, Mari." Katie sits down in her chair again and tucks her feet under her butt. She's nervous. I can tell because she only sits like that when she thinks bad news is coming. It's her go-to position for bracing against something bad.

I keep my voice calm and gentle. "So what's in this letter that has you so spooked?"

Trystan looks down at the carpet. "Bob gave it to me earlier when I asked him to help Jon. He said I couldn't open it alone. That I had to be with friends, and that it 'checked out.' I think it's about my dad."

A heavy silence settles on the room. I'm still holding the envelope. Trystan hasn't tried to take it away. He still doesn't look at me, before finally saying, "Open it. Read it, and give me the highlights."

"You don't want to read it first?" I ask, holding the paper out to him.

He shakes his head. "No, if Dad wrote it, he'll rip into me, and I don't want to know the specifics. If it's someone writing to tell me he's dead, again, I don't want to know the specifics." Trystan pushes his fingers into the sides of his hair and holds his head in his hands. He doesn't look up again.

I tear open the paper with a sense of dread. Two deaths so close together would suck. Even though with everything that happened between Trystan and his shitty father, I know his death will still be hard. Trystan's father blamed him, neglected him, and abused him. If I hadn't accidentally interrupted a beating one night back in high school, Trystan might not be here now.

I pull out the paper and scan the handwriting. At first glance, I know from the penmanship a woman wrote the letter. Each letter is a fluid curving swirl flowing into the next. As I read the note, I grow increasingly upset. If it's true, this is going to kill him.

When I'm finished reading, my eyes shoot to Trystan. He hasn't moved. Katie watches me, biting her thumb nervously. "Well? What is it?"

I'm shaking, still holding the note. My lips part, but I can't find the right words. When Trystan turns to face me, I want to cry. This story can't be true.

"Is it Dad?" Worry pinches his brow as he threads his fingers together. He's waiting, looking at me. His eyes lock with mine, and I know he feels the dread bubbling up inside of me. My stomach is in a free-fall. I don't want to deliver this news, but I have to—he asked me to do it.

I shake my head. "No, it's your mother."

CHAPTER 25

Trystan drops his hands and sits up straight. "What? How can it be from my mother? MY mother?" He reaches for the note and hesitates. His hand is in the air just above the paper, shaking. He pulls away as if burned, and jumps up quickly.

He paces the floor, and I watch a million emotions collide on his face. "That can't be. She doesn't want anything to do with me. She left us because of me. Dad said she couldn't handle a screaming baby every day. She picked up and left. She left me, Mari!" He screams the words at me and I feel the knife being shoved deeper and deeper into his stomach as he realizes the ramifications of her coming to him now.

Katie's voice is soft. "What does she want?"

I'm still holding the paper and sitting on the edge of the couch. "She says she wants to talk to you, but this could be from anyone, Trystan. There's no way to know if this woman is your mother."

He shakes his head and stops abruptly, gasping as if he'd been sucker punched, before explaining. "Bob checked it already. When he handed it to me, he said it was legit." Trystan turns suddenly, his eyes locking on mine. His lips press lightly together, and his eyes are glassy. "Do you know how long I've waited for this? Do you know how many ways I've imagined this day? But she shows up now, right after the Times printed how many millions I earn in a year. You've got to love my fucking family!" He smiles, but there's only pain in his eyes. Trystan sits down hard next to me, slamming his head into the back of the couch. He stares at the ceiling and closes his eyes.

Katie slips from her chair. "I'm going to make some coffee." She glances at Trystan, opens her mouth to say something, and then doesn't. She looks at me and leaves the room.

Trystan is quiet for a few moments, but I know what's racing through his head—he thinks she wants his money. "When I was a kid, I'd lie in bed at night and wonder what she looked like. I wanted to hear her voice, and I'd imagine her singing to me. The nights my dad locked me in the closet, I'd picture her face opening the door and scooping me up in her arms, taking me away from my father. I waited and waited for her to show up, but she never came. Why the fuck should I let her in now?" He opens his eyes and looks over at me.

My chest feels so heavy, like it's being crushed. He has to feel so much worse. I lick my lips and sit back next to him, staring straight ahead as I talk. I feel his eyes on the side of my face. "I don't know. I wouldn't know what to do if I were you, or how to decide something like this. I mean, we both had shitty parents—yours more so—"

"Your dad was an asshole, Mari. He completely ignored you until your mom died. Just because he didn't hit you doesn't mean he didn't hurt you."

I swallow hard and nod slowly. "Maybe, but before my mom died, she started making an effort to know me, to know what I liked and what I thought. It was weird at first because I didn't believe her. She'd always been so enamored with my father she didn't even see me, so when she suddenly took an interest in what I was doing, it was hard to swallow." I'm wringing my hands as I speak, recalling memories I regret—things I can't fix because she's gone.

"I remember that. She came to the play."

"She did, and I didn't know how to accept that she wanted to know me. I regret that, Trystan. I held her at arm's length because I was afraid."

"Afraid of what, exactly?"

I shrug, trying to keep the pain out of my voice and failing. "I don't know. That she wasn't sincere, that she wouldn't like me once she figured out who I was? Maybe I was just afraid I'd screw it up. After I had spent so much time alone, longing for something I couldn't have, I didn't know how to react when she tried to fix it. I left it a mess for a while. We had lunch, and she came to see my dorm room and helped me set it up. Some of my chances were stolen, but I was the one who wasted the rest." I can barely breathe. I haven't admitted this to anyone, but he knew me then and knew how hard it was. I feel his hand on top of mine. He squeezes, and I don't care that he can read me, that he can feel the regret coursing through my veins.

"Mari, there's no way you could have known what would happen."

I force a smile. "I know, which is why I feel so horrible about it. Trystan, I can't speak for you, but if I had it to do over again, I wouldn't hold back." I'm afraid to look over at him. We're poking around an old wound that never healed, a scab that never came off.

I usually protect these thoughts, shoving them down inside me as far as they'll go. These things are never said, and they aren't supposed to see the light of day. I have no idea how I admitted it, except that I know he needs to hear it.

"You think I'm afraid? You think that's the reason I wouldn't want to see her?"

I'm already as raw as I can be. I don't hold back, I don't filter my thoughts—he can see through me, anyway, so what's the point? I turn to face him and take his hand. Now he has one of mine, and I have one of his. I bite my lower lip and jump in. "I think it's easier to believe your dad than face your mother. If you meet her and she confirms what your dad told you—that she didn't want you and it's your fault she left—that would hurt worse than him just claiming that was the truth. I'd be afraid to hear that, too. But what if that's not why she left? Maybe your dad lied, or maybe he just didn't understand. Trystan, the truth is that you won't know why she really left unless you talk to her. If you don't, you'll regret it. You'll look back and wonder what you lost. I know I do."

"What if she just wants to use me? Mari, I can't handle that, not right now." The insecure way his brow wrinkles makes me want to throw my arms around him. His defenses are completely and totally down. Trystan trusts me with this, and it's big enough to destroy him.

"Trystan, you're the strongest person I know. You've lived through hell and smile telling the tale." I laugh and touch his cheek as I say it, before dropping my hand to my side. "You came to school every day and acted like you were happy. That's strength like I've never seen, not before or since. Trystan, you can do this."

He presses his lips together into a thin line and blinks rapidly. His dark lashes clump together with unshed tears. He releases my hand and stands. Trystan turns his back to me, putting his hands behind his neck and stretching. When his shirt lifts I can see a few words tattooed on the small of his back. They're small, written in script and resemble a poem. It disappears beneath his jeans. That wasn't there the last time we were together. I wonder what it says, which song it is. Knowing Trystan, it has to be a song.

Trystan drops his arms suddenly and turns around. He pins me in place with those cobalt eyes, and I wish I could take away his pain. He nods once and then twice as he shoves his hands into his pockets. "I'll talk to her."

CHAPTER 26

I've held this ring in my pocket intending on giving it back to Trystan, but I haven't found the right time. The thick band feels cool against my skin as I run my fingers over the Greek inscription not for the first time today.

I pull it from my pocket and stare at it. How did we get like this? Maybe I should have gone to him a long time ago, but I was so hurt, and it's not as if he approached me either. It really looked like he nailed me and left, just one more name in a long list of conquests. It's classic Trystan Scott.

Giving Trystan advice in light of Seth's death is making me replay a lot of my choices over the past ten years—since I lost my mother. I didn't give her a chance to make up. I mean, I tried, but I was still mad at her. That anger never really went away. It bore a hole in my chest, infected with something rancid. Now every time I think about her I feel sick with guilt. I wouldn't wish that on an enemy.

The guilt needles its way into the crevices of my mind, filling my memories with doubt. What if mom felt rejected and pushed aside? What if her attempts to fix things with me didn't go well because I wouldn't let them, because I couldn't forgive her for ignoring me for seventeen years?

From my earliest memories, she was always with Dad. If I needed something, I had to wait, because Daddy came first. She was with him at work and stayed late even when she didn't have to. She skipped my awards at school and barely showed up for anything for twelve years. From the time kindergarten started until the time I filed for early graduation in eleventh grade, she failed to show up.

Then one day, she was there. It was like someone flipped a switch and I suddenly had a mother. I didn't know what to do with all that rejection. It piled up on my shoulders and crushed my heart for so long. It felt awkward, but I tried to accept her attempts to reconcile. I wanted it. I wanted her in my life. I wanted her to accept me for who I am.

All that was stolen from me before I even knew what she thought. One day she was there and the next she was gone.

I don't visit her grave. I don't talk to her, and I try so hard not to think about her because it only fills me with remorse.

When I look at Katie's tear-stained face, I see glimpses of that pain, of that bitter regret that seeps in when someone dies too soon. I don't know how to be there for her in this, because it's becoming clear I didn't handle my mother's death well—assuming I dealt with it at all.

Katie enters the room in a black dress and wool coat. She's saying goodbye to her best friend today, and I need to be there for her. I pocket the ring, but the flash of silver catches her eye. "What is that? You keep playing with it." She speaks over her shoulder as she grabs a dark blue scarf off the hook on the wall.

"Nothing." I quickly stuff the ring in my pocket, hiding it from sight. If she's seen it, she doesn't know what it is anyway. There's no way she'd realize it belongs to Trystan.

Katie settles into her usual spot. Her cheeks are red from the cold, and her skin is pale. She smirks. "So want to hear a joke? It's kind of lame, but funny in a dorky kind of way. It's up your alley."

"How do you do it?" I shouldn't ask, but I can't help it. "How do you go on as if nothing's happened and still have a smile on your face. I didn't smile for a year after Mom died. How do you find humor in anything?"

Katie's eyes glisten almost instantly. She smiles serenely, closing her eyes for a second. When she opens them again, she walks toward me and places a mitten-covered hand on my arm. "I smile for Seth. If I couldn't smile, if I couldn't laugh after knowing him even for a little while, what's the point? I'm going to be the woman he saw in me. I'm going to be the best parts of him, so he lives on through me. And I'm going to randomly cry my ass off for no apparent reason, so stop asking me stupid questions, Cockapoo, and let's go."

I grab the entire box of tissues and follow her into the hallway. Today is the worst day of Katie's life, and yet she can see her way through the storm. She's an amazing person, and I'm lucky to have her in my life. If I say that now, though, the limo ride will be a snotfest, so I make a mental note to tell her later. I need to get out of the habit of assuming people know how much I love them. Even if they do know, they need to hear it.

CHAPTER 27

The days inch by at slug speed. When I lie down at night, I can't sleep. When I wake up in the morning, Katie is in the same spot on the chair, her thin body tucked into a ball, in the same position she was in the night before. The dark circles under her eyes are getting bigger, but there's nothing I can do besides wait with her.

We watch old TV shows, and I fix a lot of food that doesn't get eaten. Katie picks at her meals, but she's not consumed much in the past few days.

About a week after the burial, Katie pulls on a pair of jeans and slicks her hair into a ponytail. She grabs a jacket and pulls it on. "I'm going to the cemetery for a while."

I'm on the couch, not watching the show flickering in front of me. I turn to her. "Do you want me to come with you?"

She shakes her head and ties the belt tightly around her waist. "No, I need to be alone. Don't worry, I'll be okay." Her hand rests on my shoulder for a moment.

"We'll get through this."

She tries to smile, but her lips twitch and fall. Over the past few days, she's stopped joking. Once she stopped kidding around, laughing at my jokes soon followed. She seems hollow, as if what made her Katie was scooped out. My friend is gone.

I hope I can help her find her way back. I know deep down, under all that grief and pain, she's still in there. Every day is a struggle, but in the end she has to be the one to decide to keep fighting.

She squeezes my shoulder. "Call Trystan. He still doesn't know his lines."

"How do you know that?"

She pads toward the door. "Because he told me not to tell you, but he still can't remember his lines. Was he like this in high school? No wonder you wanted to kill him half the time." She grabs a scarf from the hook and puts it around her neck before grabbing her keys.

"Yeah, he was. I think he has dyslexia or something because he couldn't seem to see the script."

"Was he ever tested?"

"I don't know. When I mentioned it back then, he didn't want to talk about it. I guess it's a sore spot."

"Good thing he has you, Drill Sergeant Mari. Go beat his part into his brain." She smiles and waves as she heads out the door.

I pick up my phone and dial my old number. Trystan answers on the first ring. "Mari, what's wrong?" Music blares behind him and suddenly stops. He must be at rehearsal for his next record.

"Nothing, I'm sorry. I didn't know how else to contact you, so I used this number." I kind of like that he jumped to get the phone, even though it was a little evil of me. I did have his other number, but I assumed I'd be routed through an assistant. "I'll be quick— Katie mentioned you're still having trouble with your lines."

He makes a sound in the back of his throat and laughs, but it's too high-pitched. His voice drops as he replies. "No, that's okay. I've got it."

"You've learned them?"

"Yup."

"All of them?"

"Of course." He sounds like his mind is far away, and I can hear him picking at the strings on his guitar.

I spit out a line from the movie, "I had to see you again. To be this close and pretend you didn't exist, I'm sorry. I couldn't do it. I couldn't stay away." I wait a moment and when he doesn't jump on his line, I prompt him. "And now it's your turn."

"Something about a plane," he says in a flat voice, and I picture him sitting on a speaker in those old ripped jeans and leather jacket, kicking the scuffed toe of his boot against the floor. His hair is probably hanging in his eyes so no one can see his face and he's not smiling. He's embarrassed, but he's hiding it with humor and charm—the way he always has.

I can't help it. I laugh. "A plane? Trystan!"

"Yes?"

"Do you want help?"

"I was going to show up and improv the whole thing, but I'm guessing they'll like your idea better."

"And what's my idea?"

"Learning the script." I swear he's pouting. I hear him suck in a breath and picture him pushing his hair out of his face and smiling. "Fine, but I can't go to Katie's anymore. We need to meet somewhere else, and coming here won't be easy on you and Derrick. The press will say things he won't like. I'm not sure where else to meet."

"Let me take care of that. You finish your... whatever you're doing, and I'll give Bob an address. See you later."

There's a pause, before he says, "Mari?"

"Yeah?" My heart starts thumping all wonky like a flat tire.

The silence stretches on for a moment, and then he lets out a little breath. "Nothing. I'll see you later."

I end the call and stare at the phone in my hand. Every time I talk to him I feel like I did in high school as if no time has passed at all. But ten years have passed, and lots of things have happened.

Life occurs in segments, little bursts of time setting us on a course. Our little boat floats out into vast waters, sailing along until a storm comes to knock us off course—or worse. How many people are floating around, lost? I'm not even sure I am floating anymore. It's more like I'm trying to break my boat free from years of rot after it's been filled with sediment and settled on the ocean floor.

I'm not a bad person, but I don't like what my life's become. I go through the motions, day in and day out, and for what? At one time, I had an answer to that. Now I feel like I'll be shoveling silt out of my hull for eternity.

CHAPTER 28

When I find a place that works, I tell Bob where to drop Trystan off and what we're doing. He's relieved someone is finally helping Trystan. Bob thinks if Trystan backs out of the movie deal, everything will fall apart—that everyone is waiting to watch Trystan crash and burn. Since he's been in the crashing phase for a while now, burning can't be too far away.

Something inside me snaps into place. I feel it move from a callous, 'I don't care what happens to him' thought, to an 'over my dead body' notion. Before I have time to analyze the reason it happened, I'm convincing Bob that

Trystan won't burn at all—not while I'm around.

Is that something I can offer? I don't know, but either way, I sound confident I can prevent it from happening. Bob is partly right about the movie, but the things that could break Trystan are unseen. Things happening behind the scenes are so hard on him right now. He hasn't mentioned his mother since the night I read him the note. I'm sure that's eating at him, along with many other things.

I'm sitting at a table in a diner on Deer Park Avenue, not far from my old high school, waiting for Derrick. I have a glass of water, and I've been watching beads of condensation slide down the side.

When he walks through the door, he scans each table until he sees me. He crosses the restaurant in long, lean strides, with a grin on his face and his rarely seen dimple showing. He looks beautiful today, all decked out in a gray suit and shiny shoes. He lightly brushes his lips against mine before sliding into the booth across from me.

"So what's the occasion?" He settles in across from me, obviously wondering why I dragged him half way across Suffolk County to a diner he's never heard of before.

I hand him a menu and explain. "I'm just feeling nostalgic. I used to come here after class with Katie. I thought it'd be nice to have some memories here with you, too."

He glances around. "Ah, so this is the place where you two went and got in trouble."

I grimace. "I never got in trouble."

He laughs and scans the menu. "That's not what I heard. Your father was adamant about that, especially where your, and I quote, 'idiot ex-boyfriend' was involved. I now assume he was referring to Trystan." He glances up at me. "Is it okay to talk about that? I'm not being an asshole, am I?"

He's sweet to ask. I reach across the table and take his hands. "No, of course not. We should be able to talk about anything." It feels like we're walking on eggshells with this topic. Derrick swings from being completely understanding to beyond irritated in a blink. I'm certain it's because fame is involved. A guy's ego is a fragile thing. I don't want Derrick thinking that he's living in the shadow of a legacy. That time in my life is over.

He presses his lips together into a tight smile. "Good, that's how I feel, too. So, I need to know—"

Apparently it's awkward question time. "I mean it, ask anything." I rub his hand gently and then sit back in the booth.

He opens his mouth, makes a false start, and snaps it shut. The second time he starts over, he actually speaks. "Why did you guys break up? He doesn't seem like an asshole and, from what I can tell, you don't hate him—so what happened?"

This is the sore spot, because there is no real answer. "He left me, and it ended. That's it. I did hate him for a while, but that's in the past. I can't walk around hating his guts. It's exhausting." I laugh, trying to make light of it.

"Yeah, but you guys seem like friends again now. So everything is all right?"

"As much as it can be. I'm going to help him with his lines again later." Our food arrives, and I dig into my gigantic salad, but Derrick just stares at his sandwich. "What's the matter?"

Derrick appears as if he's thinking too hard. His brow is furrowed and there are worry lines etched into his forehead. "I think

I've been pretty supportive, but this guy is your ex. Would you be okay with me hanging out with my ex-girlfriend? By the way, she's a supermodel, incredibly funny, and rocket-scientist smart." His tone is light, but his hands are on either side of his plate and his eyes are locked onto mine, worried.

I reach out and rest my hand on top of his. "I don't cheat, and there's no way he's stealing me away from you. If he makes you uncomfortable, I won't do it. You come first, Derrick."

He shakes his head. "I'm not going to be that guy. You do what you think is best." He watches me for a moment as if trying to put his finger on a thought that won't sit still.

I shovel more salad into my mouth and feel a little self-conscious. "What? You want some?"

He smiles softly and shakes his head. "I think he did something to you, and you didn't forgive him. You're still mad about it."

I nearly drop my fork and spew salad across the diner. Derrick has never been that perceptive before. There are two ways to play this, denial or tell him the truth.

You're getting married, putz. Tell him the truth.

I frown and lean back in the booth. "You're right. He did something, and I can't let it go so there's no future for us like that. Trystan banished his ass to the friend-zone for eternity."

"What'd he do?" Derrick is careful. He knows he's poking sore spots and, based on the way he's hiding behind his plate, he knows I don't want to answer.

"Okay. I'll drop it." He doesn't push it further, just picks up his food and takes a bite. The lack of argument is anticlimactic. I want him to care enough to press me. I want him mad enough to threaten to beat Trystan to a pulp, but he doesn't. "Well, he seems like a good guy. Would it be weird if I asked him to play a little one-on-one this weekend?"

What the hell? He was just asking me to distance myself from Trystan, but he wants to be buds with the guy? Derrick seems bipolar at times. It's as if there's a great guy and a total dick fighting for control of his brain at all times.

I hide my surprise and wave my fork in the air, trying to make light of things. "Ah, so there's a bromance brewing?"

"Ha. Funny. Nah, I just thought if he's going to be around you, I should get to know him better."

I nod agreeably because I don't know what I think of the whole thing, but I manage to conceal my thoughts by focusing on my food for the rest of the conversation. My mind won't let go of the thought of the two of them being friends.

Why is that bad? It'd be like Derrick and Seth being close. That wouldn't have been weird, so why does it bother me that he wants to spend time with Trystan?

Maybe it's because I didn't sleep with Seth. I wasn't madly in love with Seth, either. That changes things. A fiancé shouldn't be all friendly with a guy that nailed his girl. It is weird and makes me feel like a concubine or something.

"Earth to Mari," Derrick snaps his fingers in front of my face. The doggie snap needs to stop. Maybe I should be glad he's not using one of those dog training clickers.

I smile and shake off the unsavory thoughts. "What? What'd I miss?"

"When are we having dinner with your father?"

I roll my eyes. I can't help it. "You're such a suck-up. I can't believe you asked his permission to marry me."

After the blow up in the restaurant I chased Derrick into the park. My engagement is embarrassing on two levels—one he initially threw the ring at me, and two, when I tried to apologize, he laughed it off and said that was his proposal. He knew we were meant to be because I ran after him. The whole temper tantrum was a test and I passed. He slipped the ring on my finger and I kept it there.

He never really asked me.

I didn't have that dream moment where the world stops as he waits for me to say yes.

To add to that mess, Derrick asked my father's permission, so Dad thinks that I had a romantic proposal. I didn't intend to hide the facts, but now they seem embarrassing. I'm such an asshat that I screwed up my engagement. There's no way to say that and have it come out right, so when people ask, I skip from the beginning of the story to the ring. Add one big ass bride-to-be smile and no one asks questions.

Derrick chews his food loudly, and takes a swig of soda. "Have you met that man? He's not someone I want to piss off for eternity. I'm on enough shitlists as it is."

"What do you mean?"

He wipes his face with the napkin and then confesses, "I haven't, um, told my mom about our engagement."

I shriek, "What?" Everyone around us stops what they're doing and stares. I wave and smile like Miss America, my face turning red.

Derrick chucks my chin. "Awh, you're so cute. But seriously, I told her about you, just not that I proposed."

Yeah, I can understand skipping that part since it was a train wreck, but not telling his mother?

I blink, shocked. "She's going to kill you. You know that, right?"

His mom lives in Jersey. I've yet to meet her, but I spoke to her on the phone a couple of times. She sounds like a cookie-baking kind of mom, busting with pride at his achievements. The apocalypse couldn't keep her away from him in an emergency.

"I know. I feel kind of bad about it, which is why I thought we should have an engagement party pretty quickly. My mom can meet your dad, and they can compare notes on how hard it is to raise kids and all that crap. It will be a great opportunity for your dad to see how much I adore you." He drowns a few fries in ketchup before shoving them in his mouth.

"And your brother?"

"He'll keep his mouth shut all night and be a perfect gentleman."

I laugh, certain that won't happen. "A party? We're going to have an engagement party?"

"Yes, with all our friends and family." He takes my hand and kisses the ring he put on my finger. "Say yes."

"Of course. Yes."

He sighs and wipes his forehead as if he were sweating. "I was afraid you'd say no. Mari is usually anti-party. That's going to be interesting when you're the bride and the center of attention. Better get used to it future Mrs. Derrick Pynea."

CHAPTER 29

"Bob, Bob, Bob." I'm saying his name over and over again, playing with the way I move my mouth. I feel like a fish. The more I say it, the more his name sounds like 'blob.'

I'm standing outside the diner, in the back parking lot, hidden from the main road by the building. Trees line the streets of the old neighborhood. My eyes rest on some little kids across the street playing at the McDonald's, fixating on this one little boy who's crying. He stands at the bottom of the slide with tears on his chubby cheeks and doesn't move. He'll stay like that until his mom comes and gets him. I didn't see what happened, but I want to watch her reaction. This moment is the kind of thing that I missed out on with my mother.

A woman a little younger than me appears wearing sweats and sneakers, her hair tucked behind her ears. She kneels in front of him and smiles, kissing his face as she scoops him up into her arms.

Something inside my chest squeezes tight and I realize something—I want that.

I never noticed it before now, but I want that. I want to be a mother and a wife. I want to offer my kid the affection I didn't have. Until now, I wasn't interested in anything but working. I put happiness on hold and buried myself face-first in books and then in work until I had no life left.

For a long time, I wanted nothing to do with marriage or babies. No, thank you. I wanted to be independent. I wanted to do things on my own terms, my own way. I didn't want to be joined at the hip with someone, and I sure as hell didn't want to get knocked up and be trapped at home with a tiny helpless human. I'm an only child, and it shows. I have no idea how to act around babies because I've never really been around them.

But watching the little boy and his mom makes me realize I've not moved forward, not in a long time. I don't think about anything except work. I only talk about patients and Dad. Until the night Trystan showed up in the ER, I'd barely taken a day off.

I pop my lips and resume my bobbing.

His voice coming from behind me scares me out of my skin. "How many times are you going to say my name? I'm not sure if I should be flattered or afraid."

I turn around slowly, smiling like a goofball. I wave awkwardly, wondering how long Bob and Trystan have been standing behind me. Trystan is wearing ripped jeans, a white t-shirt, and faded black Chucks. There's a red cap on his head obscuring his face somewhat. Bob's wearing a Men In Black suit.

I twist my hands in front of me, feeling my face catch fire. "Yeah, so, you heard that?"

"Bob, Bob, Bob, Bob," Trystan mocks, then starts laughing. He's laughing so hard he can barely stand up straight.

Bob wears a concerned look, like he's afraid I might have been hexing him. "If you're done with whatever that was, let's move on before he's ambushed by fans."

I salute Bob and grab Trystan by the crook of his elbow. He giggles and nearly trips over his feet. "This way, Mr. Scott. We have to shove you in my trunk."

"Hey!" He straightens, finds his footing, and walks toward my car.

"Nice giggle, by the way."

He smirks at me and tugs down his visor. "You liked it."

"I did. It was very manly."

Trystan chortles again and gets into my car. "Shut up, Jennings, and drive."

"It's Dr. Jennings, to you. Don't make me kick your disrespectful ass." Trystan snorts and sinks back into the seat, slouching down so he isn't as tall. It must be weird to spend your whole life hiding.

Is that what I've been doing? Hiding? Not from people, but from life. I toss the thought aside as I pull into the parking lot, and pull my car into the back of the high school. Trystan looks at me like I'm nuts. "Feeling homesick?"

"I still have a key to the basement and, thanks to Tucker, I have permission to be in the school theater whenever I want."

He sits up straight, and his jaw drops. "What? I donate piles of money to this theater department, and they didn't do that for me!"

"That's because you were a pain in the ass when you were here. Come on, loose lines. Let's nail that part into your head," I say as we get out of the car and walk across the dark parking lot.

"You had me at 'nailed.'" His lips pull up into a twitchy grin.

I elbow him and scold. "Be serious. You're running out of time. If Seth hadn't died, they wouldn't have given you an extension. So, tell me the truth—why can't you seem to remember any of this script?" We're at the side door. I pull it open and head inside. I pass a custodian and show him my badge. So, maybe I'm not really supposed to be in here, but it's not like he knows that.

Trystan follows with his head down. He's easily recognized, so he doesn't speak until I unlock the basement door and flip on the lights. They hum to life as we stand on the metal grate at the top of the landing. This is where I was standing when I heard Trystan talking to Seth about the girl he couldn't have.

The words float up to me and the past crashes with the present in a surreal way.

That girl had been me.

Trystan stands there for a moment, looking at walls covered in familiar dingy yellow paint. He puts his hands on his hips and inhales deeply. "That smell never gets old."

"No, it doesn't." It's a combination of basement aroma coupled with the faint odor of paint. Add in the old furniture, dust, and dampness, and it becomes its own signature scent. "If these walls could talk, huh?"

I feel his eyes on my cheek and glance over at him. "Yeah. The last time I was down here was with you. You patched me up and covered…" His voice trails off, and he swallows hard. "You hid the beating my father had given me the night before." The corner of his mouth pulls up, and he looks away, placing his hand on the railing. He glances down at the old couches and unused props below. Flats still line the walls and stretch from floor to ceiling.

Trystan doesn't talk about his dad, and I can't blame him. The man is scary. "Have you talked to him at all since then?"

He shakes his head and stares at the old couch. "Nah, there's nothing to say."

"Come on." I reach out to touch his hand, but stop short, hesitating. My palm hovers above his and I pull it back. He pretends he doesn't see, but I know he did because of the way he flinched when I was about to touch him.

Ignoring it, I bound down the metal steps, past the old canvas flats the school uses in productions and head over to the couch. "Is this the same one?"

Trystan passes me and jumps on it. The black pleather couch is fluffy and worn. It's been patched up with duct tape to hide signs of wear. When Trystan's weight comes down on the furniture, I can hear the air rush out of the holes in the upholstery. It hisses between the gaps in the tape. He sits up and pats the seat next to him. "Yup, it's the same one." He's grinning.

"What's that look?"

He shrugs and beams at me. "I don't know, happiness?"

"You're happy to be at school?" I offer a crooked smile. "Maybe I should have examined your head more closely when I had the chance."

"Ha! Funny girl. Okay, come on. Shove those lines into my head. Work your magic, Mari." He hands me the script, and we jump in.

This movie isn't bad. Actually, it's pretty good. It's got a lot of kickassery where Trystan won't have to speak, save a few one-liners, but those aren't sticking either.

Back in high school, Trystan was chosen to play the lead in school plays because he's so charismatic. Even then, Tucker claimed his mind was a sieve—nothing stayed in there very long.

That's not quite right, though. It was more like text couldn't get past his eyes, like there was a disconnect between printed words and his memory. There's no way for them to spill out of his mouth by just looking at the paper. I think that's why running lines with him had worked back then, but it's not working now. Adding another person and creating a connection to the text isn't overpowering whatever is occurring.

Something else is going on.

A few hours pass and we're both frustrated and tired. Trystan sits on the edge of the couch hunched over with his head in his hands. He tugs at his cap and sighs. When he sits back and looks over at me. "We tried, but this isn't working. I should just back out of this now."

"You can't. They already stalled the production timeline for you. If you back out, they'll charge you an insane amount of money." I toss the script on the table and sink back into the couch, pulling my feet up under me. I wrap my arms around my ankles and press my pointer and index fingers to my temple.

"I can afford it. It's better than dealing with this."

I drop my hand, annoyed, and unable to hide it. "It's not the money, Trystan. You're rich, and you've paid for it. Dear God, you've earned every cent you have, and you can spend it however you want, but this isn't you." My hands are out in front of me, palms up, and I can't wipe the frustrated expression off my face. "You can remember song lyrics and can dance every step of every show you've ever done, right?"

"Mari, it's not the same."

"Then explain it to me, because I don't understand how you remember all those things but not this." I'm snapping, and I don't mean to. He feels bad enough as it is, but I can't seem to shut up. "Trystan, if you blow off this movie it's going to look bad. People will say all sorts of crap and it'll damage your brand in a way that might not be fixable."

"Actors drop out of movies all the time." He pulls his cap down tighter and threads his fingers together, resting them on top of his head as he stares at the concrete floor.

"No they don't, not like this, not for this reason. Hollywood came knocking and gave you a chance along with your huge paycheck. Everyone knows. They know you're excited about the part. They know the speculation that you'll ease into the limelight there as easily as you did with singing, so how are you supposed to explain why you can't do it?"

His fingers clamp down tightly on the top of his hat before ripping it from his head and hurling it at the wall. It hits the painted cinderblocks and falls behind a couch. "I don't know! I don't know why I can't, but whatever talent I had before is gone. I thought it was you. I thought if Mari helps me, that'll fix it, but that's not helping, so that means it's me, and I don't know why." By the time he's done speaking his shoulders are up to his ears and his arms are sticking out, palms up.

I pick up the script and toss it to him. It smacks him in the chest before he moves to catch it. I push myself up so that I'm sitting on the arm of the couch. "Read it, Trystan. Pick a part and read it to me."

"Thanks, mom, but I can read fine." He throws the papers on the floor and starts pacing.

I slip off the couch and pick them up, open the booklet, and shove it back into his hands. I point to a paragraph. "Read this to me."

Trystan's eyes slowly lift until he's watching me from behind dark lashes. His heart is pounding like a cornered cat, and I know he's going to lash out—but I don't know why. I know he can read, but I'm starting to wonder if he can see.

"Mari." His voice is deep and rumbles with warning. "Don't press this. Not now."

I put my hands on the script because it looks like he's going to toss it again. I hold my hands over his and stand opposite him, pushing the script at his face. "Read it!"

He's frozen in place, his lips slightly parted, his azure eyes blazing with shame. The pit of my stomach bottoms out. "Trystan? What's happening to you?"

A tremble works its way up his arms, and he shakes me off. "I didn't hit that tree on purpose. I was driving and suddenly then it was just there. Trees don't just jump out in front of cars, but I had no explanation for what happened. I didn't see that I'd swerved off the road. You know I wasn't drunk and driving around, Mari. I wouldn't do that." His shoulders are tense as he walks toward one of the flats. He reaches out and touches it, sliding his fingers along the canvas, feeling the texture beneath his fingers.

In that moment, I feel it—I can hear his terror silently screaming across the room. I step toward him and place a hand on his shoulder. I pull until he turns to me. Those deep blue eyes are downcast and won't look at me. I put my hand on his cheek and lean in toward his face. "Trystan? Please tell me what's going on."

He pulls away from me, no longer able to meet my eyes. "I have an unusual form of macular degeneration. That's why I crashed, that's why I can't learn my lines—I can't see them. I'm going blind, Mari."

CHAPTER 30

My lower lip trembles as words fail me. "That can't be right. Are they sure? You're not even thirty! Have you seen a doctor about this, Trystan?" I'm behind him, talking to his back asking stupid questions. His white t-shirt is pulled tight across his shoulders, highlighting the toned muscles beneath.

He won't turn around. His head is lowered, hanging between his shoulders as he kicks the floor with his Chucks. "Of course. I went to the doctor the day after Seth's funeral. At first, I thought I had something dark in my eye—like an eyelash—but it wouldn't go away. It's hard and getting harder to see at night, well at all, really. In the daylight, what I can see is blurry and I struggle to make out subtle details. I'm tripping over cracks in the sidewalk, missing my marks on stage—earlier this week I didn't see the edge and took a header off the stage into the pit. I'd rather people thought I was a drunk asshole than know about this, Mari. I've been making sure everyone sees me with liquor in my hand, hoping they'll jump to conclusions." He turns to me and it feels like I'm choking.

I can't swallow or move. Can he even see my face anymore? "Trystan, who have you told about this?"

"No one. Bob noticed he's suddenly driving me everywhere, uncontested. I told him it was to avoid the press, but he senses something's up." He breathes in deeply, making his chest expand before releasing it. "Shittiest few weeks ever. I find out I'm going blind, Seth dies, and someone claiming to be my Mom suddenly shows up."

"I'm sorry." I say it because I don't know what to tell him. I usually have all the answers, but not this time. I know what macular degeneration is and what happens. I know that there's nothing to do about it—it's a disease that destroys the retina and burns a hole in the center of his vision. If he's lucky, he'll still see a little bit outside that area.

He backs up to the couch and sits on the arm. He offers a trademark Trystan Scott smile. "There's nothing to be sorry about. I'm actually glad I hit that tree or I wouldn't have seen you again. Literally."

I pad toward him slowly and stop in front of him. "How bad is it?"

His mouth is dry. He presses his lips together and tries to swallow. "I can still see the outline of your hand." He takes my wrist and intertwines our fingers. "I can catch the highlight of your nail, and I see your engagement ring. It's like it's underwater and I'm looking into a pond. It's murky, but it's there."

I place my hands on either side of his face and tip his head back. "Can you see my face anymore?"

His lips part and then close quickly. He looks away and shakes his head. "Not if I look directly at you. I can sort of see you out of the corner of my eye, but I can't see the freckles across the bridge of your nose or those long dark eyelashes you have." He chews on the side of his mouth for a moment and then stands. He leans in and kisses my forehead. "Thanks for listening."

"Of course I'd listen. So, it seems like you have two options—learn this, with me, or back out."

"I don't have time to finish filming before this turns noticeable."

I suck in air through my teeth when an idea hits me. "This isn't like a play, so you don't need to remember the whole thing, cover to cover all at once. What if they started shooting right away and I helped you with each scene, one at a time?"

"You'd have to come with me, and I can't ask you to do that."

"You don't have to. If this is your last big thing before your life changes, I want to do it with you."

He turns and looks up at me. It kills me to think those gorgeous eyes can no longer see my face. "I don't think your fiancé will agree to that."

I smile and wrap my fingers around his forearm. "My fiancé wants to be man-friends with you, and have you sing at our engagement party, so I'm pretty sure he'll let me follow you to a set for a week, especially if Katie came along. And getting Katie out of sweatpants would be an amazing thing to do right now. She spends half the day sitting next to Seth's headstone, staring at the ground."

I'm worried about her, but nothing I do seems to matter. I've been living at her apartment and trying to keep her afloat, but she's not here. She's still drowning in grief. Taking her somewhere routinely would help a lot.

"I didn't know she was that bad."

"She hides it, but she's having trouble."

Trystan makes a face. "Derrick wants me to sing at your engagement party?"

"Apparently. Can you handle it, Scotty? I know it's a little weird."

"It's fine. You know I'd do anything for you, including befriending Derrick. Should I invite him over to sleep on my couch? Order pizza and do man things?"

I snort a laugh and slap my hands over my mouth. He pries them away. "I love that sound, and yeah, man things. I like manly things." He smirks and adds, "Thank you, Mari. This has been horrible, and I didn't know how to tell you."

CHAPTER 31

Suddenly all my problems seem small. He's been dealing with this on his own. Trystan's a poet at heart. The way he makes sense of life is to take it in through his senses, filter it through his heart, and pour it out onto paper. What happens when he loses his sight?

I can't imagine. It'd be similar to losing my sight. If I went blind, the past ten years of working my ass off would have been for nothing. I'd be paralyzed in the universe I built assuming I'd be able to rely on my vision well into old age.

Trystan's a young man. It's not fair. Everything has been so hard for him.

I've been quiet for way too long. We're in my car, driving back toward a different drop off location on Route 110. It should be fairly empty at this time of night.

Trystan has one foot on top of his knee and stares straight ahead. I wonder if he can see the streaks of red and white as the cars blur past. He clears his throat and glances over at me. "So your car smells like Pop Tarts." He sniffs the air before winking at me. "Is there a sugar stash in your glove box?"

"No! It's in the backseat." We both laugh and then it goes quiet again. I hate this. I should just talk and say what I need to say. I've held in too many words for too long. "I was going to officially invite you to the engagement party, but things took a turn tonight and parties didn't seem so important."

Trystan twists in his seat until he can reach into the seatback pocket of his chair. "Score." He pulls out a silver foil packet of toaster pastries and rips open the top. The scent of cinnamon and brown sugar fills my head.

He bites into one and after he swallows he tells me, "Maybe it is a good time for a party. The moments in life that tend to hold the most meaning are the ones where everything goes wrong. In the end, it doesn't matter what happened, only who was there."

I glance over at him. "Are you going to tell anyone else?"

"Not until I have to." He bites into the other rectangle and then hands me a piece.

I stuff it into my mouth. "Okay, so we need to keep this a secret until you're ready to tell people."

"Or until there's no way to hide it anymore—like when I fall off the stage twice in a row and I'm not drunk." He lifts a Pop Tart like it's a beer mug and grins.

"That's not funny." Tears blur my vision, and suddenly I can't see. I pull the car over to the shoulder and flick on my hazards so no one plows into us. Trystan is leisurely eating the remainder of the package and avoiding my gaze.

I want to slap him and throw my arms around him. I'm torn between feeling betrayed and relieved. I smack his head with the back of my hand.

"Hey! What was that for?"

"Because you made me worry about you! You stupid, idiotic, boy!" I say it between laughter and tears. When I go to slap him again, he manages to grab my wrist. Those blue eyes lock on mine like he can still see me perfectly.

Those beautiful lips twist into a relieved smile. "I'm glad you know, and I didn't mean to worry you. I honestly didn't know if you hated me. You should have, after everything I did to you." His grip on my arm loosens, and he's about to let go.

My heart is pounding in my chest and I want to cry. A decade of emotions surges to the surface and I start babbling. Tears run down my cheeks as my hands wave around like a deranged Italian. "Hate you? I couldn't! I wanted to despise you. I wanted to see your picture in the paper and vomit, but I couldn't. There was always this place in the pit of my stomach that cringed when I saw you, and until now I thought it was because of everything that happened—that the thought of you just made me sick. And to some extent it did, but that's not the reason why—it was me. I was sick with remorse for letting you walk away.

"I never went after you. I never said a word to you—I just let you pass by. That feeling in the pit of my stomach is regret, for a decade of loss, for seeing you become an amazing man and having nothing to do with it. You went on without me and lived your life. I thought I'd never have the chance to talk to you again, but when you came into the ER—" I can't say it. The words stick in my throat, and although everything else came out in a rush, this won't pass over my lips. My face is cold and wet. My nose is running and I'm sobbing at my ex on the side of the road.

Trystan drops my wrist and leans toward me. He wraps his arms around my shoulders and pulls me toward his chest. I cry against him until I have no more tears. Trystan touches my hair lightly and holds onto me. When I pull away, I offer an awkward expression, and try to resume a normal rate of breathing.

"You're not the only one who had things wrong, okay? So don't blame yourself for what happened to us. It was my fault. I was the one who torched everything. I made sure it looked bad, like I was with someone else the day of your mom's funeral so that you wouldn't come back. I didn't know how to deal with all this, Mari. I knew I'd fall at some point, and I didn't want to pull you down with me. The last thing I wanted to do was make your life harder. I'm so sorry."

I press my lips together trying to find the right words, but there are none. Now our lives have moved on, and there is no going back. I'm lost in his gaze, watching those crystal blue eyes and wondering how much he can see. I want to lift my hand to his face and hold onto him. I want to be his rock in the storm, the way I had been so many years ago, but that time has passed. Our lives went down different roads.

"What's that look?"

I feel funny that he noticed. "I thought you couldn't see me?"

"I can see the shape of your face and that your cheeks aren't puffed up, and your eyebrows are sitting low, which means you're frowning. I've been faking it for a while, remember? Plus, we have this." He gently touches the back of my hand with the pad of his finger, and I feel a jolt of emotion from him. I know that touch goes two ways, I can feel his, and he can feel mine. "I know regret is crawling up your throat right now, but you shouldn't let it. Maybe we lost track of each other for a little while, but I'm here now. And so are you, with your dad and a doctorate. You achieved everything you set out to do when we first met."

The knot in my throat grows larger as he speaks. At one time Dad ignored me, completely. He fought with my mother in her final days, because she wanted to spend time with me instead of him—and I pushed her away.

After that shitstorm had passed, things did get better. I put my life back on the path I'd been on before I met Trystan, and I've been content. I like my job, I want to help people, and I'm good at it. I'm glad Dad and I finally found a way to get along, too. That was a long time in the making. But I still wish I hadn't lost all that time with Trystan.

He knows I can't speak, and I'm sure he senses my thoughts. At one time I would have been petrified and pulled my hand away, but now it's comforting that he knows me so well—that he can feel what I'm thinking without speaking.

Trystan's head tips to the side until I look at him. "You haven't lost me. You'll never lose me. There's a reason you were my best friend, and that's exactly what I need right now. I need you to be there with me through all this and help cover it up until I know what I want to do with the rest of my life."

I'm nodding, wishing he didn't want me as just a friend, but I clearly feel that vibe coming from him. He needs me as a friend, and I'm good at it. I want to be there for him. I squeeze his hand, and pull away. "Done. One BFF ready to take on the world with you."

"And you have one BFF ready to go to an engagement party this weekend and support you in every aspect of your life. I'll even be nice to your father." He grins devilishly and slumps back into the seat. His foot is on his knee again, and he taps out a beat.

I wipe my face off and pull into traffic. "New song?"

He's nodding his head slowly, moving it to music that I can't hear. "Yeah, it's been buzzing in my mind and I can finally make out the melody."

CHAPTER 32

Trystan resumes acting like his old self. It's amazing how he covers up the blurry vision. If I didn't know better, I'd worry he were a sociopath he's such a convincing actor. He pretends to have fun, too, but I know that's a cover. That trademark Trystan Scott smile and laugh is a mask, albeit a charming one, meant as a slight of hand so people won't look too closely. It's an amazing thing to watch him fool everyone—everyone except me.

It's been that way since high school. As soon as the gaggle of drooling girls walked away, he'd slump back into his seat, kick up his feet, and talk freely. There was no overabundant charm, no sparkling charisma. It was just him saying what he thought or how he felt. It's weird to be given such trust by a person—especially someone like Trystan who is always 'on' all the time. It must feel strange to finally just be himself, but he doesn't do it when Derrick or Katie are around. That mask is still in place, still sealing in his thoughts and distracting when they get too close to the truth or have a near miss with a sore spot he'd rather not talk about.

We're at my Dad's house, because Bob wanted to look around for security reasons before the engagement party. The early afternoon sunlight cuts through the blinds, forming slats of light on the floor. As Bob wanders the house, I grab everyone drinks from the kitchen and steal a few bags of chips. I'm a freaking hostess! I've got this down.

I walk from the enormous chef's kitchen my mother loved so much, to the vast living room with leather couches. The walls stretch high into rafters that have exposed beams. My Dad left the kitchen but redid this room. It screams manly man now, with leathers and dark rich colors.

I swat at Trystan's feet after I set down the drinks. "No feet on the table unless you want to be on Dad's bad side."

Trystan drops his legs and sits up. "I'm already on his bad side." He grins and looks at Derrick while grabbing a glass. "I'm not sure the man has another side. Have you pissed him off yet? Or made him happy? I'd like to compare notes and figure out how to make steam come out of his huge ears faster."

Derrick shakes his head and lifts a can of beer from the tray. "I'm not on his bad side. I never did anything to piss him off."

"Except put a ring on my finger." Derrick glances over at me, surprised. "Are you serious? What Dad wants to give away his daughter? Please. You're on his shit list for at least five years for that one."

Derrick squeaks and jumps off the couch. "What? How could that piss him off! You're almost thirty!"

I wave a finger in his face. "Don't even go there."

"Using the woman's age never goes well, man. I'd stop while you're ahead." Trystan puts the can of beer to his lips and swallows. When he sets it down on the table, the golden liquid is in the same place it was before. He didn't actually drink any. "Where's Katie? She's going to be your maid of honor, right?"

I nod, surprised he's interested. "Yeah, she's coming. She said she found something that would be perfect for the party. She'll be here in a little bit."

Derrick sits down on the couch and downs the rest of his beer, before grabbing some chips. "So, we're going to have the party in this room, right?"

I nod, half wanting to wait for Katie, but I know the guys have a limited attention span. "Yeah, I think we'll have the caterers set up tables over there and do a buffet style night with canapés and champagne. You know, nothing too over the top."

"Canapés?" Derrick blinks at me like I have two heads.

"Teeny-tiny expensive hors d'oeuvres," Trystan offers with a smirk. "Chick food."

I put my hands on my hips and scold him. "Cute little pastries and sandwiches. They're small and adorable, and…"

Derrick laughs, "Oh God, how much is this going to cost me?"

I make a face because he knows he's not paying for it—Dad offered to buy everything. "Don't be like that, Derrick."

He rolls his eyes and then smirks at Trystan. "I'm serious, why not set aside the money for us, and just buy snackage from Hickory Farms?"

I glance at Trystan, who jumps up and beams at me. "I think I hear Katie's car. I'll help her with that cow of a present she bought you." He darts out of the room faster than I can blink and nearly walks into the door. Trystan holds up two fingers making a peace sign, and Derrick laughs.

It's like my fiancé figured out how to flip on dick mode at the worst times. What the hell is he doing? "Derrick, this is one of the wedding events. It's not supposed to be slapped together at the last second with food we have left over from last Christmas."

He lets out an annoyed sigh. "That's not what I mean, Mari. Think about it, instead of spending sixty grand on a wedding where everyone is uncomfortable and can't wait for it to end, why don't we do a little wedding and cut down on all the pomp and circumstance.

It'll save us a fortune, and we can put that money toward a house."

I stare at him. "So, you don't want to have a big wedding? Or you want to elope?" I'm not serious about running off and getting hitched by a J.P., but he perks up.

The next thing I know, Derrick is holding my hands and smiling at me with full wattage. "Babe, that's exactly what I'd do. Then we won't have all these people around, and it can just be us. We can start house shopping and bypass all this shit."

He's so happy, so incredibly excited that I can't speak. He wraps his arms around me, holds on tight, and kisses me on the cheek. "This is why I love you. You get me. You're not one of those rich brats wanting to feel like a princess and have everyone falling all over her. That's not you. A justice of the peace— that's totally you. You're practical, and I love it. So, if this is going to be the big party, then canapés and champagne sound great. We can even go to the JP right after the party." He's rushing on, getting more and more excited as he speaks.

I finally have to hold onto his shoulders and catch his eye. "We can't go to the justice of the peace this weekend. And I can't do that to Dad. He wants to walk me down the aisle. I'll do a small wedding if it makes you happy, but—"

He waves me off. "If it makes me happy? You don't have to act with me, Mari. I know you better than anyone. All right, no JP for now, but let's set a date and talk to your dad. My mom will want to come too, and my brother. Let's make it family only and small. It'll be intimate and perfect." He leans in and kisses me. His mouth is on mine, and then his tongue sweeps over my lips. His arms slide down my back until he's cupping my butt, pulling me against him.

I don't pull away, because I love him, I do, but this blindsided me. I wanted a wedding—a real one—and now I'm not having one. I kiss him back and forget about things. I don't want to think, I just want to feel him against me. I close my eyes and get lost in the kiss. As it gets hotter, images flash behind my eyes of Derrick and our first kiss. I can see his red shirt and the stripes, and the flannel. I feel his hands on my face, cupping my cheeks and then the memory merges with another, and things shift.

I'm seventeen and kissing Trystan. I feel his soft flannel in my hands and his lips on my mouth, and when he touches me—

I pull back, gasping right when Katie and Trystan walk in the room, so it looks like I'm being shy. Derrick laughs and pinches my butt before walking over to Katie. "Hey, gorgeous. What's in the box?"

Katie is still wearing solid black, which is weird. It's like she's an Emo unicorn or something equally absurd. She has a small box in her hands, and Trystan is holding a giant crate, lugging it into the room behind Katie. His brow is covered in sweat. He pushes the package onto the carpet and then sits on it, and wipes his head with the sleeve of his shirt.

A red flannel shirt.

It's just cold feet. Every bride has pre-wedding jitters. That's all this is. It has nothing to do with Trystan or anything else. I'm just nervous, and I should be—this is a major decision. Forever is a long time.

Katie pulls off her Matrix coat and throws it on the couch, before handing me the little box. She's smiling and pressing her palms together. She lifts her hands to her face and bounces on the balls of her feet. "Open it!"

I look at the little box in my hands and frown. "It's not a dildo, is it?" That would be a Katie thing to do.

She laughs. "No! Of course not. Trystan's sitting on the fake man dick. I had to get one that was the right size." She laughs when Trystan jumps off the box and then winks at Derrick. "Good luck satisfying her. I hope you're a strapping young man." She holds up her hands about an inch apart and makes a face. "Because this will never do."

Derrick takes her hands and separates them, so they're about a foot apart. "More like this."

"You think you're this long?" She holds up her hands and shows all of us.

"Nope, that's girth, baby." He sniggers as Katie drops her hand, disgusted.

I slap the back of his head. "Cut it out."

"Sorry, I forget sometimes. No dick talk in front of other chicks. They might get jealous, huh?" Derrick leans in close and puts his arm on my waist. He pulls me against his side and slips his tongue into my ear.

I shriek and pull away, swatting at him. He laughs like it's funny, but it's not. I've known him for about nine months now, and this is the first time I'm seeing this side of him, well, when his brother isn't around. "Derrick!"

Katie glances at Trystan, but neither of them says anything. I swallow my pride and act like it didn't happen. He's just flirting, poorly. I focus on the box and open it, ripping the paper back and then opening the lid.

Inside there are several smooth stones. Each one is carved with a single Greek word.

I lift the first one.

ψυχή

Then the next.

μου

My jaw drops and I look up at her, ready to cry. "Oh, Katie."

Katie looks bashful and proud. "You have that phrase on your desk. It's still in your old room. I thought it was one of those mantras, and I know how important it is to you, so I had the words put on something that will last forever as a good luck charm for your marriage."

This is what I had engraved on Trystan's ring:

η ψυχή μου είναι η ψυχή σου
My soul is your soul.

It means that no matter what life threw at us, we'd be there for each other. He was wearing the ring the day he came into the ER, so I know he knows what these rocks mean— what they say.

I hold the stone in my hand and run my thumb over the word, soul. I never explained this saying to Derrick, and he doesn't react well now.

He takes the box and laughs. "You seriously got us a box of rocks?"

Katie frowns. "It's symbolic." She's not one to take crap from people, but she does this time.

Derrick teases her. "I think I would have preferred a dildo. Unless it's a diamond, a rock isn't much good when it comes to marriage."

Katie's jaw locks and I know she's holding back a slew of words.

Trystan doesn't move. He's behind everyone, back by the large box that was very heavy. I wonder what's in it.

Derrick tosses the box on the table and a few of the stones bounce out and clatter on the floor. "I know a gag gift when I see one. The real present is in the box. Let's open it! Come on, Mari." He rushes past Trystan and pulls off the white ribbon that was sitting on top.

I glance at Katie, feeling embarrassed and upset. Derrick is usually a sweet guy. This isn't like him. I walk over as he's tearing into the gift, and whisper in his ear, "No matter what's in here, you are going to love it. I haven't seen Katie smile in weeks until just now, and your comments killed it."

"Mari, you're overdramatic. She's smiled, and it was a gag gift." He stops talking when he has the top of the box unsealed. The container is about as high as his waist, and square. He flips back the lid and only sees white packaging peanuts. He laughs, sifting through them. He suddenly pulls his hand out, swearing. There's a gash on his palm, a thin line of blood.

"I sliced my hand. What the hell is in there? A chainsaw?" Derrick cradles his palm and squeezes it to stop the bleeding.

Katie looks pale, and the corners of her mouth are falling further. "I should go." She grabs her coat and heads toward the door.

Derrick stops her before I can. "No, don't leave. This was my fault. Stick around."

Katie glances over at me, uneasy. Her chest rises and falls a little too quickly, and I wonder what she's done, what's in that box. Katie nods and puts her jacket down.

Trystan clears his throat. "Why don't you cut it open? The box is really heavy anyway. We can pick up the Styrofoam after. And Katie always gets kickass presents. I can't wait to see what it is."

"She does. I love these." I hold the stone up and smile at her.

Katie smiles back, but it doesn't reach her eyes.

Derrick pulls a knife out of his pocket and opens the blade. He carefully cuts the box and dances around it like a kid on Christmas morning. When the front two seams are cut, he holds the panel of the box in place. "All right, everyone ready for the big reveal?"

I clap and whistle. Trystan does the same, as Katie sits there quietly with an expression on her face that makes me nervous.

"Here we go!" Derrick drops the front of the box and the packaging peanuts flow out. Behind the cascade of plastic snow, there's a shiny black thing with flecks of red—and the same phrase: η ψυχή μου είναι η ψυχή σου

Derrick's face pinches as he kneels down to look at it. "What the fuck, Katie? Was it a buy one get one free sale?"

Trystan is looking over Derrick's shoulder. "It's a bloodstone, asshole. It's not cheap."

Derrick ignores Trystan and makes a face at me. I'm in awe and reach out to touch it. "Why did it cut Derrick's hand?"

Katie swallows hard after watching me for a moment. "There's a small knife in there. I heard about this tradition where you take a bloodstone, and the bride and groom both put a drop of blood on it. It's like a talisman, and I added the engraving because, well, I assumed it was important."

Derrick turns around and stares at her. "Why would you think that had anything to do with me?"

"Since when is your marriage just about you?" Katie makes a face, and I can tell she's out of patience. "It should mean something to you because it's important to Mari. It means so much to her she had it engraved on your wedding band. Why are you acting like such an asshole?"

He shakes his head and grips the sides with his hands. He's yelling at her. "We didn't pick out bands yet. What the hell are you talking about?"

"I saw it. Mari keeps it in her pocket. Oh my God, I'm sorry—I thought he knew." Katie's big eyes meet mine, and she has no idea what she's done.

But Trystan knows. He figures it out quickly and speaks before I can tell the truth. "Katie, it's okay. Derrick, Mari has your ring in her pocket. It's been there for a while now. I guess she didn't show you yet."

I mouth Trystan's name in a silent plea. He can't do this. That ring was his. He can't give it away.

Derrick softens and walks over to me. His head tips down and he catches my eye. "Really? You already have my wedding band? Can I see it?"

I pull Trystan's ring out of my pocket and show it to him. Derrick takes it and sees the inscription. He smiles softly. "I had no idea you did this. It makes Katie's weird presents make sense, a little bit."

"They're sentimental, asshole, not weird." Katie is really upset. She walks over to me and apologizes. "I didn't know he didn't see it yet. I'm so sorry."

"It's okay. It's not your fault." I comfort my friend and stand next to my fiancé, watching my ex from across the room.

That ring was a promise that I would always be there for him. I shouldn't have kept it. I should have given it back to him that night. Now Derrick thinks I bought it for him.

CHAPTER 33

I'm at Katie's apartment for the night. After we finished cleaning up at Dad's, I took the little rocks and left the bloodstone behind. I want to tell her what happened, that the verse was something for Trystan, but she feels bad enough as it is.

Katie is folded into a ball in the chair again. She has her knees tucked under her chin, and she's staring at me. "Did you know that for the first three months of a relationship, both parties fake who they are, one hundred percent?"

I'm on the couch. We're eating popcorn and watching an old black and white Audrey

Hepburn movie. I glance over at Katie. "I think I've heard that."

"So you know at six months you start seeing parts of the person and at nine months, their full personality comes through—that around nine months you can actually see who the person really is. You know that already." She rests her head on her knees and looks back at young Audrey with super long hair. "I love this movie."

Roman Holiday was her debut film. It's a great story, one of my favorites. "Me too. And yeah, I know that it takes time to get to know someone. Where are you going with this?"

Katie smacks her lips together a few times and then her face scrunches up. "I find it fascinating he hadn't noticed your attachment to that verse. It's equally strange the man claims not to even have a soul—those are made up—while his fiancée is convinced he's her soul mate. Do you see where I'm going with this?"

"No, I really don't. Katie, let's just watch the movie." I shove another fistful of popcorn into my mouth, but I can feel her green eyes tearing a hole in my face. I groan and grab the remote. I press pause and yell at her. "What? What do you want me to say?"

"That the ring was for someone else. That you wrote that little poem for someone else, someone who likes old stuff, someone who appreciates poems, someone that would think Greek and rocks are cool! Someone that would understand why I spent a fortune buying you a big ass bloodstone!" She drops her feet to the floor and jumps up. Katie pads over to the couch and sits down hard next to me. "That ring was Trystan's, wasn't it?"

I'm going to be sick. "No."

"You might as well tell me the truth because I'll find out anyway." Katie glares at me until I look at her. "I'm not doing this to be mean, Mari. I promise. It's just that I know you and the man that I saw tonight isn't the Derrick you fell in love with. That was an asshole frat boy who has no appreciation of sentiment, art, or anything. Trystan said Derrick wanted to have your engagement party catered by Hickory Farms! What the fuck, Mari? You seriously want to spend the rest of your life uncovering more of those types of gems?"

"Katie, he's just nervous. Everyone gets nervous before a wedding."

She opens her mouth, snaps it shut, licks her lips and shakes her head. "No. You know what? That's bullshit. Seth and I weren't nervous. I wanted to unbury who he was and learn things about him that I didn't know. I wanted to find out how the real Seth was, and the more I found, the more I loved him. Sometimes the opposite occurs and as the dating façade is chipped away, you realize you don't want to know the person underneath. That's not bad. It just means you guys weren't meant to be together."

"You don't know what you're talking about. I love Derrick." I get up and storm into the kitchen. I don't want to have this conversation, and if she pushes me toward Trystan, I'm going to bite her head off.

She follows me in her fluffy socks, nearly skating after me on the floor. "I didn't say you didn't. I just want you to consider what you saw, and what he said. Like with the wedding—are you really going to elope? I thought you wanted the dress and the church? I thought you wanted to walk down the aisle to Pachelbel. When did you change your mind?" She's leaning against the counter as I dig through the cabinets looking for something I don't need.

"It doesn't matter. It's a party, and you know as well as I do that I hate being the center of attention. We talked about it, and I agree with him. We should elope." I'm saying these things like I believe them. I come out from behind the cabinet door to find Katie with her arms folded over her chest and a frown on her face.

"When were you planning on telling me that I wasn't invited? That you didn't need a maid of honor? That there was no wedding?" She lifts her hands palms up. "Listen, I don't want to fight with you, but you shouldn't have to throw away your dreams, and the things you want because they don't line up."

"I didn't! We're having a big ass engagement party, the way I wanted and so, I thought it would be a dick move to insist on a huge wedding, especially since I don't really want one. It's not worth fighting over. I can still wear a white dress and my dad will be there—"

Her gaze meets mine, and I feel the weight between us. "But I won't be there. I'm your best friend and I'm going to miss the most important day of your life because he wanted it to be family only and you said yes. And that's okay, if I freakin' believed it was what you wanted, but I don't!" She throws up her hands over her head and storms away.

"You don't know what you're talking about! I'm not you!" I follow her into the living room.

Katie stops before her bedroom door and turns around, breathing fire. "No, you're not. You gave up on your dreams and walked away from your friends, but who am I to judge? Maybe I don't know you that well after all." She walks into her room and slams the door.

CHAPTER 34

I want to fight back and tell her she's wrong. It's like she flipped the crazy switch and I can't turn it off. The only thing to do is prove her wrong. She isn't right about this. I grab my keys and coat, and head to Derrick's house.

When I get there, I pull up to the duplex and notice his brother's car and a car I don't recognize. I get out and rush up the walkway. I ring the bell and when Derrick opens the door, I throw myself into his arms. I take his face in my hands and kiss him hard. He's all too happy for the PDA and kisses me back, despite the protesting coming from behind us.

Breathless, I pull away and ask, "Can I stay here tonight?"

"Yeah, baby. Anything you need." Derrick puts his hand on the small of my back and walks me inside. His brother is there along with a woman I've never seen before.

She smiles at me warmly. "Is this Mari?" She said my name right, so they must have been talking about me.

I nod and extend my hand. "Yes, I am. And you are?"

"This is my mom. I invited her here for the engagement party." Derrick puts his arm around his mother and kisses her on the cheek.

She's about five-foot-six with reddish brown hair and big blue eyes. I see the resemblance between her and her sons. When she smiles, the corners of her lips pull up in the same way, and I can make out a shallow dimple behind the lines etched in her skin by time.

She swats away my hand and throws her arms around me. "You're going to be my daughter-in-law! I think we're past a handshake." She kisses the side of my face and then steps back. "Let me look at you. Oh, you're so beautiful. Derrick's descriptions didn't do you justice." She smiles at me as she holds onto my shoulders. The woman has a killer grip.

I smile awkwardly and look at my fiancé. "Why haven't I seen a picture of her before?"

She releases me. "Oh, I don't like pictures. I'm sure he has a few that he snuck, but there's nothing formal. Not even a family picture. I always look like I'm having a colonoscopy." She makes a face, and I laugh loudly.

Jared groans and covers his face. "Mom, you can't talk about your colon with someone you just met. Mari will think you're mental."

She laughs it off. "If you can't find the humor in life, you're doing it wrong." She swats a hand at her son and asks me, "Would you like some dinner? We were about to sit down."

"Yes, thank you. Can I help you with anything?" I feel a little awkward, like I intruded on a family event to which I wasn't invited. I tuck my hair behind my ear—old nervous habit—and force a smile. I hope it looks serene. When I'm nervous, my mouth pulls into weird expressions, and adding a smile just makes it more noticeable.

"I've got it covered. I'm sure you had a long day at work. I'm so glad to finally meet you. Derrick has told me so much about you." The corners of her eyes wrinkle when she smiles. Her face is slim, and her skin has a weathered look. There's something about her lips and the way they curve that makes me feel welcome. She seems sincerely glad to see me.

"I hope what he told you matches what you find."

She waves a hand at me. There are no rings on her fingers. I wondered if she'd taken it off. Derrick said she never really got over his father. He died in a car wreck, and she'd brought up her two sons alone. "Oh, I'm sure it'll be great. Sit and tell me about your job. It must be exciting. Did you always want to work in an emergency room?"

I pull out a kitchen chair and sit while his mom walks over to the counter and resumes chopping vegetables. I don't want to explain Trystan or that little detour from my otherwise perfectly planned life, so I hedge. "It's not really exciting, but it does keep me on my toes. I like a challenge. I've wanted to help people since I was a kid, and this has been a really great way to do it. Coming to the ER isn't something anyone plans for and lots of life decisions are made there. It's a turning point for many people, and I try to help in any way possible."

"You sound like Derrick when he was a little boy. He'd come home from school with a new thought every week on what he wanted to do with his life, but it always revolved around helping people." She looks over at her son, who is standing in the doorway. His arms are folded across his chest, and his body is stiff, tense.

"Awh, cute baby Derrick must have been adorable."

"Oh, he was. He had great big ears and chubby cheeks." She stops chopping and turns around. "I'll pull out the baby books later, and you can look through some pictures."

Derrick groans as his brother cackles from the living room a few feet away. He pushes off the doorframe and walks toward me, and slips into a seat. He takes my hand. "Is everything all right with Katie?"

"Yeah, we just had a bit of a fight." My stomach twists. I didn't plan on talking about this with other people listening. I don't want to make Katie look bad either, or cause the jealous green monster to arise again.

That's a strange thing—jealousy. When I was younger, it drove me crazy when a guy acted jealous. It was hard to stay with someone when they were like that, always sneering at other men and oozing testosterone from every orifice. It gets old. But Derrick's lack of jealousy with Trystan bothers me. We did date. I did sleep with the man. I don't understand why it doesn't bother him. It must be an act for my benefit. It sounds silly, but I wish he'd tell me that it bothered him—just a little—that Trystan is around. Instead, Derrick and Trystan are shopping for BFF charms. I'm not sure how that happened. It's what I wanted, so I should shut up, but still.

"Mari, is Katie going to be in the wedding?" The sound of the knife slicing through carrots and tapping on the cutting board draws me back to the present. "I heard she's your best friend. Derrick speaks highly of her."

My eyebrows slide up my face and disappear under my bangs. "He did what now?"

Katie and Derrick have never been chummy. She always saw him as a placeholder, and he knows it, so this is a little weird. Derrick smiles and leans in and bumps my shoulder with his. "She's teasing you, Ma. Of course I like Katie."

Jared fake-sneezes something that sounds like bullshit.

Derrick ignores it, as does everyone else. "Katie's had a rough time. Her husband recently died in combat."

"I remember you mentioning that. I'm so sorry. That must have been horrible." She dumps the veggies in a pot of boiling broth and turns to face us, resting a hip against the counter. "Did you know him well?"

"Yes, we went to high school together. Seth was the kind of guy you couldn't miss and didn't forget. They hated each other at first, and then something changed." I can't help but smile as I think about it.

"Mom, wasn't it like that with you and Dad?"

She has a far off look in her eye and nods her head. She grabs a raw chicken and starts deboning the thing quickly and tossing the meat into a hot frying pan. It sizzles on contact. She adds a few spices and the kitchen suddenly smells delicious.

Derrick goes on to tell me the story of how his parents met. It's not as love/hate as Katie and Seth, but they had an awesome story. She explains, "No one thought we'd be a good pair, but I knew." She has a far off look on her face and then continues. "We'd both had hard lives and had to learn to trust again, but that was all it took. Trust is an important thing in a marriage."

Derrick and I sit, chatting with her until dinner is ready. Jared joins us for soup and fried chicken with cornbread. Apparently it's their favorite. The two of them are so close in age I sometimes forget Derrick is older.

I'm just starting to feel at ease when things get really weird. Derrick's mom sits at the table, silently eating her meal, making pleasant conversation while the guys start ribbing her. It seems like they're having fun at first, but the tone shifts, and I know her smile isn't real anymore.

The backhanded compliments flying from Jared's mouth are alarming. Derrick says nothing in her defense, laughing and joining in as the mood strikes him.

Jared picks up a piece of chicken. "Dinner is pretty good, Ma. Oh, you remember when Dad used to make this meal? It was so good, Mari. There's just something about food when a guy cooks it. No offense Mom, but you know what I mean, it can't be replicated."

Derrick agrees and stuffs his face with the cooking he's saying is subpar. "Yeah, Dad made this meal for years, Mari. It had this extra kick. It's hard to explain, but you remember, right Ma?"

She nods and pokes a carrot with her fork. "I do. Your father was a good cook."

Jared jumps conversational tracks. "So, who's going to be chained to the stove when you guys are married? You or Mari?"

I laugh, not taking it seriously, but Derrick is confident. "Mari. Wait, you don't want to cook for me?"

"Sometimes, but I work long hours, Derrick. It's not going to be an everyday occurrence. We've talked about this."

He gives his plate a grumpy look and stabs a piece of chicken. "I thought you were kidding."

"The wife's place is in the kitchen," Jared says as if he has three wives chained up somewhere baking him a feast.

"Funny." I point at him and then turn to his Mom. "This is delicious. My mom never cooked anything like this for me. Your boys are lucky to have you."

She smiles weakly and doesn't answer. There's something going on here I'm not seeing. What sucked the wind out of her so abruptly? Before I can pinpoint it, she's up and cleaning. Derrick and Jared don't clear the table or offer to help. They just sit there bitching about some game on TV last night.

I smack Derrick's elbow and scold him. "Get up and help your Mom."

His face twists in that are-you-nuts expression. "She likes doing this for us, right Ma?"

"Of course. Why don't you all go into the living room? I'll put on the coffee."

The guys leave, but I linger. I start clearing the table, and she doesn't say anything. It's not until I'm standing next to her scrubbing a pot that she speaks. "So, things with Derrick are good?"

"Yeah, we get along well."

Her face crumples, but she doesn't look over at me. "That's good. Sometimes he seems so much like his father." She says that like it's a bad thing but doesn't elaborate.

The conversation shifts to the wedding and our new plans of having a small gathering with close friends and family only. By the end of the night, I'm exhausted, but I don't want to stay here. There's a weird tension in the air.

Around midnight, I push off of Derrick's chest. "I think I'm going to head home. Katie should have cooled down by now."

"Why don't you stay?" He kisses my forehead and pushes my hair out of my face.

Jared groans and covers his face with a pillow. "Don't make out in front of me. I'll have to burn my eyes out, and no one wants anything to happen to these beautiful babies." He drops the pillow and blinks at his brother. Jared is sitting across from us on a beat up chair.

Derrick puts a hand behind my neck and pulls me in hard, crushing his mouth on mine and leaning me back into the couch. I fight him, because I don't like kissing in front of other people, and Jared is hard to swallow on a good day. I smack his chest with my hands, pushing him back.

His lips are locked on mine as he crushes me with his body. I squeal and shove him hard. He doesn't stop until his mother is in the doorway. Derrick gets a sheepish look on his face, sits up, and grins.

I shove him. "You can be an asshole sometimes, you know that?" Jared brings out the worst in Derrick. It's as if the two of them are constantly trying to one-up each other on the dick scale.

Before Derrick can reply, his mom is standing next to me. "It was lovely meeting you." She leans in and gives me a hug, and whispers in my ear, "He really adores you." When she pulls away, her hands are on my shoulders, and she walks me to the door with Derrick following.

He holds the door open and lets me pass through, then walks me to my car. "Sorry, I didn't think you'd mind."

"Well, I did." My arms are folded tight over my chest, and my fists are shoved into the crooks of my elbows.

"Got it. I won't try to kiss you again." He sounds pissed.

"Derrick, don't be like that. You know I don't like having an audience, so don't make me."

He nods. "Right, sorry. I mean it. I don't want to make you feel uncomfortable." He's sincere and charming, but something feels off. It's nothing huge, just this little sensation in the pit of my stomach. I don't know why it's there. Guys can be assholes, and everyone knows when two guys are together, their assyness increases. But they pretty much attacked their mom tonight, and she didn't fight back. It's like her spine was sucked from her body. She morphed from one woman into another, and then back again.

Maybe she's going through something.

"Love you, babe. Be careful driving home. Call me when you get there, okay?"

I agree, and I'm pulling away, thinking about everything and not specifically thinking about anything. I drive past my exit and don't realize where I'm going until I'm entering the Brooklyn Battery Tunnel. The yellow lights whoosh by as I enter Manhattan around 2 am. I find a place to park at the end of the block and head toward his building. I stop in front of the glass doors and stare. I want to talk to someone. Katie's mad at me and that leaves Dad or Trystan.

I shouldn't be here. He's a guy. I'm getting married. Shouldn't I be talking to Derrick about this? I would, but since it's about him and his mom, I can't. I'm not going to Dad. Although he's tried to fix things between us, he's still a novice on the parental card. I think about it for another second and turn away. I can't bother him in the middle of the night about another guy. That seems wrong to me.

It shouldn't.

But it does.

I slam into a hard chest and splay my hands on a worn leather jacket, and pry my body away. "I'm so sorry."

"Mari? What's wrong?" Trystan is standing in front of me with tousled hair and rosy cheeks. His gray shirt is sticking out from under his jacket, and I can see the seams. It's inside out. He was with someone.

My bottom lip curls down and my lower eyelids fill with tears. Before I can speak, his arms are around my shoulders, and we're walking inside. "Mari, what's wrong? Are you hurt?"

I shake my head and silently cry on his shoulder. When we're in his penthouse, we pass the foyer and head straight to the couch. He sits me down and by the way he's acting, you'd think there was nothing wrong with him. You'd have no idea his eyes betrayed him just like everything else in his life. Trystan crouches in front of me, his hands on my knees, and he's looking at me from the side of his eyes.

"Don't cry, Mari. Talk to me."

"Why are you so great? Compared to you, my problems seem like nothing, and yet you drop all your worries to help me. I didn't even have to ask." My voice is soft and scratchy. I blink rapidly, trying to hold back tears.

He's looking at me, and that gaze bores into me. For once, I'm not afraid. I let it. His hands find mine, and he rubs his thumb along the back of my hand, looking into my eyes like he can see my soul. The corner of his lips pulls up. "You never have to ask."

"Why? Why do you know what to do and what to say to me? You always know, and he doesn't. Katie doesn't. No one understands me the way you do, and being here makes me feel guilty." All the thoughts merge and come out as one sentence with a single rush of air. I try to lower my head, but Trystan leans in closer, and I end up pressing my forehead to his.

"I think you know why and I'm just glad it's there. I can still see the shape of your face, but I can't read your eyes anymore. If I touch you, I can feel your thoughts. I know what you're feeling. I don't know why I have that with you, but I wouldn't trade it for anything. You shouldn't feel guilty for having a friend." He squeezes my hand and pulls away, moving to sit on the couch next to me.

"That's not what I mean. I can't be here and dump this on you. I don't even know what we are..." the question hangs in the air like a grenade with the pin pulled. I shouldn't have said that. My jaw twitches and before I can bite it back, the question is out of my mouth. "Do you still care about me?"

Trystan is still, barely breathing. We're not touching, not invading each other's thoughts. I'll only know the answer to this if he chooses to tell me. The silence stretches on until all the hairs on my body are standing on end.

I stand, ready to run out, but Trystan is up and grabs my wrist. He pulls me back to him roughly and puts his other hand on my face and threads his fingers through my hair. "Why are you asking this now? What happened?"

"Nothing. I don't know." Tears slip out of my eyes without my consent and roll down my cheeks. "I shouldn't be here."

"You keep saying that like something bad is going to happen if you stay. Are you afraid of me?" His voice trails up as he asks as if he's surprised. My lips part but I can't answer him. My heart pounds like I'm going to die and I'm trembling. Fear is racing through my veins and making me act like someone else. He drops his hands and steps away with a hurt look on his face. "I see."

"Don't do this to me, not now." My neck is so tight I can't swallow, and I feel close to having a full-blown panic attack.

"I'm not the one doing it, you are." He steps away, and walks to the kitchen. He grabs a glass from the cabinet and a bottle of water from the fridge. He fills it and walks back to me. "Here, calm down. Try to trust me. I won't hurt you, Mari. You're safe. I promise."

I take the water, chug it, and then hold it between us, like it can prevent me from feeling any of this. Trystan keeps his distance but doesn't sit. We're both standing a few feet from each other, neither of us speaking. I wish he'd step closer. I wish he'd wrap his arms around me and let me cry until I fall asleep.

"Thank you." My voice is weak, nervous.

Trystan is watching me, and it doesn't matter that he can no longer see me because it feels like he can see through me. He takes a few steps, closes the distance, and takes the glass from my hand. He sets it down on the coffee table and swallows hard. He opens his arms wide and stands there, waiting for me. "Of course. Come here. Cry, get it out of your system, and we can talk tomorrow."

I'm frozen in place. I should be able to go to him. I want to, but my feet won't move. The longer Trystan stands there, the lower his arms move. They inch down little by little until it's clear I'm not taking his comfort. My skin feels like ice, and I want his hands on my arms to thaw me. I want to drop my defenses and see what's left of the girl I was, because I felt like she died with my mother, but when I'm around Trystan I'm not so certain.

When I fail to move, Trystan turns around abruptly. He sits, pulls off his boots, and shucks his leather jacket, leaving it on the couch. "I'll show you the guest bedroom. You can sleep there and take a shower. You'll feel better in the morning. I promise." He pads down the hallway and opens a closet, grabbing an extra pillow and blanket, before opening a door that leads to a room with a queen bed at the center and dark wood furniture all around. The floor is hand-scraped hardwood in wide, dark planks, and next to the bed is a white shaggy rug. The room looks new, untouched. Trystan puts the things on the bed. "The shower is through there. Oh, hold on." He disappears for a moment, and when he returns, he has a pair of flannel pajamas.

He puts them on the bed and tells me, "These should fit and they're really comfortable. I'm going to head out—"

I don't let him finish. I walk up behind him and act on the impulse floating through my mind. I hold onto that toned arm and press my body against his, wrapping my arms around his back. I hold on tight like the world is floating away, and he's my rock.

Trystan hesitates, but his arms finally wrap around me. He tucks his chin, so I'm nestled under it and against his chest. His heart pounds faster and faster, as his arms cover with goose bumps. He holds me like that for the longest time. I don't move, and we don't speak. I breathe in deeply and try to calm down. His scent fills my head as I stare at the seam at his neckline. He's living his life, loving as he wants, yet I still feel paralyzed by fear. He holds me until the world seems calm once again and I think I can manage to let go. My arms slip from his body, and I step back, ashamed to look at him.

He catches my chin and lifts my gaze to his face. "You never need to feel like that with me."

I know he can't see me, so I don't hide my thoughts. I let the bipolar emotions I'm feeling bubble up within me and overflow. The tragedy he's lived through, the unfairness of it all can send me into a blind rage if I fixate on it. His father hated him, his mother abandoned him, and everyone close to him has died—save Jon Ferro and me. How is he still standing, smiling, and going on? How did I become so weak in comparison? Why can't I live as bravely, as independently? When did I get so weak that I need to cry with people and ask for help?

The pit of my stomach is in a free-fall and I'm barely breathing. My heart beats too loud, and I'm hyperaware of my body, of my breathing. My skin tingles as if covered with ice, and I know his touch will thaw me. I know his lips are soft, and his arms are strong. I feel caught in the undertow, drowning, but a pair of blue eyes and strong hands pulls me to shore. I've lost myself, and I didn't even know until Trystan came around again.

I'm not the woman I want to be, and I don't know how to backtrack to find her.

The pressure in my chest builds as I stare at the smoothness of his lips, and the dark stubble around his mouth. He was with someone. His lips are still swollen and so very pink. His cheeks flush and his breathing is shallow and quick. Does he feel this? Does he know what this is? Because I don't.

Without warning, Trystan steps away, once then twice. The distance between us puts so much tension on my heart it feels like it'll break. His lips part and he releases a rush of air before dropping his head. Trystan stares at the floor and runs his hands along the side of his head and then down his neck. He stays like that, for a moment, and when he looks up, I get that fake smile. "I need to get some sleep. So do you. I'll see you in the morning."

H.M. WARD

Without another word, he's gone.

CHAPTER 35

~TRYSTAN~

I'd rather rip my heart out my chest and feed it to a dog than live like this. Mari walks up to me thinking I can't see jack shit, but I can. I can make out the curve of her mouth and the slope of her cheek. Even if I couldn't, I can still feel her thoughts barraging me in an endless stream.

Something set her off tonight, first with Katie and then again with Derrick. No one is good enough for Mari, so I didn't say anything, but maybe I should. No, I can't do that to her. She's finally happy. She found someone. I can't say that I haven't been trying to move on, I am.

I was with this woman who had it all, amazing voice, great curves, gorgeous breasts, and a brain—and when we were half naked, I felt so guilty I blew her off and walked away. I made my decision, so what the hell is wrong with me?

Fuck it. I need a cold shower and to raid the fridge. I peel off my shirt, toss it aside, and pad into the bathroom in my jeans. I turn on the shower with the remote, thankful the crazy designer insisted on this particular unit. It has eight jets, all with custom controls that can adjust anything from the temperature to the flow of water. It's amazing. And I can talk to it if I want to change a setting, which is a lifesaver.

"Eighty degrees, steam on." The control panel on the shower beeps after accepting the command and the water comes on.

After tossing my jeans and boxers, I step into the steam and put myself directly beneath the stream. I shiver as it bounces off my body, chilling me. I put my arm on the wall and lean forward, placing my head on my wrist, letting the water roll off my body. The warm air and the cold water is a combo that is refreshing and puts my nerves at ease.

The shower turns off, and I grab my towel. I wrap it around my waist, enjoying the heated warmth around my hips. I should probably grab a robe, but Mari should have passed out already. I chance it and hurry to the kitchen, grab a bottle of Coke and handful of Blow Pops. When I turn around, I see her standing in the doorway, blocking my exit. Damn.

My hair is dripping water into my eyes, and she just stands there, silent. I can see the baggy shape of the pajama shirt on her curvy bottom, and it's really clear that she skipped the pants. Those legs. Dear God. The curve of her calf all the way up to the top of her thighs is outlined in light. I remember holding her there, pulling her to me, and pushing inside of her. Shit, stop it. You're wearing a towel, and she's not blind.

I turn toward the counter and think of something that'll make it less obvious that I'm thinking about her in a non-friendly way. "Mari, what do you need?" My voice is too high. Jesus, she's going to notice.

Her voice comes from over my shoulder. She's stepped into the kitchen. Dear God, don't come closer. I don't know how many times I can avoid kissing her in one night. I'm not going to be that guy—the one who ruins a relationship and turns a great girl into a cheater. I have to hold it together and keep her away.

"I wanted some milk. I'm sorry, I didn't mean to startle you." Her voice is so soft, so warm. It's like a caress, and I miss it so much. I'm like a junkie with her—there's never enough.

"Yeah, there are a few bottles in the fridge—in the drink drawer."

She pads past me. "Thanks. I'll grab this and get out of your way. Nice dinner, by the way. Blow Pops and soda. Are you five or something?" She has a smile in her voice.

I turn toward her and smirk. "Dinner of champions. Besides, I'm feeling a little nostalgic tonight."

"Me too."

No. Say no. Be an asshole and push her away. I'm not doing this to her. She has to go back to Derrick. I change the subject abruptly. "I need to get to bed. I'm supposed to meet someone in the morning. The woman that claims to be my mother is coming to brunch. I need to look halfway decent."

"Wow, you called her?" She sounds surprised.

"Yeah, last week. We set up a time to meet, no expectations, just a meeting. I'm going to see what she's like. I've always wondered about her." I hide the hopeful look on my face and bury my chin in my chest before I remember I'm wearing a towel. Right, I need to get past her and back to my room. "Stick around as long as you want tomorrow. I've got to be up pretty early."

"Right. Good luck, Trystan. I wish I could say something that would make it go amazingly. I hope she's everything you hoped for."

As I pass by, I'm pulled to her. I have to rip my guts out to keep walking. My pulse is hammering in my head as I pad back down the hallway to my room. I need to be more careful. Something has made her think she's fragile, but I know her—she's not. It feels like we're skirting a bomb, waiting for it to explode.

I need to talk to Mari and make sure she's okay, but now isn't the time to do it. She's too emotional, and I'm too smitten. A hug will turn into more and I can't do that to her. She'd never forgive herself if she cheated.

First, I have to meet my mother. Then help Mari. Tomorrow is going to be a long day.

CHAPTER 36

It takes a long time to master the nondescript hobo look, but after nearly a decade, I've got it down. No logos, nothing with distinguishing characteristics, sunglasses, ball cap, and clothes so faded they no longer belong to a specific color spectrum. For example, I beat the shit out of this ball cap after ripping the Yankees emblem off. I washed it in bleach, transforming the once navy blue cap to a slate blue that's easily confused with gray.

I tuck my hair under the hat and slide a pair of mirrored sunglasses on my face. I forgo my leather jacket and instead grab a beige hoodie from Goodwill with bleach splatters at the cuffs. Coupled with a plain pair of jeans and a white t-shirt, I look like any other guy walking the city streets this afternoon. Scratch that. I look like any other man walking the city streets working for the sanitation department or perfecting his aptitude for becoming homeless. The only people who don't work in this city are socialites. Although I never had to beg, I consider it work. Being reduced to a shadow of a human being, someone who can't even afford to eat, humbling himself enough to ask a stranger for spare change—I'd rather starve, but at some point I would have done it. If Sam, the guy who owned the deli, hadn't given me a job while I was in high school, I would have been screwed. There were times I came close to asking for a handout, but I never hit that point. For that, I'm glad, but at the same time I've experienced what it feels like to have nothing, to go to bed hungry and to wake up starving. I remember being cold because we had no blankets and no heat. I've spent nights in the dark because the electricity was shut off, and there were nights I spent outside because I couldn't risk being around Dad. When times got tough, he had a tendency to blame me, and his fists quickly reminded me of the burden I was.

I'm not a preacher or a welfare advocate—I just know how hard it can be and some days, trying isn't enough. I continue my life knowing I'm lucky, and I never forget where I came from, either.

Bob drives me within a block of the café, and I feel like I'm going to puke. It's a blessing and a curse that I won't be physically able to see her. My vision is getting worse, and if she looks anything like me, I'm not sure if I could do this.

Bob's voice breaks through my thoughts. "I'll be here. Call if you need me."

"You mean if I need you to save me from an elderly con-woman?"

"I think she's the real thing, or you wouldn't be here. I checked her out and—"

Shaking my head, I put up a hand stopping him. "I don't want to know. I don't care where she's been or what she's done. She left me and didn't look back. I'm here to put this to bed and never see her again, Bob."

"Of course. If you need me, you know where I am." The man's voice drops and I know he wants to tell me more, but I don't want to hear it. This woman blew any chance she had of claiming me as her son. She's too late.

I kick open the door, and duck into the swiftly moving crowd on the sidewalk. No one pays attention to the car or me. I keep my head down watching for changes in the color of the ground. That's been the easiest way to spot broken pavement.

I stuff my hands into my pockets and cut right, shouldering my way past people. I grab the silver door handle and yank it open before walking inside. This part is going to be tricky. If I talk to the hostess she might recognize me, so I decided to get here first and have Mom come and find me. God knows I won't be able to see her.

The café is busy, and there's a dull murmur of people talking, glasses clinking, and the smell of fried food filling the air. Something with a sweet strawberry scent hits me hard, and I smile because it reminds me of Mari. I resist the urge to pull off my cap and run my hands through my hair.

When I get to the podium, I don't have to say much. A woman with big brown hair and a thick Jersey accent asks me, "One?"

"Two."

"Ah," she smacks her gum and doesn't look at me twice. "Alrighty, hun. I'll put you over here, so you're a little easier to spot." She drops the menus on a table close to the door and turns away to get the next person in line.

I slide into the booth and try to calm down. My palms are wet, and I feel like I'm about to hyperventilate. Part of me wants to bolt, but there's this nagging feeling I should be here—like my life will go to hell if I don't talk to her. It's weird, like an omen.

A waitress comes by, and I don't look up from the menu. She has that rough sound to her voice and an insanely thick Long Island accent. "Cauwfee, hun?"

"Yeah." One-word answers tend to work well, although I usually avoid public places. All it takes is one fan to recognize my profile and I'm fucked.

She pours the hot liquid into a white mug. "I'll come back in a few." She disappears, taking care of other tables while I wait.

I have one question that I want an answer to before I leave. I don't want to hear her life story or know what her hobbies are—I don't want to know her at all.

I swallow the lump in my throat and down some of the scalding black coffee. I stopped putting sugar and cream in it to hide my vision problem a little bit longer. I can find my face to take a drink, but I can't always pour without spilling. The whole thing got awkward, so I switched to black coffee, surprising the hell out of everyone. Previously, I enjoyed the beverage with more cream and sugar than coffee.

I'm holding the cup in my hands, focusing on the warmth radiating from its sides when I hear her voice for the first time. "Trystan? I'm Lynn. I'm the one who sent the letter." She stands there at the edge of the booth. Her voice quivers when she speaks.

The scent of her perfume hits me. It's something juvenile, like vanilla and spices. From what I can see of her, she's tall and thin with dark hair—and she's incredibly nervous. Anxiety is wafting off of her tidal waves.

She stands there shaking enough that even I notice, waiting for me to reply. I don't say much. I've got my guard up, and I'm not dropping it—not even for a second. I don't care if she's afraid—she should be mortified by what she did. I hold out my hand, palm up, toward the seat opposite me. "Sit."

She slides in, and I notice a nervous tic, she's done it twice already, and then a third time. Her left hand runs through her hair at her temple and then down behind her ear, tucking the long strand in place.

I do that.

Frequently.

I have to remind myself that this could all be bullshit. I've had people do all sorts of things to get close to me, some even learned my movements so they could mirror them—so I'd think we had a lot in common and become instant BFFs. I could attract crazy before becoming famous, but after I became a household name, holy hell—it was like strapping a beacon on my body because the crazy chicks came out of the woodwork.

Guys say don't dip your stick in crazy, and that's accurate, completely. It always bites you on the ass. Horse girls are the worst—you know the type, the ones who found out unicorns weren't real and switched to horses. After that, second place is tied between models and chicks named 'Holly'—they're both completely insane, just in different ways.

Back to reality, back to the woman who left me and I know nothing about. I spit out, "What do you want?" I don't look up at her. I don't need to look to know she's got big eyes that are ready to spill tears on her cheeks. I can hear it in the ways she breathes, in her voice.

She does that hair twitch thing, tucks the strand that's already tucked, and laughs nervously. "I didn't think this was a good idea, that too much time had passed, and now I'm too late—but I didn't want to regret never trying to see you."

I can't talk. My jaw locks and I feel my fingers tighten involuntarily around my mug. I'm practically strangling the thing. When I don't speak, she continues, "I thought you'd think that I wanted something from you—everyone must want something."

"And you don't?" I sound so fucking jaded it's almost cruel. I keep my chin tucked and my eyes on the mug.

"No," her voice is soft and careful. "I don't want anything from you, and that's the last thing I wanted you to think. That's the main thing that kept me away after first seeing you in the press." Her voice fades and her jaw flaps a few times. I don't help her out. I show no compassion. "I always thought I'd find you again, but I never expected this."

I can't help it. I'm laughing in her face, bitterly with a smile sharp enough to cut glass. "Really? Well, I never expected to have a mother who abandoned me suddenly show up and want me back, and since you didn't appear until I'm way past my teen years, should I assume you had an aversion to teenagers as well as babies? Or do you just hate kids in general and you waited for me to grow up?" I'm on my feet, sliding out of the booth. "You know what, this was a bad plan. I should go back to resenting you from a distance, and you can go back to being the woman who abandoned her only son because he cried too much." I'm out of the booth and ready to dart past her when she grabs my wrist.

I freeze even though I want to rip my hand away. "What are you talking about? I didn't abandon you. Trystan, I never left your side from the day you were born until the day your dad ran off with you. I spent every day of my life looking for you. He said I left you?"

It feels like someone shoved a hot iron into my chest, each new word pushing it painfully deeper and deeper. I growl out the word, "Yes." I stand there, perfectly still and her hand drops.

"I understand why you're so angry, then. That makes sense, but that's not the way it happened."

I grit my teeth together to hide the pain coursing through my body, and slide back into the booth. I wave a hand at her while wearing a plastic smile. "Then tell me the truth, and don't leave a damn thing out, because God knows I have the means to verify every last detail, and if you lie to me—even a tiny bit—I will find out and I'll never speak to you again."

She nods and tries to hide her shaking hands by folding them together. I hear the pain in her voice when she speaks, but I'm too raw to do more than notice. Every time she speaks it feels like being clawed apart. I want to scream at her for leaving me, for letting Dad abuse me, and humiliate me. I bite my tongue and sit. I tell myself to sit and hear this story.

She takes a shaky breath and dives in. "I need to start before the day you disappeared. Things weren't always bad. Your father wasn't always horrible. When I first met him, he was sweet. He doted on me. But then we got married, and things changed. I thought that was the way it was supposed to be, you know? Everyone says the first year is the hardest, so I thought things were normal, but his temper flared up hotter and higher. By the end of that first year, I was in tears more often than not. Then I found out I was pregnant with you, and I was thrilled—we both were until you arrived. After that, everything went to hell. It was like your dad resented you, and at times I thought he hated you. I wasn't sure why, but it frightened me so much I planned to take you and run."

I sit there as this story spills out from her heart. I can hear the pain and sorrow, and know this tale is full of heartbreak and misery. If I could see her face, her eyes would be glassy, and the corners of her mouth would droop in a permanent frown—I can hear it in her voice. I want to believe her, but it's so easy to blame dad.

"You were going to take me away from Dad?"

"I was. I had the car packed with everything we needed, and we were going to take off before he got home from work. I had enough cash that we could get away, go somewhere he'd never find us, and it took so long to save that money. He didn't let me keep any money around and only gave me a debit card for groceries and food. I could deal with the controlling issues he had, I would have stayed if he only screamed at me in a fit of rage, but he did something to you."

My heart is pounding, and I want to tell her that she doesn't need to say more, especially since I think I already know, but I can't save her from retelling this story. "What did he do?"

"You were crying. You had an ear infection, and you hurt when I laid you down. I'd been carrying you all day, and I was tired. Your dad wasn't helping me and, frankly, I didn't want him to, but I needed to lay you down just for a moment. When I came back from the bathroom, your room was completely silent, and he was standing there over your crib. Your crying had stopped and when I looked at you to see why…" Her voice breaks and she swallows hard, choking back tears.

I can't keep being an asshole to her. Whether she's legit or not, she thinks this was real. I can sense her horror. I can feel her agony. I reach out and touch the back of her hand lightly. "You don't have to say the rest. I'm sure I already know."

She puts her hand on mine. "I have to tell you—I wouldn't have taken you if he hadn't, but Trystan, when I came back in the room he had a pillow over your little body. Your tiny hands were tearing at it trying to pull it away, but the movement was so slow and erratic. I thought I'd lost you. I rushed over and ripped the pillow away. You started crying, and so did I."

"Dad said I cried a lot."

"You did, but you had reason to—babies cry when they hurt, and you were hurting. He was so jealous of you. You took up all of my time. He'd work and come home, and you were there. He'd want to take me on a date, but you had to come. He'd want me in bed, but you needed me more. These were all things I'd expected, but he hadn't, and the older you got, the more resentful he became. I couldn't risk staying there, so I packed up our things, but the day we were going to leave went wrong."

She squeezes my hand hard then pulls away to dig through her purse for a tissue. She lifts it to her face, patting. "Your dad came home early and saw the car packed with you in your car seat. He ripped the keys from my hand, ran inside and saw that your things were gone. He was furious. There was a lot of yelling, and he shoved me. I fell and hit my head on the driveway, unconscious long enough for him to drive away. Everything I needed to take you and start over was in that car. He took my money and my son, and I never saw either of you again." She laughs nervously, tucking that piece of hair behind her ear again.

I'm slow to speak and want to get this right. Her story meshes with Dad's version in places, so I don't think it's total crap. "I'm sorry you went through so much. I hate to add to your burdens by not taking your story at face value, but I can't."

"I understand." She dabs her eyes with the tissue again. She must be crying. That's got to be why the waitress hasn't come back.

"People have made up things that sound believable before, and other women have showed up claiming to be my mother. I need to verify this, all right?" I feel like such a dick for saying it. When those other people spoke, something felt off, but this doesn't. Everything from the way she describes dad on a good day to the way she pegged his outbursts, to his undying love for her—it all feels right.

"Of course." There's understanding in her tone, something the other people lacked. "Even if this is the only time we meet, I'm glad you listened. You didn't have to, and honestly, I'm surprised you stayed. Everyone has one chance to tell their story, and I'm grateful you listened to mine. You've had a hard life, Trystan, and I know that man, I'm sure he blamed you for everything."

I nod, not wanting to say more before I know for certain. "Listen, I'd appreciate it if you didn't tell anyone about this yet. It's a lot to come to terms with, and I don't want the press around right now—not for something like this. This story is between you and me, okay?" She probably has another life by now. It's a selfish thing to ask, but I have to say it. I don't want the pap around to harass the crap out of her before I get a chance to know who she is. They'll taint everything.

She nods slowly, dabbing her eyes. "Of course. I've not told anyone, for several reasons, that being one of them. I'd like to get to know you without expectations or cameras. I know I can't make up for lost time, but—"

I stop her. There's enough guilt in her voice to drown us both. "Time is our friend now—there's lots of it. Let me check some things and I'll contact you again." I pull out a bill and put it on the table. "Please order lunch on me. I need to head out before someone recognizes me, but you should take your time. I'll be in touch."

I walk away feeling like a louse. It feels like I walked out of a meeting negotiating a new record deal, not like I finally met my mother.

CHAPTER 37

I tell Bob the basics and ask him to confirm her story when I get in the car. As we drive away, I have the fierce desire to go back. It feels horrible, and I can't understand why. There's this sense that something bad is going to happen, like the other shoe is going to drop with a spike on the toe. My stomach has been uneasy for days now, and I've not eaten much, besides candy. I feel like shit. I slump back into the seat and cover my eyes with my arm.

Bob has been looking at me in the rearview mirror. I can feel his eyes on me.

"If there's something you want to say, say it."

"What if this all checks out? What does she want? Did she say?" Bob knows how much this means to me.

I haven't said much about my missing mom over the years, but he knows damn well it's a sore spot, and there's always that need for closure. Besides, I already have one parent that hates me. It'd be nice to have one that actually liked me. "I'm not sure. It sounded like she wanted to talk to me, and she didn't expect to get to tell me anything. It was almost like today was all she hoped for. It's kind of sad." I drop my arms and sit up. I pull off the ball cap and toss it on the seat, and run my hands through my hair and stare at the floor, thinking.

"It is. If you believe all that crap about mothers being genetically tied to their children, it must have ripped her heart out when your father kidnapped you."

"By crap, you mean science?" Bob laughs and looks over his shoulder at me. "Yeah, I read. Just because I can't see shit, doesn't mean I stopped listening. That was in the news recently—that moms have their babies DNA. I know stuff." He's quiet, maneuvering the car through rush hour traffic. I should have taken the helicopter, but that wouldn't be inconspicuous. At the same time, being trapped in the city at this time of day sucks. "He kidnapped me, didn't he?"

"Sure sounds that way. But your mother was going to do it first."

I work my jaw and sit back against the seat, splaying my hands on the Italian leather. It feels cool and smooth under the pads of my fingers. "Check to see if the kidnapping was reported."

"I will, but it could have been filed under a domestic dispute, or not at all—it depends on what your mom wanted to do when she found you. If you'd been my kid, I'd have tried to steal you back and drawing federal agents to that fact wouldn't be pretty. Besides, your dad had custody of you, so there probably isn't a paper trail, Trystan. I can contact her friends from back then and talk to them. A neighbor might have seen something. Is that the main thing you want corroborated? The day your dad took you?"

"Yeah. That's the point that makes everything stick or turns it to bullshit."

"There's one way to find out today if she's telling the truth."

"No." I don't want to hear the suggestion. There's no way in hell I'm asking my father for a damn thing.

"He'd know."

"Even if he did, he wouldn't tell me. The man is a classic asshole and likes to make me suffer. He'd tell a version of the story that rips my heart out and makes her look like Satan." Dad's great like that. "Plus he's still pissed about the whole jail thing."

"What'd he expect? You can't beat the shit out of people and not get your ass taken down a notch. He was already in deep shit before he hit that cop."

I don't even want to think about it. That night was so fucked up. It wasn't long after announcing I was Day Jones when Dad decided to try and beat my ass publicly in front of a gathering of fans at a local music store. There was an undercover cop there with his daughter. Dad showed up intending on beating me to a pulp and before I could swing at him, the cop stepped in between us. Dad didn't pull his punches, even after seeing the badge. The little girl's screams still ring in my ears. Dad had blood on his mind that day, and he beat the shit out of the cop. The fight only stopped when I hit my father in the back of the head with a metal rack. It tore the flesh at the base of his neck. Blood spewed everywhere. I thought I killed him, and I didn't think twice about it. As soon as Dad stayed down, other people helped the cop, and I went over to the kid. Her face was wet with tears, and her tiny cheeks were white. Her hands trembled, and she was hysterically sobbing. I held her hands, wanting to comfort her—I knew what it was like to be terrified like that without a parent, plus it was my dad who hurt her father—and she threw her little body into my arms. I held her like that until her Mom showed up. Her name was Becky.

"He didn't care at that point." That was the truth. He didn't care about anything except ruining me.

Bob nods to himself, then blares the horn. The traffic is stop and go, but mostly inert. I could walk to the other side of Manhattan faster than it's going to take at this time of day.

Bob flips someone off, as he shoves the car into another lane. "Give me a few days. I'll find someone." He turns onto East 34th Street and grins. "I got you a ride. Your helicopter is waiting on the tarmac."

"Seriously?"

"Yeah, seriously. I know you—you'd walk before you remembered you have that sick machine." I bought a Sikorsky S-76C a few years ago for about 12 million and change. It's the same model the military uses, but they make a few luxury models with posh seats and all the bells and whistles. Bob has a serious man crush on that machine.

The Sikorsky was one of those purchases that seemed too out there for me at the time. Looking back, I see why I needed it. Getting around the city is a pain in the ass, and I can't miss a performance because I couldn't get to Teterboro on time. Bob's right. I'm an idiot.

"I want to fly it." Bob laughs and looks back at me with a huge smile across his wide face.

"Learn to fly first and I'll let you. We can ditch the car and fly everywhere. No one would mind if I landed in midtown, right?"

"Shit, no! It's Trystan Scott. People would want you to fucking sing, or something. You'd have to be ready to give impromptu performances for the rest of your life."

"Yeah, now you know why I usually jump out of the car and walk." Unspoken words hover in the air, and we both know the opportunity won't last much longer. "Thanks, Bob."

He nods as he pulls through the gate and drives straight onto the tarmac, stopping close to the helicopter. "I don't know what you believe—we've never talked about God or the purpose of life—but I believe bad shit doesn't come without something seriously good. You're a good person with a big heart, and lots of people have tried to take advantage of that over the years. Another man would have become bitter, but not you. Fame didn't change you. Not many can say that."

I tip my head forward and lift my eyebrows, pointing out the window. "Bob, I have changed. That's a helicopter, and it's not in a video game."

"I know you don't like to hear it, that you think it's bullshit, some false flattery or something, but it ain't. You have the markers of a very successful man, and you had a shitastic life. The highs are super high, and the lows are in hell. You managed to hold on to who you are through all that. You see what I'm saying? You're good people, Mr. Scott."

I'm beyond uncomfortable, so I accept the compliment. "Thanks, Bob, for everything."

CHAPTER 38

When I'm inside the Sikorsky, I pull on the headphones and sink back into the chair. There's a glass of scotch waiting for me on the little table. I pick it up and hold it in my hand, wanting to knock it back, and wanting to toss it out the window at the same time. This shit poisoned my father. It turned a mean man into a cruel bastard.

I stand and put the glass down in the mini bar and dump the contents in the drain. We hit a bump, and my ass hits the seat hard. The pilot comes on and apologizes. "About fifteen minutes out."

"Thanks, James." He's ex-military, but retained the curt, no-nonsense demeanor. Add that to the New Yorker thing, and I love him.

He speaks like he was taught to talk by tweeting and doesn't use more than one hundred and forty characters per thought. I've tried everything I can think of to send him on a rant, but he never bites.

I look down at the city and the tall steel buildings jutting up out of the ground like glass gods. The windows reflect the dying sun as it sinks, and there are thousands of lights below from homes, offices, and cars. It's still surreal to fly this close to the ground, alone.

I thought the only time I'd be in a helicopter would be going into battle with Seth. I regret it so much it stings. The memories of him aren't bittersweet, they're painful. It's like trying to swallow razor blades with a smile on your face, and I just can't do it.

Before he died, I wasn't around much. He and Katie had graduated to the baby stage, and I was so far from their world, I barely showed my face. Now, it's too late, and there are no words to make it better. I fucked Seth over, and I ruined Katie's life.

Seth wouldn't have been there if I hadn't planned to enlist. He would have attended college. He wouldn't have signed on for another tour. Part of me thinks there's no way to know that, but that's bullshit. I'm trying to shirk blame even though it's my fault.

I push the thoughts away for another day.

CHAPTER 39

When I get back to the apartment, Mari is gone. I didn't expect her to stick around all day, but she seemed so upset I thought she'd want to talk more. Maybe it's cold feet. Certain I'm alone, I'm stripping off my jacket and shirt when my phone buzzes. I pad over to it and see it's ringing.

I swipe my finger across the screen, swallowing a mouthful of regret. "Yeah?"

"It's me. Katie. The most bodacious babe you've ever had the privilege of befriending. Will you call down and tell your guard to let me up? He thinks I'm a rogue groupie here to do you." She pulls the phone away from her face—I can hear her as she chastises the guard, "As if I'd even try coming through the front door if I wanted to nail the guy. Service elevator, hello? Fire escape, laundry shoot, the roof! Are you totally new at this——?"

I hang up and call down before Katie can make the man cry. After two rings, he picks up. "Hey, this is Trystan Scott in the penthouse. That lunatic in the lobby is my friend. You should let her up before she castrates you."

The guy sounds young and star-struck. "I believe you. They left directions not to let anyone up, so I was following——"

"Who said that?"

"Your bodyguard. I would have called if——"

I cut him off. "It's okay. Let her up, and I'll talk to Bob later. He's probably not back yet to check IDs and all that. You can send her up." I still hear Katie in the background scolding the man when I hang up. I wait next to the elevator doors with my arms folded over my chest. I'd normally grab a shirt, but the elevator is already moving. Better not to have a pissed off Katie roaming through my house looking for me.

The doors chime and slide open. Katie is standing there in a solid black dress that comes to her knee, a black swing coat that's cinched at the waist, and a pair of biker boots that stop just below her knee. Her makeup is heavy with dark eyeliner and her hair looks wild, as if she'd been standing too close to the helicopter.

I smile at her. "Nice to see you."

She grumbles and breezes past me, throwing her purse on the couch, and then spinning around to face me. "I hate that man! I can't stand him. I have to vent, or my brain will explode. If I don't get it all out, I'll shoot my mouth off to Mari—which is the worst thing I can do." She takes a moment to breathe and I can feel her looking at me. "What, do you think I'm going to drool over your abs? Put a shirt on!"

Wow, something really got to her. I push off the wall and head back toward my room with Katie on my heels. "New tattoo? I haven't seen that one." Her finger touches a spot on the small of my back, and I jump. A rather unmanly shriek comes out of my mouth at the same time.

Katie laughs. "Holy crap! Is that a poem? Did you have a poem tattooed on your ass?"

"It's my back and stops at my hip."

She chuckles. "Good thing you don't write long poems, huh?" She waggles her eyebrows mischievously before her mood snaps back to mad. She stomps over to my bed and throws herself on it, ranting while staring at the ceiling. "He's an asshole. I can see now. I'm kicking myself for not noticing until now—that man passed the initial boyfriend test, and it's hard!"

"I know." I say, walking into the wardrobe and pulling a long-sleeved white cotton shirt from the hanger. I pull it over my head, and when I come out, she's still ranting. I cut her off. "What'd he do? And to be clear—are we talking about Derrick?"

"Yes! OMG, weren't you listening at all? He's got this evil vibe, and I swear to God he's an asshole."

I don't say anything because I don't like him either, but for a totally different reason than Katie's. I doubt she wants to slip Mari out of her clothes and hold her close to her chest. I'm assuming my reason for hating Derrick is tainted, but I can't tell Katie that.

I stand at the foot of the bed. "What'd he do?"

She makes an annoyed sound in her throat and sits up quickly. "He's fake. There's something about him that's off, and I can't put my finger on what it is—but have you seen him with her? Derrick is sweet until something happens, he freaks out with uber-asshole style, and then he completely backs down. It doesn't matter why or over what. His temper flares and then he puts it out cold."

"Isn't that a good thing?"

"No!" She yells at me like I'm an idiot. "It means he's hiding who he really is, and a temper like that followed by a complete one-eighty is a red flag. It's a big-ass red flag, but if I say anything to Mari now, she'll just be pissed. She won't listen to me. I already told her I didn't like him." The corner of her lip curls up as she looks down at her nails, and picks at the polish. "I may have told her he was a clone of you."

"What!" My eyes get huge, and I grab the sides of my head. "Why would you say that?"

"Because he is! Have you seen him?"

No, not really. Dark hair, tall, a little thicker than me. That's it. The guy could have a baby face, and I wouldn't know. "Yeah, but a clone isn't possible." I get her to laugh.

"Nope, there's only one Trystan Scott, thank God! The world couldn't handle two of you. Back to the issue at hand—Mari's marrying an asshole. What do I do? Stand by and smile? Or blow everything up and make sure she knows? Those are the only options I can think of, and neither sound good. I need a drink. Please tell me you have something stronger than Kool-Aid?"

"Yeah, I do. What do you want?"

She puts a finger to her lips and pauses while tapping it, thinking. Then she smiles, I can hear it in her voice. "A chocolate martini! With a marshmallow. Or whipped cream. I'm guessing you have whipped cream. Vats and vats of it."

"Yeah, yeah. Come on. I'll make you something resembling that." After trying to find something to substitute for just about every regular ingredient, I emerge from the kitchen thinking I nailed it. In terms of being close enough, at least.

I hand Katie a mug. She takes it, and looks into it, "This isn't a martini glass."

"It's not a martini. It's the next best thing."

She hesitates, and then takes a tentative sip. "Holy crap! What is that?" I can see her mouth open and shut and hear her laugh. "It's got some mega-burn."

"Don't drink it too fast. Liquor is quicker, and that's probably two-thirds booze."

"What's the other third?"

"Marshmallows soaked in booze."

Katie pops one in her mouth. "It's squishy. Is this vodka?"

"Yeah, vodka, schnapps, and a massive amount of Swiss Miss—which I nuked, so it would be hot. It's probably disgusting cold." I sit on the chair at the end of the coffee table, adjacent to the sofa where Katie's perched.

The tension in her voice has subsided a bit, and I make my way back to the reason she showed up. "So, you hate Derrick."

"Check." Katie tries to fish out another marshmallow.

"Did something happen last night? Mari showed up really upset."

"That would be me. I told her what I thought of him, and she ran out. Apparently, it's no longer open for discussion. The thing that pisses me off most is that I didn't see it. He's faking, right? No guy can put on a perfect act forever. The closer they get to the wedding, the more I see the real Derrick the Dick shining through. A guy with a temper that lashes out is bad news."

"You're preaching to the choir, Katie. What do you want to do?"

"I don't know. I was hoping you'd know, because I really don't. If Seth were here, he'd concoct some elaborate plan to trick the guy into showing his true colors. I'm not good at stuff like that." Her head hangs between her shoulders and, as I watch her, I notice the black slash across my field of vision is no longer a line—it's more like a hole.

I really want to tell her, but Katie has enough stuff to deal with right now. I inhale deeply and slide back into my chair. "What if we did the obvious?"

"And that would be?"

"Tell him she spent the night here. A jealous guy with a temper is going to react to his fiancée spending the night with her ex, no matter the reason." It'd be a dick move on my part, and I don't want to hurt Mari, but if Katie's right I need to know. Mari needs to know. The thought of someone hurting Mari makes me insane. My fingers are gripping the arms of the chair so tightly my nails are bending back.

Katie's been watching me, silently sipping her drink. "What's with you?"

"You'll have to be more specific?"

"Why? So you can deny it? Come on, Trystan. Something's up with you. You've been walking around drunk, falling off the stage at work—yeah, I heard about that—and, when it comes to Mari, you're cold. Don't you care about her? Don't you want to keep her from getting hurt?"

She's poking my buttons with a sledgehammer. Subtlety is a quality Katie has never possessed. I sit up and glare at her. "Don't ask me questions you can answer already. You're not that dense. Figure it out."

She laughs once, bitterly. "Dense? Nice, Trystan. Tell you what, I'll explain what I see, and you tell me when I'm wrong, okay?" She ticks off one finger. "First, you're still in love with Mari. Second, you hate Derrick, but think it's because you're still sweet on Mari. Third, you didn't tell Mari you still love her because you have some deranged idea you're not good enough for her. And Fourth, and final, all the drunkenness that has you falling, tripping, and crashing your car is a hoax. You're hiding something."

My jaw tightens as she speaks. Her words feel like barbs in my chest, finding their mark and sinking in. I want to yell, but I swallow back any emotions. I'm not ruining Mari's relationship. If the guy is really a dick, she needs to walk away because she sees it—it can't have anything to do with me.

Katie places her mug on the table and walks over to me. I stare at her, unblinking. "Mari informed me she and I will follow you to your movie set. Why on earth would she do that? What would make her risk pissing off Derrick to help you remember a few lines? Hey, Trystan?" She leans in close to my face, and her eyes are swallowed by the black hole. I only see her mouth, wavering in front of me.

"What?"

"Really? No reaction?" I'm about to push her away, when she says, "What about this?" She leans in and presses her lips to mine. I jump out of the chair and practically fall on the floor trying to get away from her.

I wipe her kiss off and yell, "What the hell are you doing?"

"Trying to figure out what the hell is wrong with you! Either you don't care, or you can't see. I'm betting on the second."

I swallow hard and look away. My heart is still pounding in my chest. "I'm going blind, Katie. I didn't want to dump this on you now." I explain what's happening, and how I've been hiding it.

"I noticed. I've seen you hold a drink. That's all you do—hold it. So, what are you going to do?"

"Deal with it, I guess. I don't have many options."

She puts her arm around my shoulder and hugs me from the side. "Well, I'm glad you weren't acting weird because you had the hots for me. That would have been awkward since you're like a loser little brother and all."

"I'm glad we cleared that up."

"Yeah, so, I'm thinking we try to bait Derrick at the engagement party. With you." Katie then tells me what she thinks will piss the guy off, and I'm suddenly glad I've not angered the woman recently.

CHAPTER 40

The engagement party comes quickly. The closer we get to the wedding, the sicker I feel about the whole thing. If Katie's right, I can't let Mari marry him. But if she's wrong? God, this is fucked up.

I know Mari didn't tell Derrick she spent the night at my apartment. It wasn't a lie, she didn't bring it up, and he didn't ask.

Bob is driving Katie and me to Mari's Dad's house. When we arrive, the front lawn looks beautiful. White lights and silver balls make the trees look like a winter wonderland. A white carpet is rolled out from the curb to the front door.

Katie takes my hand and squeezes it tight. She leans in close to me and whispers, "Watch your step, the carpet buckles just past the curb." She laughs lightly, kissing my cheek. She's been great since I told her about the stuff with my eyes. She didn't ask me anything else, she just made note of times I seem uneasy, and she stepped in to help. I don't worry about being unable to read the menus, cracks in the pavement, or a thousand other little things I used to deal with on a daily basis.

Thanks to her, I was able to try someplace new for lunch the other day—a place I didn't have the menu memorized. She sat next to me and read the entire menu to me. Discreetly. Seeing how close she's been to me physically, everyone thinks she's my new girlfriend. She's always holding my hand or whispering in my ear. No one guesses it's because she's helping me not to trip or quietly reading something to me.

"Thanks, Katie."

"No problem. And remember, I'm the one that will tell Derrick. I'll put you with Mari and then go to find him. Either the shit will hit the fan, or not. Then this will be over. God, I hope I'm wrong about him." Her voice is tight, and I know she's worried. Katie and Mari have been best friends for as long as I can remember. I know Katie can't afford to lose that support right now, and I admire how she's put Mari's needs in front of her own.

The front door is open, and a woman is there with a clipboard. Katie gives her our names, and she welcomes us inside. "The bride-to-be should be downstairs in a few moments."

Katie leans in and whispers in my ear, "Can you make it up a flight of steps without falling on your face?"

"Yes, I'm not an invalid. I just can't see very well."

"Just checking. I'm going to torch this mofu. Burn baby, burn." She goes into a chorus of a song and dances a little bit as she leads me to the back stairs on the other side of the kitchen. I used to sneak up these steps in high school. "Go get her, killer."

The lights are off, which makes it more difficult to see, but everything is the same as it was when we dated. I follow the railing up, turn onto the landing, and go to the end of the hall. Mari's door is cracked. I put my hand on it and push it open a little allowing the light to spill out onto the darkened hallway floor.

"Mari?"

"Trystan? You came!" She sounds excited.

"I wanted to see you, I mean really see you. I can't do it downstairs."

She's up and walking toward me. Mari pulls me into her room, and closes the door. "I know what you mean. Go ahead. I spent half the day straightening my curls. It feels like unicorn hair," she says, giggling.

She guides my hands to her face, and I move slowly, feeling the curves of her cheeks before slipping my hands back through her silky hair. One side is pinned back, and the other is down. "You look beautiful tonight." I let her locks fall through my fingers and put a hand on her shoulder. "Are you happy?"

"Yeah, why?" Her voice says the opposite of her words.

"Nothing, it seems like you're nervous, that's all."

Mari reaches out and takes my hands in hers. Tingles shoot up my arms and my heart is engulfed with the emotion streaming from her body. "What does it feel like to you?"

I have no clue. Something is making her feel loved and excited, but there's fear and guilt swimming around in there, too. "I know you think I can read your mind, but I can't. I only feel what you feel. I'm guessing, and even that is open to interpretation. So you tell me. Use your words, Mari. Come on, girl, you can do it." I tease her and get treated to a laugh before she shoves me lightly.

"You're an ass."

"Yeah, but I'm a cute ass."

"Oh, I have no doubt you know that already, so let's not inflate your ego any bigger. Tonight is my night. I'm supposed to be the one who's walking on sunshine."

"Does it feel good?" I'm joking, but her demeanor changes as she considers the question seriously.

"I'm not sure. Half the time I feel like I'm going to puke. Is that normal? I've asked a lot of people about cold feet, and everyone says it passes, that it's fleeting. I'm sure that's all it is, but it's scary, you know?"

I feel like an asshole for adding to her misery tonight. It's too late. The plan is already in motion. Katie is telling Derrick that Mari slept at my place earlier this week. She's going to let it slip like she wasn't supposed to say anything. I am supposed to distract Mari until it's done. Katie will text me and let me know.

"Life is scary at times. That doesn't have to mean anything. Mari, you know how you feel about this guy, right? He's one hundred percent what you want, right?"

She laughs it off. "One hundred percent isn't possible."

Wait. What? Before I can ask her about that, my phone buzzes. It's Katie. She's done it.

Mari takes my hand. "Let's get downstairs before people wonder where we've been."

"Mari…" I place my other hand over hers and look into her fading face. Our eyes lock and that strange pull feels stronger than ever, beckoning me to her. I'm so close it wouldn't take much to lean in and kiss her. I banish the thought, but before I can blink her bedroom door flies open. It hits the wall so hard the knob busts through the sheetrock.

"Nice. You're up here with your ex-boyfriend while I'm downstairs telling people how much I love you." Derrick growls at her. I want to step between them, but I can't. This is what Katie worked to set into motion. I need to wait.

Mari laughs him off. "Trystan is one of my best friends. He wanted to see me before the party."

"I'm sure he did." Derrick glares at me while pumping his fists at his sides. "Was it fun? Nailing my fiancée behind my back?"

Mari scolds him, "Derrick, it's not like that."

He rounds on her. "Then what's it like? Because sleepovers with an ex this close to a wedding aren't usually a good thing."

"I didn't sleep with him." She laughs nervously and shakes her head. Her arms fold over her chest, across that white dress, and she holds tightly onto her arms. I want to intervene and end this, but I can't. This is what we were looking for, and I admit—this sounds bad and looks bad. "Derrick, I've never given you a reason to doubt me."

"You lied to me! You said you were sleeping at Katie's, not at his place! You didn't ask me if you could spend the night with your ex. You hid it from me! Tell me why. Were you having an orgy? Were the Olsen twins there?"

I try not to laugh. I have no idea what this guy thinks I do in my spare time, but orgies aren't my thing. "She had a fight with Katie and asked for a place to sleep. Damn, man. You could trust her a little bit, okay? Mari's not the cheating type."

Derrick is vibrating. He's ready to blow. The guy sucks in air and presses his eyes closed. He willfully pries open his fingers and breathes a ragged breath. "Sleepovers with your ex-boyfriend are off the table."

"You don't trust her?"

He gets up in my face. "I don't trust you. I see the way you look at her, how you're always trying to touch her. I thought we could be friends, and I'd see that you were like that with everyone, but guess what? You're not!" He screams the last two words in my face, spitting a little as he does.

I blink, and he steps back. "Yeah, well, she loves you. She's marrying you, and I don't fuck around with betrothed women. You won, man. Back off."

Derrick is in my face again, and I know how badly he wants to put his fist in my face. The feeling is mutual. Every inch of my body is charged ready to fight. But Mari pulls on

Derrick's arm. Her voice is calming and soft. "He doesn't feel like that toward me. We're friends. That's it." She wraps her arms around his neck and kisses him.

When she steps away, Mari seems happy. "I'm heading downstairs. Come down in a second and we'll pour the champagne." Mari disappears through the door and I'm left alone with Derrick.

He steps within an inch of my face. "If you even think about her, I'll tear your balls off." Derrick turns and slams his fist into the wall, cracking it. He shakes out his hand and smiles. "Next time, that'll be your face, so stay the fuck away from her."

He disappears through the doorway.

A few minutes later, Katie finds me sitting on Mari's old bed, staring at the wall. She rushes through the door and turns around. Her jaw drops as she spots the hole in the wall. "He flipped out?"

"Yeah, he did, but not in front of Mari. You're right. The guy is unbalanced."

"She didn't see this?"

"No, he did that after she left the room and said that would be my face if I tried anything with her."

Katie pouts. "We can't use that! It sounds like normal boyfriend pissy territorial crap."

"I know."

"What do we do?" She sounds truly worried, and the truth is, so am I.

"I don't know."

CHAPTER 41

After Katie helps me get down to the party without doing a header on the staircase, a passing waiter shoves a flute of champagne in my hand. I find a corner to watch from, ignoring the murmuring and staring from other guests. Katie finds a spot next to me. She leans in when she speaks, the top of her head nearly touching mine. "This blows."

"I know."

"I'm going to have to make a speech or something. She invited me to do it. I can out him."

"I can't let you do that. Mari will never forgive you and he'll hide it. No, we need him to lose it in front of her."

The high pitch of a champagne glass chimes and I hear Mari's voice. "Thank you for coming tonight. As you know, this is the reception slash engagement party for everyone. The wedding will be in a couple of weeks, and we wanted to keep it small and intimate..."

Katie frowns, murmuring, "Derrick wanted that, not her. Mari always wanted a big-ass wedding. She has a three-ring binder from when we were kids listing out exactly what she wants in a wedding—straight down to the twelve bridesmaids, four flower girls, a fairy, and a dog ring bearer."

I try not to laugh. "A fairy?"

"Yeah, that's how I can tell you're a guy. Most women scoff at the dog."

"I'm pretty sure there are other ways to tell I'm a guy."

"Shut up! Derrick's about to make his toast." She elbows me in the side, and I nearly fall over.

"Damn it. Did you file those things?"

Derrick clears his throat. "There are very few things in life that present themselves with complete certainty. The day I met Mari, I knew we were meant to be together."

Katie coughs softly and covers her mouth with the back of her hand, whispering, "Stalker."

I smile and listen to Derrick tell the story of how they met, ending with how much he adores her. "If you'll raise your glasses and toast with me. To Mari, the best wife a man could ask for."

Everyone toasts and glasses are clinked together. Katie is brewing next to me, ready to pop. "He sounds like he won a trophy."

"Yeah, I noticed that. His wording was a little interesting."

Derrick gets everyone to settle down and introduces the next speaker. I'm not paying attention until I hear her voice.

"Ever since Derrick was a little boy…" Her voice is soft, confident, easy, and very familiar. She's too far away, and I can't really see her.

"Katie, who is that?"

"Derrick's mom."

That can't be right. "What's her name? I need a name. Now." Katie can tell I'm panicking, but she's not sure why.

"I don't know. He didn't say. Trystan, what's wrong?"

Before I can rationalize anything, my feet are moving, and I'm walking toward her. I can't hide the shock on my face. The crowd parts for me until I'm standing a few feet from her.

She had a smile on her face and a drink raised in her hand until she sees me. "Trystan." She says my name as a curse.

"Lynn, what is this?" My mouth moves, but I can't fathom what's happening. Did she lie to me? This woman can't be my mother. She's Derrick's mother. She has another kid here, too.

But she answers me. It's her, the woman from the diner. "My son is getting married. I didn't know you'd be here. Do you already know each other?" Worry pinches her voice, and the room is creepy silent.

Derrick's voice slices through the silence. "Ma, why is he talking to you? How do you know him?"

Jared materializes from somewhere, flanking his brother. "I think you should go, Scott."

"Lynn?" Mari's voice is high, fragile.

Disgust crawls across my face. "I should have known you were another gold digger. Mari, this guy had his mom pretend she was my mother. I met her, remember? I believed her. It turns out she's just a really good liar and your boyfriend is a bastard. He used you to get at me."

Mari seems frozen. She doesn't move.

Derrick is rushing toward me with his brother close behind. "No one says shit about my mother."

Lynn tries to speak, but no one is listening. Derrick's fist comes flying at my face. I dodge it and swing back, hitting him in the side. He swears and doubles over. Jared lands a punch in my side and connects with my kidney. Cheap shot.

I don't hold back. I go for him. My arm pulls back, and I'm about to let my fist remove his teeth when I hear Mari's voice, "Stop! Don't!"

I think she's speaking to me, so I pull my punch and turn. She wasn't talking to me at all—she was yelling at Derrick. He was behind me. I turn in time to get a fist in my gut, and a flash of silver catches my eye as I go down. My arm is screaming, burning and I realize that asshole cut me.

Derrick rushes at me, his foot ready to kick me in the gut. "You stupid son of a bitch! You tried to steal Mari, and now you're talking shit about my mom! You're going to remember what happens when you fuck with our family!" As he swings his foot to my gut, I let him. When it connects with my body, I roll, and he goes down. I manage to punch him in the face once before his kid brother pulls me off.

He tosses me back to Derrick. Suddenly, all three of us are standing, staring each other down.

Lynn rushes between us, her eyes full of tears. "I should have told you—I should have told all of you—but I didn't. Trystan is your brother. I'm his mother. If you want to hurt him, you'll have to kill me first." She positions herself in front of me.

Derrick is livid. His face is bleeding, and he's screaming. "You're making shit up to protect him! Get out of the way, Ma. This guy isn't going to mess with our family ever again."

"He is your family! Get it through your head, Derrick. Think for once. I told you that you had an older brother. His father kidnapped him when he was small, and I couldn't find them. Trystan is that baby! Trystan is your brother! I contacted him a while back, and we met for the first time a couple of weeks ago. There was a time I would have done anything to have you all together, but not like this. Not here, not now."

CHAPTER 42

~MARI~

I stand there, stunned. Is this really the woman Trystan's been talking about for the past few weeks? The way she's placed herself in front of Trystan is telling. She chose her relationship with him over her other two boys, over Derrick.

I thought he was already mad, but this gesture seems to catapult him into crazy land. His nostrils flare as he breathes. The veins on the side of his neck are incredibly huge, and the pulse point on his temple is pounding like it's going to pop. His hands are still in fists at his sides. He glares at his mother as he rages. "This is the brat you chased after all those years? The kid that vanished never to be heard from again? Half-brother or not, I don't ca—"

She cuts Derrick off, stepping closer to him. "He's not your half-brother—Jared is his half-brother. You and Trystan share the same father. After he had taken off with Trystan, I discovered I was carrying you."

Jared isn't angry. He's confused. He's shaking his head. "But, Ma, who was the man who raised us?"

"That was your father, and he was a good man, a good father to both of you."

"This is bullshit." Derrick is grinding his teeth together and grimacing so hard I barely recognize him. "This guy is just another one of your charity cases."

"Derrick, he's not. He doesn't need me. I reached out to him expecting him to ignore me or shoot me down, but he didn't. He listened, patiently, which is more than you're doing now. Your father stole my firstborn child from me, and I finally have him back. I won't let you chase him off with your uncontrolled temper!"

Derrick's hand flies and connects with the side of his mom's face. The sound is deafening. Lynn stands there with her spine straight and tears in her eyes. She's been through this before. Trystan's father is a horrible man. When I think about the night I found him beating Trystan, I lose it. No one should hit their mother. No one.

I'm screaming incoherently, launching myself at Derrick. I claw at his eyes before jumping on his back and pounding my fists into the sides of his head. I'm like a fly on a bull, my hits doing very little except annoying him.

A pair of strong arms pulls me off. It's Trystan. He sets me down and calmly turns to Derrick. His voice sounds so deep, so scary. His finger lifts toward the door. "Get out before I make you leave."

Derrick laughs. He pushes his hair out of his face, folds his arms over his chest, and looks at Jared. His younger brother shakes his head and puts his hands up. "You hit mom, you dumb fuck. I'm on his side," he says, jabbing a thumb toward Trystan. "You crossed the line, and I'm going to make sure you never do it again."

Jared steps next to Trystan. I feel Lynn reach for my hand. She laces her fingers through mine, trembling. I squeeze gently without looking at her. Katie is watching, horrorstruck from the corner—along with the rest of our guests.

At that moment, Bob comes rushing through the door, out of breath. "Awh, shit. You ruined her party?"

"No, Derrick did that all by himself." I pull off my engagement ring and run over to the front door, and launch it into the air. It hits the pavement outside with a metallic noise. "I'm not marrying you."

"Get the fuck out of my house before I shove my shoe up your ass and surgically remove it from your throat." Dad is standing in the kitchen doorway, still in his scrubs. His eyes are thin slits, fixated on Derrick. He takes a step toward him and Derrick bolts. He rushes out past Bob and doesn't stop to find the ring.

Dad comes up behind me and puts his arms around my shoulders, kissing the top of my head. "I'm sorry I was late, Mari."

I release Lynn's hand and turn to face him with tears in my eyes. "No, your timing was perfect. Thanks, Dad." I wrap my arms around his neck and hug him hard.

I start crying, and he peels me off. This is well past his comfort zone. He glances around, searching for someone to hand me off to, and places me with Trystan. "Here. Fix this."

Trystan laughs and pulls me close. "Your Dad is… I have no words."

"Neither do I. Thanks for convincing me not to give up on Dad all those years ago."

Dad turns around abruptly. "That was you?"

Trystan seems uncomfortable, but answers. "You only have one set of parents, sir, and, the way I see it, they'll make mistakes, but as long as they aren't bashing your face in with a brick, they're worth fighting for."

Dad stares at Trystan like he's never seen him before. Regaining his composure, he turns toward all the guests left murmuring around the room. "Party's over, get out! If you brought a gift, please take it with you. I'd rather not have any tokens to remind us of this night. It's bad enough I'll have the bill."

Several guests chuckle uncertainly, thinking he's kidding, inciting him to throw up both arms and yell, "GET OUT!"

Bob lets out a belly laugh and starts ushering people out of the house. "You heard the man. Get going."

CHAPTER 43

Soon, only Trystan, Katie, Dad, and Lynn remain. Lynn intended to leave with Jared, but Dad asked her to stay. He looked over her cheek and gave her ice.

"I'm sorry about that, about Derrick. He's…" She can't finish her sentence. There's an ugly reddish-purple mark on the side of her face, and I'm sure it will appear black by morning.

"He's got issues that aren't your fault." It still hurts, but I'm kicking myself for not seeing this side of him. I glance over at Katie. "They're no one's fault, and I'm sorry I didn't listen to you when you tried to warn me."

Katie's eyes are glassy. She smiles at me. "In all fairness, I didn't know he was THAT unhinged. I'm sorry, Mari."

Dad cuts off any more sappy apologies. "Lynn, do you have somewhere to stay?"

"I was at Derrick's until next week. I live in New Jersey."

Dad scratches his cheek and then picks up his empty coffee mug. He pads over to the sink and talks with his back to us. "I have a guest bedroom, and the house is empty most of the time. You can have Jared move your things here until you're ready to go home."

I blink at Dad's back, shocked. Hospitality isn't his thing and neither is kindness. Exhibiting them together is shocking.

Lynn is grateful. "That would be wonderful. You have no idea how stressful this has been."

"I don't. But I want you to make yourself at home here. I'll set up the guest room with fresh linens. And Trystan," Dad waits while Trystan looks over at him. "I made you an appointment with a specialist." Dad clears his throat, nervously running his hand over the back of his neck. "I'm sorry. I wish I could do more."

Trystan nods and looks away. Lynn keeps her gaze on the table and from the way Katie is staring at her mug, she already knows. I'm about to change the subject, when Trystan says to Lynn, "I haven't told many people yet, but I'm losing my eyesight."

Katie looks at him like he's crazy, and then addresses Lynn. "If you tell anyone, I'll personally hunt you down and—"

Trystan cuts her off. "She won't tell anyone. She's my mother." He smiles at her, and she smiles back, eyes full of tears.

"Did you confirm it? Did the papers come back?"

Trystan shakes his head. "I don't need the papers. I already know you're my mom."

CHAPTER 44

A few weeks pass. The winter is melting, and spring is coming. It's one of those unusually warm days where all the kids cut school, and the adults find a reason to leave work early. I'm wandering the paths at Belmont Lake with Katie and her new puppy, Gilbert.

He's a floppy eared lab mix. He's got huge paws and is always in trouble. She tugs at his leash, trying to get him to stop pulling. "Gilbert, be good!"

"I can't believe you named him that."

"Uh, what else would I name him? I mean look at him? He's Gilbert Blythe!" She picks up the dog and snuggles him. "He's got a sexy smirk, and dark hair. Plus all the girl doggies love him. When I have enough money, I'll adopt Anne, and we can be one big happy family."

I snort laugh. As she puts Gilbert down, he darts all over the path, and between our legs, tangling the leash. I step around and over, trying not to step on the little animal. Good thing he's quick.

Katie hasn't asked much, but I know it's coming. "So, how are things?"

I shrug. "Same as usual. I'm working like crazy and have no life."

"Have you seen Trystan much?" She turns around and steps out of the leash that tangles her legs. Gilbert barks at a gaggle of geese sunning themselves on the path ahead. He pulls against the leash so hard he gags.

"No, not since the party. He's got a lot going on, and it felt like I was intruding." I feel my lips moving weird and glance at Katie from the corner of my eye. She's too preoccupied with Gilbert to blast me.

"I'm surprised he didn't call you."

"Me too." Actually, that's why I backed off. I thought he'd come around more. But he didn't. Things are back to the way they were before the crash. It's as if Trystan Scott vanished from my life again.

"Gilbert, stop it. Yuck! Spit that out!" Katie picks up the puppy and pulls a half-eaten worm from his mouth. "You're so gross."

"I think he can eat those." I know he can eat those.

"Gilbert does not eat worms." She says it the way Anne would. We're talking all overdramatic, nose in the air, and snooty—from back before she liked Gilbert she would have said the opposite. I think Katie's been watching the series on Netflix at night. She still doesn't sleep. The puppy is a good thing for her, and she loves doting on him.

"Have you heard anything from Derrick?" She strokes the dog's head as we walk.

"Yeah, actually, I did. He sent me a bill for the engagement ring."

Her jaw drops. "He did not!"

"Yes, he did. Dad responded with a bill from the engagement party, and he actually got Trystan's ring back. I'm glad I wasn't there for that conversation. Derrick backed off after that."

"Your dad is scary."

I smile. "Yes, he is, and this is the first time that worked in my favor. Hey, you know the—" We're walking past the geese at the moment, and Gilbert decides to bark. One gigantic goose jumps up and charges us, honking like a crazy son of a bitch with its neck fully extended. We take off running, and when I look back over my shoulder, the entire gaggle is chasing us.

Katie tries to run with the wiggling puppy while he claws at her, persistently trying to get down on the ground. He thinks it's dinner time and wants to eat them. He doesn't know these geese will eat him. I'm pretty sure they feast on human flesh at night. That one big goose is insane. I now remember I usually avoid this path because of him.

Katie is laughing and scolding Gilbert. "Stop barking! Ah! Shut up, Gil!"

We're away from the lake and back around by the parking lot. The only goose left is the lunatic bird. It stops suddenly and rears back, fanning its wings and squawking.

Katie is panting hard when she finally stops running. She turns to the goose and yells at it. "You ruined girl time with Mari! You suck! Bad goose! Bad!"

It's like he can understand her because the goose charges again. We both scream and run for the car. I get out the keys and click the unlock button. "It's not opening!"

"I don't want to die!" Katie scream cries and keeps laughing.

I'm laughing too hard to breathe. Trying to laugh and run is a bitch, especially with a rabid bird on my heels. "You're going to make me pee! Stop it!"

"Open the door!"

We're almost to the car, and it finally unlocks. We yank open the doors and dive inside. Once the doors are closed hysterical laughter ensues, until something hits the windshield. Gilbert barks as we scream. The goose is on the hood hissing at us.

Katie doubles over laughing. Tears are rolling out of the corners of her eyes. "Oh, my God! Drive! Drive!"

"I can't. He's in the way." I turn on the windshield wipers and spray. Katie laughs harder, and the goose finally backs down.

She comes up from the floor for half a second and takes Gilbert's paw in her hand. She makes the coordinated movements with her badass talk, "Take that, bitch."

BROKEN PROMISES

Gilbert's tongue flops out, and he smiles. We both laugh until we can't breathe.

CHAPTER 45

"Katie, where are we going?" She shushes me and slaps at my hands when I try to peek from under my blindfold.

"I had this whole bachelorette party planned for you, and then you all ruined it and stuff. I thought it'd be a fun way to spend a Sunday night." She whoops and a horn blares. "That was nothing. You don't need to look."

"I'm going to die."

"Nah, that's tomorrow night's fun. We can Thelma and Louise it off the Verrazano–Narrows Bridge, as long as we have money for the toll. It's like $14 now! That's insane!"

I snap my fingers in Katie's general direction. "Focus! Where are we going?"

"I can't tell you because it's a surprise. Duh! Wait until we get there. Then I will unmask you, and we'll party like it's 1999."

I go for the blindfold again, and she swats my hand away. "No! Bad Mari!"

"You use that tone with Gilbert."

"Only when he's bad. Come on. We're almost there."

"How about a hint?"

She makes an overdramatic sigh. "Fine, there's music where we're going. How's that?" The car slows, and she cuts the engine. She opens my door, takes my hand, and I have no sense of direction at all. There are no sights or scents to clue me in as to where we are.

"Come on, this way." She holds my hands and takes me inside. We're walking down hallways, and I suddenly feel like I'm in the hospital, but it's too quiet. "You didn't take me to work, did you?"

"No, that would suck. I'm not a sucky friend. I'm your BEST friend. This is the best present ever!" She tells me to wait a second, and I hear metal on metal and something click. She pulls open a door and moves behind me.

"This part is very important, and if you do it wrong, you die."

"Katie!" I'm about to rip off the blindfold, but she shoves me forward.

"Two steps and sit. No more, no less, and sit on your ass." I'm bitching as I do it, but I take the steps and sit down. The floor is cold and hard—it's metal. There are little holes in it, like a grate. A musty scent fills my head, and I realize where I am.

When I hear the door latch shut, she shouts, "Blindfold off!"

"Katie?" I pull it away and see I'm in our old high school at the top of the stairs leading to the basement. "How is this fun?"

"Go down the stairs, you twit! Your present is at the bottom."

I walk down slowly and catch a sound. "Hello?" Someone is down here. My heart speeds up, and as I round the landing, I see Trystan, outlined in a bright light on a stool with his guitar in his hand. "Trystan?"

I haven't seen him in a few weeks, and from the way he isn't quite looking at me, I know he can't see.

"Mari?" He sounds surprised. "Where's the photographer?"

I smile and shake my head. "How much can you see?"

"Not much. Katie set up this shoot with a new photographer she likes. She wanted to give him a chance at the big time by giving him an exclusive shot. Why are you here?"

"Katie said it's girl's night and then blindfolded me. She told me not to fall down the stairs, and that's about all of it."

"She said you guys got attacked by a goose."

"We did. I still cringe from it. I had a dream last night that I couldn't run fast enough to get away from that thing. I was in my dad's house in my bedroom, and the thing was squawking as it climbed out of the toilet."

He laughs. "Nightmare."

"I know. Toilet water and a killer goose. So, what's going on in Katie's head with this?"

Trystan sighs and puts his guitar down. "So there's no photographer coming, right?"

"I don't think so."

"Did she lock us in?"

I run up the stairs and try the door. It's locked. I bang on it. "Katie!"

"Yes?" She sounds saintly.

"Are you going to let us out?"

"Did you kiss and make out? I mean, make up?"

"We're not fighting. Open the door." I'm a little annoyed and suddenly feel really nervous. Being around Trystan was fine when I knew I couldn't have him, now that I can—it scares the hell out of me.

"I will. First thing in the morning. And don't bother trying the other door, I chained it." She laughs, and I can hear her voice fading in the distance.

I stand on the landing with my heart thumping. I peer over the edge and can see him sitting down there. I might have been avoiding him, but he's not made an effort to speak with me either.

"She's not coming back, is she?" He shouts up at me tipping his head back, as if he's looking at me. His long dark hair tumbles back, and I can see his face wears a warm uncertain smile.

"Nope, not tonight."

"Like old times, huh?"

"I'm sure that's what she's hoping for." I make my way down the stairs and walk over to the couch to sit down. I'm holding my head in my hands, knowing he can't see me freaking out.

"And what are you hoping for?"

When I glance up at him, his eyes lock on mine and the pit of my stomach drops. I don't know if it's the words or the way he's looking at me, but it sets me on edge. I feel like a cornered cat.

I try to make light of it. "I'm hoping for a nutritious dinner of Blow Pops and Kool-Aid."

"Then you're lucky because both are in the cooler with some sandwiches. Katie stopped at a deli and bought us food, well, me and you since she ditched me." He laughs and stands, looks left then right, then back at me. "I can still see you a little bit, you know?"

I shake my head uncertainly. "You can?"

"Yeah. You're wearing a white shirt, and your hair is pulled away from your face, but you're missing something."

"I am?"

He reaches into his pocket and holds out his hand. In it is a pink tube of strawberry Lip Smacker, the lip balm I used in high school. I smile and take it from him. "I used to love this stuff."

"I know. I remember it. There are some things that remind me of you—that's one of them."

"Yeah, what are the others?"

"That first song, and this." He points to his back, to the tattoo I caught a glimpse of the other day. The corners of his lips pull up and fall quickly.

"I saw that, well part of it. What does it say?"

His dark lashes lower and I swear his cheeks burn. "It's the kind of thing that makes me feel incredibly happy when you're not around, and incredibly embarrassed when you are. I thought you already saw it."

"I didn't look." I had wanted to look, but I kept my grabby hands to myself. "I figured you'd tell me if you wanted me to know."

He nods slowly and when he lifts his face he's all smiles. "So, let's bust out the deli feast."

Got it. Not going to tell me.

CHAPTER 46

After I stuff myself with fried chicken cutlet on a roll, followed up by a fried pie—yeah, I eat those sometimes even though they're totally unhealthy and a million calories—I sit on the floor and squirm in the uncomfortable silence.

Trystan lies back on the couch, and I think he's going to sleep until he starts talking. "I'm sorry about you and Derrick. That must be hard." His arm is draped over his face. I watch him for a moment and envy the way he always seems to be relaxed. I can't even fake it.

I pick at the crumbs of icing in my Hostess wrapper and pop a piece into my mouth. Mmmm. Sugar. "Better now than later."

"I suppose, but aren't you sad?" He drops his arm and props himself up on his elbow. "This used to be a lot easier when I could see you. Do you mind coming over here?"

My heart slams into my ribs and falls into my toes. I try to maintain the distance between us, but I know what he wants—he wants to see me with his hands. I'm sure it's platonic, but my feelings toward him are not. I'd be an asshole if I told him no, so I nod and then remember to talk. "Yeah, I can do that."

Trystan sits up the rest of the way. The expression on his face doesn't change. His dark hair dangles in his eyes in a way he rarely allowed when he could see. I have to block the urge to push it back. Actually, I have to resist a lot more than that. I ball up the wrapper and toss it in the trash before sitting down next to Trystan on the old couch.

He reaches for my hand but doesn't take it. As his palm hovers, he asks, "Are you sure you're okay with this? I mean, I know it's you and I'll sense a lot more than with other people."

I know what he means, and the truth is that I'm not sure about anything anymore. I don't answer. Instead, I take his hand in mine and lace our fingers together. "What'd you want to talk about?"

"I want to know how you're doing. I haven't heard from you in a while—since the party actually." His hand is warm in mine. I feel his thumb rub gently over my skin and my stomach flips in response.

"I know. I had to work through some stuff. You didn't call me, did you?" I don't think he did, but I don't want him thinking I blew him off if he needed me. I would have dropped what I was doing and went to him no matter what was happening. Friendship is like that—bad things happen, and they're usually at the worst time. A real friend shows up. I promised myself I'd always be there for him.

"No," he breathes. His head hangs between his shoulders as he continues to talk. His thumb moves in slow circles, and I swear I can feel him thinking. "I planned on it, but then things—my eyes—got a lot worse. It was like someone flipped a switch and everything vanished. Within a week that little spot engulfed most of my vision. I can't see much anymore, and what I can make out is so difficult to see that it might as well not be there at all." He lets out a rush of air before putting his other hand on top of mine, enclosing my hand between his hands.

"I wish I could fix it." I want to wrap my arms around him and cry, but he doesn't want that. It's not pride. It's more that he's accepted what life threw at him and is done sobbing over it. Even though he is, I'm not.

"I know." He bites his lower lip a few times and then turns toward me. He takes my cheeks in his hands and gently turns my face toward him. "The doc your dad set me up with determined the cause, and I've been wrestling with it. At first I wanted to lash out at him, but now—I don't want to waste another second of my life thinking about him. My father stole my mother, my childhood, and my future. One too many blows to the head and he fucked me over for life. I didn't call you then because I needed to wrestle with this on my own. Katie came by, and I told her I was okay and sent her away, too. She probably thought I was going to flip out."

His hands gently hold my face as he speaks. When I reply, his touch lightens and makes me shiver. Goosebumps erupt on my arms, and I have to fight the urge to pull away. Talking to him like this makes me feel stripped bare. "We were worried about you, but I understand wanting to figure out how you feel about it before people tell you how you should feel. That's pretty much the same thing I was doing with Derrick. I've replayed all those months with him, finally seeing the snippets of his true character only after he went nuts at the party. It makes me question everything—like I shouldn't trust myself anymore."

Trystan can't see me, but part of me suspects he can because his eyes lock on my lips. I'm squirming inside, wishing I could pull away and keep my secrets, but part of me doesn't want that at all—I want him to know.

He drops his hand, sliding it down my cheek and brushing his thumb over my lips. Trystan's head tips to the side slightly, his dark hair falling into his eyes. "I know what you mean, but you can trust yourself, Mari. I know you. You consider every scenario ten million ways before you make a decision. You think you can run through every option, good or bad, and determine which path to take. Sometimes, no matter how much you consider something, you still can't see the bad coming. Sometimes the only way through the fire is directly through the center—we can't skirt it, and that's not our fault."

My heart races faster as he speaks and that thumb sits on my lower lip. Trystan leans in close enough to kiss me, but he doesn't. He lingers there halfway between friendship and something more. It makes me want to scream, cry, and laugh all at the same time. I finally act on the urge to push his hair back and rest my hands on the back of his neck and rest my forehead against his. "My dad likes you now."

Trystan smirks. "Damn, and I was trying to get the other Dr. Jennings to fall for me. I hit the wrong one with my sexy man charm." He laughs, and I can't help it, I giggle softly.

"Man charm? Is that what this is?

"Honestly, I'm not certain since I can't see what I'm doing." He tries to hide a smile and pulls back a tiny bit.

I feign shock. "So you think you don't have what it takes to make a woman notice you anymore?" Emotion rips through me in a wave of panic, so raw and desperate that I know I hit a sore spot—a wound that's still open. The smile fades from my voice. I reach for him and hold his face between my hands. "Are you crazy? You're Trystan Scott. For the longest time, every man has wanted to be you, and every girl wants to be with you. This," I lean in and kiss the corner of one eye and then the other, "is part of what makes you incredible. It's what makes people look up to you and find strength when theirs is gone. You've had a hellish life, and you still live with a smile on your lips. Trystan, if anything, you're more attractive now."

His eyes become glassy, and he pulls out of my grip. He blinks rapidly trying to keep the tears from falling, but they roll down his cheeks anyway. "Why? Why should I believe you and not think that it's bullshit made to pity me? I can't stand pity, Mari. How am I supposed to go through life with people looking at me like that?" He mashes his lips together and stops talking abruptly.

I put a hand on his knee so he can sense my sincerity. "It's not pity—not from me and not from anyone else—it's awe. You inspire people. They see your strength and want to be like you. I want to be like you. And as for me, it adds a layer to you that wasn't there before."

He laughs bitterly. "What? Blindness? Gee, thanks."

"No, it strips that cocky façade away and forces you to be vulnerable. You don't like it because it wasn't your choice, but isn't that the way it's always been with us? I mean this—" I take his hands in mine and hold them between us, lacing our fingers together. A wave of emotion hits me hard, and I drop my guard in response. He's afraid, and I know it has something to do with me.

"Even this isn't the same as what it used to be."

I lick my lips and carefully tread across a minefield. It feels like we're standing on a sheet of thin glass and one wrong move will destroy everything. "No, it's not. I feel it too. It's different, stronger. You never needed your eyes to read me, Trystan. Focus on this, on the touch and forget the rest. What do you feel?"

My heart is wide open with nothing protecting me. If he says something, it'll destroy me, but fear erodes his confidence, betraying him. I matter the most to him. I can feel it. What I think about him matters so much that he's scared to hear what I actually think. The truth rolls off like lies, and he won't hear it—but if he feels how I feel, how I've felt all along, he'll know.

Trystan's grip tightens, and he keeps his face lowered so I can't see, but I don't have to see him to know what he thinks. That is my point.

I close my eyes and focus on his skin, on his touch. I sense the chasm between us shrinking alongside the terror I feel in facing him like this. Last time I gave him my heart, he stabbed me. I shove the thought away and replace it with what I know of him now. I accept the whole thing, who he was, who he is now, and whatever comes next.

Emotion swirls in my chest until I can put a word to it. All that hope, faith, and trust point my mind toward one word. Fear juts up from somewhere within and I try to pull away, but Trystan holds on tight.

He clamps down on my hands and pulls my hands to his chest, so we're face to face. "Were you trying to hide that?" He's breathless but calmer than before.

"I didn't know." I didn't know that I love you. I didn't put it to words until now, and the realization makes me want to run away. What if he doesn't feel the same? What if this ruins our friendship? What if…?

Trystan drops my hands and lifts them to my face. He spreads them across my cheeks and leans in so close. His lashes lower and I can feel the warmth of his breath on my lips. "What if I told you I still think about you? What if I confessed that losing you was the worst mistake of my life? I love you, Mari. I always have, and always will. Do you love me?" He knows the answer to that question already—he can feel it filling my body from head to toe.

I blink rapidly, trying to put my feelings into coherent words. "I," my jaw flops like a docked fish, and I can't speak.

Trystan leans in and wipes the tears from my eyes with the pads of his fingers, gently pushing them away. Then he leans in and presses a kiss to each eyelid, slowly, softly. "I love the way you see the world, the way you live in it and change it for the better. I love the way you fight for kids and people who need someone to look out for them."

"How'd you know—?"

He smiles. "You're an advocate for the poor, typically children and the elderly. You're the hospital liaison, the only one who willingly stands between the corporation and the people each year. You volunteered for that job. You protect those who can't protect themselves."

"Trystan, that's not public knowledge."

"I've got people."

I grin and try to pull away, but he holds me tight. "Bob?"

"He's the size of two people, so sure. Let's say Bob's been following your career for a while and maybe telling me about it. What's worth noting is what you said about me—that people find strength when they hear my story—that's what happens every time I hear about you. You're the one who gives me the strength to keep going. It's always been you, Mari."

His hands suddenly drop from my face, and he pulls away.

There's only one thing holding me back, and it's fear. It shouldn't be there, but I need to hear him say it. "Promise me one thing, when life gets hard, never set me free again. I know you were trying to be selfless, and give me a quiet life, but if you're not part of it—"

He offers one of those cocky smiles and glances at me over his shoulder. "I'm sorry. I'll never do that to you again. I promise. There's one thing I need from you?" He picks at his callous on his left hand as he speaks.

I scoot closer to him, so our hips are touching. "What's that, Day Jones?"

"I need to hear you say it because this is unbelievable and when I wake up, I'll think it was a dream." He bumps his shoulder against mine. "Three little words, Mari Jennings, Dr. Kiss Ninja. Let me hear you say them."

My stomach swirls like I swallowed a tornado. I want to laugh hysterically while simultaneously crying, and my entire body tingles like I ate an entire bag of Pixy Stix. It's like Christmas morning, but it won't end when I unwrap the present.

I lean in close to his face and say what he wants to hear, kissing his lips softly as I say each word, "I. Love. You."

CHAPTER 47

The words hang in the air while we both sit there in shock. Trystan is breathing hard, gripping his knees like he might tear his jeans off. He doesn't look over at me when he speaks. "So."

I laugh nervously. "Yeah, well, this is weird."

"It is. I admit that if I could see you, I would have kissed you by now—maybe more."

I laugh. "Are you confessing that you have speedy issues? Because, I love you, and I'll deal, but—"

That breaks the strange tension. Trystan reaches for me, placing one hand on my stomach and the other on my waist and tickles. I try to push him away, but he's relentless.

"I do not have speedy issues! How could you even think that?" His fingers find my belly button, and I squeal.

Swatting at his hands, I fall off the couch and land between the couch and the coffee table. Trystan holds out his arms and closes his eyes, "Marco?"

I start laughing so hard I can't move.

"You're supposed to say, 'Polo.' Come on Mari." Trystan feels his way to the place where I am on the floor. He puts one leg on each side of my body and lowers his face to mine, then grabs my cheeks in one hand and mimics my voice. "Polo!"

I'm laughing so hard my entire body is shaking. I bite at his hand and catch it in my teeth. He seems shocked for a second and then shrugs. "If you're into that, then so am I." He laughs for a second, seeming truly happy.

He lowers his body on top of mine, and I can feel his heartbeat, the warmth of his skin, and the scent of his cologne filling my head.

He's propped up on his elbows with his hands in my hair. He lowers his lips to mine, slowly, kissing me so softly, with so much yearning and devotion, that every giggle inside of me transforms into bliss.

I wrap my arms around him and thread my fingers through his hair. I want the kiss to be deeper, harder, but he lingers lightly stroking my lips with his tongue before pulling away. He sits up, straddling me, and laughs. "Mari, this is—" He tips his head back and laughs at the ceiling like this is a cruel joke.

"Hey, it's okay. We'll figure it out. You already know the basics, or so I've heard." I rest my hands on his hips to make sure he doesn't move.

"I can't see you. I don't know if I'm even doing things right, touching the right places, because I can't see it." He sounds pained, like he doesn't want to mess this up and doesn't know how to go forward.

"Hey, we don't need to see to do this. Here." I push him off my lap and shove his shoulders back until he's on the couch. I flip off the light switch behind his head, and the room is plummeted into darkness. "Now, we're even. I can't see my nose. Or my hand."

I'm waving my fingers in the air in front of my face and hit something.

"That's my nose." His voice still sounds pinched.

"Then I'm a little too high, huh? Hold on." I don't say what I'm doing, I feel around in the darkness for him and find his shirt. I peel it off and then place my hands on his chest and slide them over his body, admiring every toned muscle. The rise and fall of his chest increases and I feel him lay back against the arm of the couch.

The pads of my fingers follow the lines of his body, tracing his neck, to his nipples, to the Y that begins slightly above the waist of his jeans. When I reach for the button, he stops me, flips me over and copies my movements. He tosses my shirt across the room and pushes me back into the couch. Leaving my bra in place, he uses his fingertips to see me. Ten fingers touch me lightly, starting at my neck and trailing down over my bra, and stopping at my stomach. I inhale sharply, pressing my hips up into him.

His hands are different than last time. The calluses are still there from playing so much, but the way he touches me is so soft, so careful—like he doesn't want to miss a thing. He slides his hands up the center of my torso and does it again, this time unhooking my bra and tossing it.

I wait for him, butterflies swirling inside me, wondering what he'll do next. When his hot body presses against mine, and I feel those lips on mine, I melt. It's a kiss that defies reality. It's soft and precious, and as he sweeps his tongue across the seam of my lips, lights flicker behind my eyes. Something sizzles to life inside of me, and I can feel him in a way that can't be real. His heart beats in sync with mine, our breathing is in rhythm, and I swear I can feel his soul touch mine. It's a kiss, a perfect kiss at the perfect time.

When he pulls away, he's breathless. "Did you feel that?"

"Yes, I did." We laugh nervously, like a couple of kids that haven't done this before. This part is unique, something that only happens with him.

I pull his lips to mine and kiss him softly. The sensations swallow us both, and we stay in each other's arms through the night.

CHAPTER 48

I'm half asleep in Trystan's arms when I hear the screech of a metal door in serious need of oil. I dart upright. "Someone's here."

Trystan groans. "It's Monday morning, the entire school is supposed to be here."

"Yeah, but there shouldn't be any morning classes down here. Drama is an afterschool activity here." I check my shirt to make sure it's not inside out and look at Trystan. He's all sexy with his shirt clinging to that body and his jeans still undone.

"You might want to button up."

He grins, remembering last night. "Anything for you." He fixes his jeans and walks toward the sound of my voice, wrapping his arms around my waist from behind. He kisses the back of my neck, and my knees nearly give out. "I love you."

I turn toward him and hold his face in my hands. "I love you, too." I press a kiss to his lips when a flat comes crashing down, and daylight blinds me.

"Awh! It worked! Bitchin'!" Katie's silhouette is in front of me, but I'm still temporarily blinded. "So, I demand you to name your first baby after me. If it's a dude, then he'll have to take one for Aunt Katie."

"You!" I laugh and stumble toward her, nearly tripping on the canvas flat. Katie enters the room through a side door leading directly to a stairwell that exits into the school parking lot. "This was my bachelorette party present?"

"Well, yeah." She snorts. "I knew you weren't going to marry Derrick. He's a dick."

I blink rapidly, ready to start scolding Katie when I notice another shape appear behind her.

It's a man, his broad shoulders and strong muscles filling out a trim set of desert-camo combat fatigues. I blink again, not believing what I'm seeing, but then he speaks. "Who's a dick? Usually, I own that accusation."

Trystan senses it and stiffens behind me, and he's as shocked as I am.

My jaw drops and I cover my mouth, choking back a sob. "Katie." I point at him like he's a ghost.

Katie turns slowly, and it's like time freezes. Her lip quivers when she realizes who it is. "Seth? Seth!"

He runs to her, picks her up, and twirls her around. He buries his face in her neck for a moment and holds her tight, breathing her in. "Babe, it's so good to hold you again."

"I thought... They said..." Katie sputters and slaps him in the chest. "They said you were dead! I went to your funeral!"

Seth laughs and pulls his cap off, revealing a shaved head. "Yeah, they didn't find my remains because I wasn't dead. My convoy was blown to bits, but a buddy of mine and I didn't die. I'm here, babe. I told you I'd come back for you. Nothing could keep me away." He smiles reassuringly at her.

Katie breaks down into tears and slams her fists into his chest. "I thought you were gone! I thought you were dead! I bought a puppy, and he ate the apartment last night. Gilbert is a bad dog! Oh, my God!" She pulls back laughing with tears on her cheeks. "You're alive. Thank God." She presses her lips together and looks at him.

Seth pulls her close to his chest again, glances over her shoulder at me, still smiling, and mouths, "Who the hell is Gilbert?"

EPILOGUE

Katie snaps a picture. "You look like butterflies are going to shoot from your nose." She looks at the back of the camera and makes a face. "I thought brides were supposed to be all calm and lovely on their wedding day."

I laugh at that. "Where did you hear that? I'm sure it's not from your day as Bridezilla."

She turns her head to the side and sits down, folding her hands and placing them neatly on her lap. "I don't know what you're talking about."

We both laugh. Katie was a terror on her wedding day. Me, I'm more trying not to cry. Mom's not here. No matter what I do, it's painfully obvious she's gone. Instead of talking with her right now, I'm with Katie—who I love—but it's not the same.

There's a knock at the door. Katie rushes over in her ice-blue dress. The hem billows around her knees as she hurries, emphasizing her bulging baby belly perfectly. It would be a pretty picture. "No guys allowed!" she barks and then laughs silently and points at the door like we are in junior high.

"It's Dr. Jennings." Dad's voice comes through the door. "I'd like to see my daughter before the ceremony."

"Let him in, please." I have the jitters, and everything seems surreal. I'm not nauseous like I was during my engagement to Derrick—I'm excited. I want to run down the aisle, say I do, and get a move on starting our life together.

"Fine," Katie whines, pulling the door open. After Dad passes her, Katie rests her hand on her belly and takes a seat in the corner of the room.

Dad glances at her. "Uh, if you don't mind, I'd like a moment alone with my daughter."

Katie is nearly ready to pop and overwrought by expectant mommy hormones.

She looks like she's going to cry, so I pull Dad by the wrist into the adjoining room and close the doors.

He clears his throat and looks at me appraisingly. "Your mother's dress turned out well."

Dad gave it to me when Trystan and I got engaged. He gave permission to alter it however I wanted, so I had a costume designer Trystan knows merge the wedding dress I loved with my mothers. Now it's uniquely mine. "It makes me feel like she's here with me. Thank you for giving it to me."

He nods, seeming nervous. He rubs his hand over the back of his neck, tips his head to the side, and reaches into his pocket. "These were your mothers, also. She wore them on our wedding day, and I know she would have given them to you today."

He places a necklace and matching earrings in my hand and closes my fingers over them, before leaning in to kiss my forehead. "I love you, Mari. I'm proud of you, of the woman you've become. I like Trystan, he's turned into a good man—but if the day comes that he hurts you, I will put my foot up his ass."

I hear Katie snort from the next room.

I lean in, put my arms around Dad's neck and kiss his cheek. "Thanks, Daddy."

He nods awkwardly and turns on his heel, vanishing without another word.

The wedding is beautiful. Trystan let me do whatever I wanted, but he insisted on choosing the wedding march. When the doors part, I have no idea what music is going to play, so when I see him sitting on a stool at the end of the aisle with a guitar on his lap, I can't help but smile.

He speaks into the microphone before him. "There's a song I wrote a long time ago and swore I'd only sing it at this moment, for my beloved Mari. So many things were against us, and I lost her once. I never thought I'd get to sing this song, so I had the lyrics tattooed on my side to remind me that love is what you make of it." He smiles softly, adding, "Please rise for the wedding march and forgive me if it's a little too slow."

Trystan's acoustic guitar fills the church as the people stand. Friends and family don't know if they should watch him or me. Their heads go back and forth as I place my hand on Dad's arm, and we walk up the aisle together, listening to Trystan pour his heart out. The words vibrate within me, touching me in a way I can't explain. The moment seems surreal like it'll change everything, and it will.

He strums the final chord as we reach the altar, letting it fade into silence. I'm covered in chills as he stands and hands the guitar to Seth. The past few months have been hard for him. Transitioning as he lost the remainder of his eyesight has been difficult, but he takes it in stride with a smile on his face. You'd never know so much has been taken from this man. You'd look at him and think he had life handed to him on a silver platter, that he never knew misfortune a day in his life.

Trystan carries his head high, and his family loves him for it. On his side of the church, his mother, Lynn, and his half-brother, Jared, share the first row with Bob—who is a sight to see in a tux. The man looks like he might rip it apart with his muscles.

Dad kisses me on the cheek and steps toward Trystan. Admiration flows from Daddy in waves. Trystan told his fans that this wouldn't end his career—if they'd have him, he'd deal with it and keep going. Trystan was met with a resounding yes. It wasn't until

Trystan needed help that Dad saw how hard he works. Dad slowly cut my hours back at the hospital until one day he suggested I travel with Trystan and be his on-staff medic. His only request was that I maintained my position as liaison between the hospital and the impoverished.

I never expected so much to change so quickly. I've been interviewed a half-dozen times since Trystan announced his condition, and they all ask the same question, "How do you handle the bittersweet reality that your life together will bring?"

I don't see it that way, not at all. If Trystan hadn't lost his sight, we wouldn't have ever gotten back together. Fate took one hideous event in his life and forced him to make a choice: he could become bitter about his loss, or he could keep fighting for everything he wants. Trystan didn't back down.

Dad slides my hand into Trystan's, and we turn to face the altar. Super pregnant Katie beams at me as she waves her bouquet. Seth is so proud of Trystan he looks like he might burst.

Gilbert is sitting with a pillow in his mouth and a little top hat on his head. I skipped the gaggle of bridesmaids, but I couldn't pass on the ring dog. I am wondering how Katie got him to sit and not eat the pillow and the rings, but he remains where he is, wagging his tail happily.

Trystan squeezes my hand and leans in close, brushing a kiss on my cheek. "I love you, Mari."

In giddy excitement, I squeeze his hand hard and beam at him. Whispering in his ear, I say, "I love you, too. And I'm having enough trouble paying attention without you kissing me. I'm going to miss it."

"Miss what?"

The pastor clears his throat, and repeats, "Doctor Mari Jennings, do you take this man to have and to hold from this day forth until death do you part?"

I giggle and kiss the back of Trystan's hand and say in a hushed whisper that's way too loud, "That part! Stop talking to me!" A few giggles rumble through the church as I scold my husband-to-be. I look straight at Trystan and hand Katie my bouquet. I place my hands on the sides of his face and he mirrors me, doing the same to mine. "I do."

He grins. "Yeah, we can't skip that part. That's important."

I try not to laugh. "It is."

The pastor smiles down at us. "Trystan Scott, do you take Mari—"

Trystan cuts him off, "I take Mari Jennings to have and to hold, from this day on until death parts us, and beyond. My heart was only made for one woman, and she's standing in front of me. I do. I always will."

Everything after that becomes a blur. The only thing I can see in that moment is Trystan. I feel his hands on my face and sense the conviction of his promise, and when he kisses me, it's like a dream.

Want to learn more about Trystan?
Read his backstory in:

THE SECRET LIFE OF
TRYSTAN SCOTT

Available now!

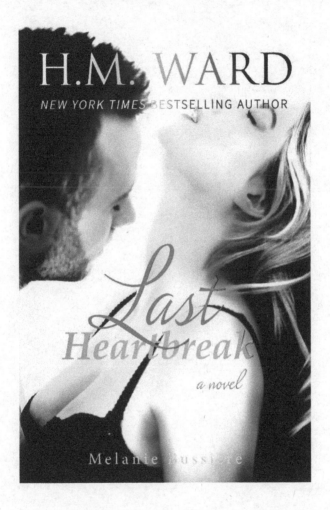

MORE FERRO FAMILY BOOKS

JONATHAN FERRO

~STRIPPED~

*****

BRYAN FERRO

~THE PROPOSITION~

*****

SEAN FERRO

~THE ARRANGEMENT~

******

PETER FERRO GRANZ

~DAMAGED~

******

NICK FERRO

~THE WEDDING CONTRACT~

******

MORE ROMANCE BY
H.M. WARD

SCANDALOUS

SCANDALOUS 2

SECRETS

*THE SECRET LIFE OF TRYSTAN
SCOTT*

DEMON KISSED

CHRISTMAS KISSES

SECOND CHANCES

And more.

To see a full book list, please visit:
www.HMWard.com/#!/BOOKS

CAN'T WAIT FOR H.M. WARD'S NEXT STEAMY BOOK?

★★★★★

Let her know by leaving stars and telling her what you liked about

BROKEN PROMISES

in a review!